When
WE WERE US

KEEPING SCORE
★ BOOK ONE ★

TAWDRA KANDLE

Cover Design: Covers by Robin
Formatting: Champagne Formats

The Trio. That's who we've been since birth: Nate, Leo . . . and me, Quinn, the token girl. Our mothers met in a prenatal class and became best friends, which meant that the three of us hit every milestone together, from the first day of school to the very first kiss. And beyond.

I've always been caught in the middle between the two boys. I've been in love with Leo since I was eight, even though he doesn't see me as anything but his pal. And I know that Nate's hung up on me. I see the look in his eyes. I wish I could say I felt the same, but I don't. It's getting harder and harder to keep him in the friend zone, though.

Things between the three of us aren't easy anymore. Leo's popular, the football team's star receiver, and the object of every girl's fantasy. I know he doesn't mean to leave us behind, but now Nate and I are just people he used to know.

What used to be so simple is suddenly messy and complicated. Leo is all I've ever wanted, but even if I had the chance to be with him, how would Nate would handle it?

When that chance does come along . . . in the most unexpected way . . . I'm helpless to resist Leo. What was always meant to be is finally happening . . . but will it come at the risk of losing both my friends?

Other Books
by the Author

The Perfect Dish Series
Best Served Cold
Just Desserts
I Choose You

The One Trilogy
The Last One
The First One
The Only One

The Always Love Trilogy
Always for You
Always My Own

The Seredipity Duet
Undeniable
Unquenchable

Recipe for Death Series
Death Fricassee
Death A La Mode

This book is dedicated to you.

Yes, you.

You, in all your perfectly imperfect beauty,

Your quirky humor,

Your absolute uniqueness . . .

You are wonderful, gorgeous and a complete original.

This world is a better place because of you.

★ One ★

Leo

I KNEW FIFTH GRADE WAS GOING TO BE DIFFERENT THE minute I stepped onto the playground that first day.

In our town, there were two huge elementary schools. The kids went to Marian Johnson Primary School from pre-K through fourth grade and then moved onto Herbert Andrews Elementary from fifth through seventh grade. It was cool to change schools, I guessed, but in a way, it meant we all started over three times before we graduated from high school, because there was also a junior high. We went from being the big men on campus back to the bottom of the barrel three times.

So when I stepped onto the newly-recovered asphalt at Herbert Andrews—everyone called it the HA school—I had to admit, I was a little nervous. At MJ Primary, I was a pretty popular kid. At least I had a lot of friends, and the teachers liked me. I didn't know how it happened, but I was able to get good grades and not be labeled as some kind of dork. I think it was mostly because we hadn't gotten to the point of labeling each other. We'd all been together since kindergarten—or pre-K, for some of us—and there was a kind of sweet acceptance that was doomed to end.

I saw it slipping away almost immediately on the first day of fifth grade. I was still standing on the edge of the playground, kind of taking everything in, when I noticed a cluster of kids over to my left, standing just beyond the swings. They weren't just hanging out; I saw a few glancing carefully over their shoulders, watching out for teachers or other adults just the same way my dog looked when he was getting into the trash.

I was curious, and I wandered over that way. I recognized a couple of classmates from fourth grade. But as I got closer, my heart sank. In the middle of the crowd, looking more confused and frightened than I'd ever seen him, was Nate.

Nate had always been smaller than me. His arms were thin and gangly, and his face had a pointed look that had been cute during kindergarten but now only had the effect of making him seem hunted. His hunched shoulders made it worse.

He was surrounded by five boys who all towered at least two heads above him. They were grinning, but not in a 'hey, let's all go play ball' way. I saw one of them reach out and shove against Nate's shoulder. Always just a little unsteady, he teetered for a moment, but to my relief, kept to his feet.

I was close enough now to hear their voices, the jeering. And for a minute, less time than it took me to realize I was thinking it, I was tempted to just turn around. Turn my back and pretend that I hadn't seen it, hadn't seen Nate in the middle of that mess.

I wouldn't have done it. I was really sure about that. But before I could prove it—to myself or anyone else, I guess—a blue tornado streaked past me.

"Hey! Get away from him. What are you doing?" Her voice ringing with the righteous indignation of the young, Quinn pushed through the little knot of boys and stood in front of

Nate. With hands on her hips and curly brown hair flying in every direction, she stood only a little taller than Nate, but she stared up at the boys with fury and challenge.

The biggest of them looked at her with a mixture of disbelief and annoyance. "Leave it alone. Go back and play with the little girls. We're just welcoming our new buddy to HA."

"You're all bullies." Quinn always did cut right to the chase. "You're mean, and you're stupid and you want to hurt Nate just because he's different from you. Go away. Leave him alone, or I'll go get a teacher."

I held my breath, waiting to see what the boys would do. I saw them exchange glances, and then the leader shrugged. "Whatever. You're not going to be around all the time. We'll catch up with him later." Turning, he stalked off, pushing through the swings and sending them flying.

The other boys melted off, leaving Quinn and Nate standing together, alone. I stalked over, ready to yell at Quinn for getting in the middle of that, when she turned and spotted me.

"What's wrong with you?" she demanded. "Didn't you see what was happening? They were going to hurt Nate!"

"I—I was—" I looked at Nate, my eyes pleading for some back up, but he was just staring off into the distance, beyond Quinn, beyond me.

"I was heading over here," I finished lamely.

"Yeah, by the time you got here, they would have pushed him down and gotten in some good punches. What were you waiting for?"

"I don't know." I pushed a hand through the hair my mom had so carefully combed an hour ago. "It just happened so fast. I saw it was Nate, and then before I could even get in there, you ran past me."

"It shouldn't have mattered who it was. They were big

kids, picking on someone smaller. You should have stopped them no matter who it was. But then when you saw it was your friend—" Quinn glared at me meaningfully. "Your *best* friend since before you were born, you should have run to stop them." *Like I did.* She didn't say it, but I could read it loud and clear in her eyes.

"Nate." I could see I wasn't going to get anywhere with Quinn, so I turned to the small boy hunched between us. "What happened? Why were they ganged up on you?"

He shrugged, still not meeting our eyes. "Mom dropped me off early," he finally answered, softly. "I asked her to. I thought I could get in here and look around, be ready when you guys got here. I was just sitting on the bars over there." He jerked his chin toward the rainbow climber, now covered with kids. "But then I saw there was an empty swing, and I thought I would grab it for Quinn." At last he looked up at her. "I know you like to swing."

Quinn sighed, the merest breath. "I do like to swing. Thanks for thinking of me, Nate."

He nodded and continued. "I was just trying to get across the playground to them, and then this one kid grabbed me, and the next thing I knew, they were all standing around." He swung his eyes up to me. "Matt was there, too. Did you see that, Leo?"

I sighed, but I didn't say anything. Matt Lampert had been in our class last year, and he had hung around with Nate and me. I would've said we were friends. I hadn't seen him over the summer, but that wasn't unusual; his family lived on the other side of town and belonged to the community pool, which was where he spent most of his days between school years.

"Why do kids act like that?" Quinn stomped her foot against the concrete and winced. I tried to hide a smile, but she looked at me and rolled her eyes. She had a tendency to strike out physically, forgetting that hitting hard surfaces hurt.

"They're just . . . I don't know. Stupid, like you said, I guess." Nate still seemed far away, and I gave him a light punch on the shoulder to get his attention. He turned his bright blue eyes to me, and I flinched at the pain there.

"You okay, Nate?" Quinn stole my line and laid a tentative hand on his arm. To my surprise, he shrugged it off. I hadn't ever seen Nate rebuff Quinn's affection—not ever.

"You shouldn't have gotten in the middle of it," he said in a low voice. "Now it's only going to be worse. They're going to think I'm a wimp, that I have to count on a *girl* to protect me."

Quinn raised her eyes to mine. She was surprised and not a little hurt. "I'm sorry, Nate. I thought. . .I didn't want you to get hurt." She bit her lip and added, "I know if it had been me they were picking on, you would have stopped it."

"That's different. I'm a boy. I'm supposed to do the defending."

Quinn stepped back, looking even more lost. "Since when does that matter? I thought friends stuck up for each other, no matter what."

"We're not babies anymore, Quinn," Nate said, more gently. Whatever angst he had been dealing with was passing, and he looked more himself. "I can take care of myself." He hesitated and then added, "Besides, if it had been Leo in the middle of those boys, would you have run to save him?"

Quinn flushed pink. I stared down at my feet, kicking at the line of white paint on the bumpy asphalt. This was a total Nate thing. Whatever crossed his mind was pretty much what he said. Quinn and I were used to it, but lately, it was making both of us more uncomfortable. Sometimes we didn't know how to answer him.

Now Quinn's mouth twisted as she tried to say the right thing. "Of course I would. You're both my friends, and I wouldn't let anyone hurt you if I could help it."

"Maybe," Nate said bleakly. "But Leo wouldn't need your help. That's what you're thinking, isn't it?"

The bell rang at that moment, and we all automatically turned toward the school building. Nate began moving in his normal jerky gait. Quinn didn't follow him right away. I couldn't read the expression on her face, but I could tell that she wasn't happy.

"C'mon, Mia," I said finally, using the special nickname I'd had for her as long as I could remember. "We don't want be the last ones in. Do you know where to line up?"

She shrugged and started walking. Nate was far enough ahead of us that I didn't think he could hear our conversation.

"Do you think he's right?" Quinn asked me. "Was I wrong? Should I have let them beat him up?"

"No. I don't know. I don't think they were going to beat him up. They were just, you know, trying to be cool or whatever. They were mostly teasing."

"What if it *had* been you?" she persisted. "What would you have done?"

This was a harder question. No one had ever bullied me in school. I slid a sideways glance at Quinn, wondering how much she really wanted to know.

"I guess I would have just talked to them. Tried to get them to cool it. They'd probably stop if someone stood up to them."

Other kids were forming lines that snaked out along the brick walls. Quinn and I caught up with Nate, and we paused, trying to figure out which line we were supposed join.

"Fifth graders on the far left!" A pretty young teacher was standing on the concrete steps, calling out instructions to the milling crowd. The three of us walked to the left, keeping our steps slower to match Nate's.

For the first time, we were all three in different classes. At Marian Johnson, there were only two classes per grade, so every year at least two of us were together. We separated into our assigned lines. Nate never looked back at us. He stood in the back of his line, his eyes fixed on the hair of the girl who stood in front of him. Quinn looked from him to me and back again. She was still worried.

I caught her eye and shrugged. There wasn't any mid-morning recess at Herbert Andrews Elementary, so we'd have to wait for lunch to see each other again. Quinn's class was the first to go into the building, followed by Nate's line. I watched them leave me behind.

★ Two ★

Quinn

WHEN NATE, LEO AND I SAY WE'VE BEEN FRIENDS since before we were born, it's true. Everyone thinks we're exaggerating or being funny, but we're not. See, our moms all went to the same birth class, where people go to learn what it's like to have a baby. For my mom and Nate's, it was their first time having a baby, so they really needed the class. But Leo's mom already had two boys, so she always said she was just there for a refresher course. I guess she had forgotten how to do it, which sounds weird, but why else would she go back to a class?

Anyway, it sounds like a movie, but our moms got talking and sort of became friends. They went out for coffee or whatever pregnant women drink (because I think they're not supposed to drink coffee), and they were going to do it again, like every week, but then Nate's mom ended up having him early. Not just a few weeks early either; my mom told me once that at first they weren't sure Nate was going to live. He was in NICU, which is a really scary place for babies, my mom said, for like two months. So all during that time, while my mom and Leo's were waiting for us to finally be born, they helped out Nate's parents. My mom used to make food for his family and drive his mom to the hospital to sit with Nate.

That's why Nate is different from Leo and me. Something happened when he was born that early, and it left him with a lot of health problems. I can actually remember when Nate started walking. His legs were weak, something to do with the muscles, and we were four by the time he could really move around by himself without this walker he used to have. He was always smaller than us, too, even though he's the oldest.

I didn't realize how different Nate was until we started pre-K. Nate had been in special schools when we were younger, but by the time we were four, he was able to come to school with us. I was glad we were all going to be together, and I was really happy that Leo and I were finally going to school. I had been a little jealous of Nate up to then, because he would talk about people he knew and stuff he did at school. It sounded like a fun place, even though Nate didn't always want to go.

In pre-K, though, it was easy to see that Nate wasn't like the rest of the kids. It wasn't just his special way of walking, which in those days was a lot worse than it is now. He would almost throw himself from one leg to the other. Leo and I were used to it, and we always walked on either side of him, at just the same speed he did. The other kids in pre-K definitely noticed that. They also saw that Nate was smaller than the rest of us. But what really made him stand out was his way of talking.

I guess it wasn't really how he talked so much as what he said. Leo's mom said once that Nate didn't have a filter. For a while I thought that meant there was something else that was wrong with him from when he was born, but then my mother explained that it meant that Nate just said whatever he thought.

"I thought that was telling the truth," I said.

My mother sighed and thought for a minute. "Quinn, if I asked you how I looked in my new dress, what would you say?"

This was easy. "I would say you looked pretty."

"Okay, thanks, but what if I didn't? What if it made me look fat or something?" At the look on my face, my mother laughed. "That's what I mean. See, you're trying to think about how you can tell the truth and not hurt my feelings, right?"

I nodded.

"All right then. Nate doesn't understand that. He doesn't mean to hurt anyone's feelings, but he just says whatever he thinks or feels, without considering how it might make other people feel."

And in pre-K, there were probably lots of kids who didn't worry too much about how other people felt, but it was really bad with Nate. He would tell the teacher about every mistake she made. He told the other children they couldn't read well or counted wrong or didn't know how to tie their shoes. It was never mean-spirited; it was just matter-of-fact Nate.

As we went through school, Leo and I tried to gently tell Nate that he couldn't share every thought that came into his mind the minute he thought it. He never understood, although I think he learned to tone it down a little. Sometimes Leo or I would give him a look, and he would realize he was going too far.

By the end of pre-K, though, everyone knew and accepted Nate. No one ever picked on him or called him names. That lasted through fourth grade, until we changed schools and moved over to Herbert Andrews Elementary. On the first day, as I walked onto the playground, I saw Nate in the middle of a bunch of bigger kids, and it didn't look like they were planning a game of tag. Nate was doing his swaying thing, which he only did when he was really nervous. No one else really noticed it, but I knew what it meant.

Right before I took off to help him, I saw Leo. He was standing between me and Nate, and I knew he saw what was happening. But before I could really wonder why he wasn't doing anything, I saw one of the boys shove Nate. He almost went down. And if he went down, I knew it wouldn't be good.

So I sprinted across the playground. At Marian Johnson, the ground surrounding the school building was a dusty field. But at HA, the whole thing was asphalt, painted here and there with maps and other pictures I guessed people thought were educational. All I knew was that I wanted to get to Nate before those kids knocked him onto that hard concrete. And I made it. I didn't plan how I was going to stop them. They were all much bigger than me, and I never was any good at that kind of fighting anyway. Leo always said I used my words better than he used his fists. I wasn't sure my words were going to make much difference here, but I guessed they did something, because the boys backed down.

After they were gone, I expected . . . well, I don't know what I expected. I guess maybe I thought Nate might say thanks. And maybe Leo would think I had done a good thing. But they both acted like I was the one who'd almost beat up our best friend. And I thought Nate was actually mad at me.

Things didn't get any better for Nate the rest of the year. We were dealing with more than just the kids who had always been in our class; now we were at the bottom of the school ladder. Fifth graders overall were easy pickings for the older kids, and Nate was an especially attractive target.

But what really made things hard was what happened with Leo. As the year went on, it seemed like Leo was moving farther away from Nate and me. He didn't always hang out with us on the playground in the mornings. He ate lunch with us, but then afterward he would sometimes go off with other boys and run around, play whatever game they put together. Nate and I sat on the bottom rungs of the monkey bars or on swings if we could get to them before they were all taken. We talked about school and about our families.

It was cool, and mostly I didn't mind hanging out with Nate. He listened to me, and he didn't think what I said was silly. And I liked hearing him talk about the stuff he was reading, his latest visits to the doctors and what he learned there, and about his mom and dad. But sometimes I would look out at the other kids, running and climbing and playing, and I would want to be a part of that. I didn't understand how Leo could just leave us there, but at the same time, I wished sometimes that I were out there playing with the rest of our classmates, too.

If Nate knew what I was I thinking, he never said anything. Which of course makes me think he didn't know, because as I said, Nate didn't hold anything back, especially with Leo and me. Even after he learned to stop saying everything that crossed his mind in front of other people, he always told Leo and me what he thought. I thought I was pretty good at hiding how I felt. And Nate never said anything bad about Leo either, even though sometimes I saw his eyes follow whatever game everyone else was playing.

One day toward the end of the year, Nate missed a whole day of school. That was pretty unusual; not that he didn't have a ton of doctors' appointments and stuff, but his mom always made sure to make them either first thing in the morning, so he got to school before lunch, or right after school. He didn't want to miss any classes he didn't have to, because he almost always got sick at some point in the school year and had mountains of work to make up. So he avoided missing any days that weren't absolutely necessary.

In fifth grade, though, Nate was amazingly healthy. He was in school every day until that week in late April, when he had to go for a whole day of tests at the children's hospital in Philadelphia. He didn't want to go, and he was grumpy the entire day before, even though I promised I would get all of his work and bring it over as soon as he got home that afternoon.

That morning, Leo was waiting for me at the bicycle rack. "Hey."

I brushed my hair back out of my face. It was curly and long and always in my way. "Hey," I answered. "Nate's not going to be here today."

Leo frowned. "He sick?"

I shook my head. "No. Tests. Doctors appointments, you know."

Leo nodded. "Yeah. So . . . we're going to play kick ball at lunch. You wanna be on my team?"

I thought for a minute about Nate. I almost felt guilty for wanting to play kick ball, like I was being disloyal to him. But then I thought about all those days of sitting on the swing watching the rest of the school play.

"Sure," I said to Leo. "I'll play."

★ Three ★

Nate

MY FIRST CLEAR MEMORY IS OF QUINN AND LEO. WE were at my house, because that was almost always where our mothers met in those days. Our house had everything I needed in it, all my medicine and my nebulizer, and there were ramps so that I could get around with my walker.

We were standing at my train table, which was my favorite place to play in those days. Trains were my obsession. Whenever I heard the whistle in the distance, I demanded that my mother take me to the crossing that was a couple of miles from our house. Sometimes she would, if we were going out anyway or if she were feeling especially guilty. But mostly she would tell me to go play with my own trains.

In those days, these were the chunky plastic toys that I could easily move and run around the tracks. Later, when my fine motor skills had improved, my grandparents bought me a more sophisticated set. But it was the first set that I remembered so well with Quinn and Leo. Playing trains was what we did together. When they got to my house, they might ask if we could go outside or watch a movie or play with something else, but we always ended up with the trains. I never thought until much later that maybe they didn't enjoy it as much as I did.

I was running my favorite blue engine around the outside track when it ran over Leo's finger. He yelped just like my grandmother's dog did when Grandpa accidentally stepped on its tail, and he pulled back his finger, sticking it in his mouth. Quinn's face puckered.

"Are you okay, Leo?" she asked, her voice sweet and high. I loved the sound of Quinn's voice.

"My finger hurts." Leo spoke around the finger in question, still in his mouth. I could tell he was trying not to cry. He wasn't a crybaby at all, so I guessed it really did hurt.

"Do you want me to get your mommy?" Even then, Quinn took care of us.

Leo shook his head.

"He shouldn't have had his finger so close to the track." This sounded reasonable to me as I said it. It was true; the train hadn't moved to run over Leo's finger. He had put his hand in its way.

"Nate, it wasn't his fault," Quinn protested. "It was just an accident."

"It wasn't an accident," I insisted. "He put his hand down on the track. He saw the train coming."

Leo scowled at me. "Who cares? Trains are stupid."

Quinn gasped as though Leo had just spoken high treason. She glanced at me, but I didn't react. Actually, what Leo said didn't matter to me at all, because it was so clearly not true. Trains could not be stupid. People could be stupid, but not trains. Now if he had said that trains had square wheels, I would have argued with him.

"Leo, don't say that. Nate's trains are really fun."

"They're stupid and I don't know why we always have to play with them."

"*You* don't have to play with them," I said. "Quinn and I are playing."

"No, Leo didn't mean it, Nate. We can all play. Come on, Leo."

But Leo had stomped off into the other room. Quinn watched him go, distress and indecision on her face.

I resumed playing with my trains as though nothing had happened. "Quinn, you run the red train now. You can make it go over the bridge and stop at the station."

Quinn obeyed without speaking. When the red train had stopped at the station, we both loaded the passengers onto it.

"Leo and I really like your trains, Nate. Don't be sad about what he said. It was just because his finger got hurt."

"I'm not sad," I answered. "Quinn, let's make the trains race." We ran the trains alongside of each other, but Quinn didn't say anything else.

A few minutes later, Leo stuck his head into the room. He didn't look at me at all. "Quinn, my mom says we can go outside and play on the swings. Let's go."

Quinn took one step away from the train table and then turned back to me. "Nate, come outside with us."

I was still absorbed. "I don't want to. I'm playing with my trains."

"But don't you want to play with Leo and me outside?" she persisted.

I shook my head. "No. It's too hot outside. I want to stay in here."

"Come *on*, Quinn," Leo called. She took another step toward the door. I watched her out of the corner of my eye.

Finally, she said, "Go on out, Leo. I'm going to stay inside with Nate for a while. Maybe we can go out and play in a little while."

Leo didn't answer, but a few seconds later we heard the screen door slam. Leo's mom jumped up and yelled at him not to bang the door, and she apologized to my mother, who just laughed.

"He didn't mean it, Lisa. That door is so light, I'm always forgetting and letting it slam behind me." I heard the edge in her voice, which usually meant that I had done something that made her sad or uncomfortable. It was the same thing I heard when the doctors were telling us about new tests I had to have or when we talked about my walking.

Quinn came back slowly to the train table. She picked up one of the people waiting to board my blue train, and she turned him over and over in her hand. As we played, I saw her glance out the window more than once, and I knew she wanted to be outside. It never occurred to me to say that to her, though. I was always happier when Quinn was playing with me. I liked Leo, too; they were both my best friends. But Quinn made me feel special in a good way. It was like she didn't see my walker or my spindly arms. She saw the real me, inside.

Leo was my friend, too, and usually the three of us hung around together. But I didn't think Leo ever understood me the way Quinn did until the first day of fifth grade. That day, standing on the playground with all those boys standing over me, I was scared for the first time in many years. I wasn't so much afraid of what they were going to do to me as much as how embarrassing it was going to be, how I didn't want to be humiliated in front of Quinn. I didn't know if she was there yet, but I knew she would be soon. The idea of her seeing me on the ground, dirty and maybe worse, made me sway in nervousness, something that I hadn't done in a long time.

But then a bad situation got even worse. All of a sudden, Quinn was right there in the middle of those boys, and she was yelling at them. She threatened to go get a teacher, and pretty soon they all left. Then it was just Quinn and me. Before I could say anything to her, Leo was there with us, and she was yelling at him for not coming to help me.

I knew Quinn thought she did the right thing. She couldn't understand why I wasn't thanking her and why Leo wasn't praising her. But she was a girl. She couldn't see that not letting me stand up for myself—no pun intended—made everything worse.

It was kind of funny that my first memory was of Quinn choosing between Leo and me. That didn't really happen again until later, when we started fifth grade. That year, when Leo started playing with the other kids at lunch, I knew Quinn would rather be running around with all of them instead of sitting on the monkey bars every day with me. But she never said it, and she never left me. And I never said she should.

Maybe it was selfish, but I guess that I felt like my whole life was a little unfair. Quinn made up for some of that. If it was selfish to want her to stay near me and be my friend, I was okay with that.

★ Four ★

Quinn

I THOUGHT STARTING OVER IN A NEW SCHOOL FOR FIFTH grade was hard. It was nothing compared to moving to the junior high for eighth grade. At least in fifth grade, we were still kids. Lunch time on the playground was the most stressful part of the day. But in junior high, suddenly everyone started breaking off into groups, and there were cool people . . . and then some who weren't considered so cool. Some people called them dorks or whatever, but it was really just someone's opinion. In eighth grade, there were a very few people whose viewpoints matter. I wasn't one of them.

Somehow over the summer, all the girls who had played Barbies and doll house with me morphed into strangers who wore lip gloss and worried about their hair. I missed that memo, I guessed. I still liked to play with dolls, and I didn't care what my hair looked like, as long as it was out of my way.

Add to that the fact that my two best friends were boys, and I was practically an outcast. But it didn't matter to me at first. I had Leo and Nate. If Leo had grown away from us a little in fifth grade, he'd made his way back over the next few years.

That was mostly because Nate and I began playing kickball at recess. Even though he couldn't really run, Nate could kick the ball. The other kids let me be his pinch-runner, and together we were a great team. Leo stopped being embarrassed by his two friends who sat on the monkey bars every day. He always chose us first for his team.

When I got to school on the first day of eighth grade, Nate and Leo were already standing in line against the building. This was junior high, and there was no playground anymore. Instead we waited outside the glass doors until the bell rang, and then we filed inside and hoped to find the lockers we'd been assigned.

I joined the boys, smiling my greeting. Nate returned my smile and greeted me. "Hey, Quinn! You look really pretty." This was high praise from Nate, who rarely paid anyone a spontaneous compliment. I smoothed the denim skirt my mom had made me wear that morning and thanked him and then snuck a look at Leo.

Most of the boys in our class were still scrawny and shorter than the girls. They could have easily passed for a year or two younger than thirteen. But not Leo. He had sprouted up three inches over the summer, and the lawn mowing business he ran with his two older brothers had given him muscled arms and a light tan. He grinned at me from his spot against the wall.

"Hey, Mia," he said. "Your mom make you wear that?"

Irrationally his words irritated me. It was true that I didn't wear skirts or dresses very often, but couldn't he have said something nice, like Nate had? Instead he had to tease me. I suddenly hated the skirt more than I had this morning when my mom had handed it to me.

"Of course," I snapped. "Didn't *your* mother dress *you* today?"

Still grinning, he shrugged. "Sure. I don't care about clothes." His eyes wandered along the lines of other students, and I saw them warm with appreciation. I followed his gaze to a pretty girl in a short cotton sundress and heels. She looked older than we were, but I didn't like the expression of admiration on Leo's face. I was pretty sure he wouldn't tease *her* about wearing a dress.

"Bet she can't play kick ball or anything in that dress," I commented. Leo jerked his attention back to me and flushed a little when he realized I'd seen the girl. I rolled my eyes at him.

"No more kick ball, Quinn. Least not at school. We're not babies anymore."

I became aware that Nate was watching both of us very closely, and I turned slightly to include him.

"How was your vacation, Nate?" I asked. His family spent the last two weeks of every summer at a rented cabin in the Poconos while my family stayed at the beach for a week. Leo usually stayed in town.

"Good," Nate answered me. "We went fishing. And canoeing. My dad says if I keep working at it, maybe I could do something like that, rowing or whatever, in high school and college. It would help build my upper body strength."

"That would be cool," I agreed. "Does the high school have a rowing team?"

"No," Leo answered for him. "But I think there's a local club. Your dad's right, Nate. It would be good for you."

Nate smiled, pleased that both of us had responded so positively. He looked up at me. "Did you have fun at the beach, Quinn?"

I opened my mouth to tell them about the days I had spent building sand castles and playing in the waves, but before I could say a word, I heard a soft voice behind me.

"Hey, Leo."

I recognized the girl in the dress, the one who Leo had been staring at earlier. Her name was Sarah, I remembered now, and she was very pretty, with black hair and huge brown eyes. She was gazing up at Leo as though he were a luscious chocolate ice cream cone.

"Hi, Sarah," Leo replied, and I realized to my amazement that he was flustered. He pushed off from the wall and shoved his hands into his pockets. "You ready to start school?"

Sarah giggled as though Leo had made a witty comment. I barely refrained from rolling my eyes again. "I guess so. Not going to be as much fun as summer, though, right?"

Leo laughed, too. "Yeah, I don't think so. Not unless they let us run through the sprinklers here, too."

"Oh, I know! Can you believe how soaked we got?" Sarah had moved closer, effectively edging out Nate and me.

"My mom asked me if I had stopped at the pool on the way home," Leo confided. "I told her it was a sprinkler inspection that went bad."

That sent Sarah off into more peals of laughter, the last of which was thankfully drowned out by the bell ringing, signaling the beginning of the school day. We all moved toward the doors and into the building.

I stayed near Nate, making sure he didn't get jostled in the crowd of kids. Our lockers were on the same hallway, and we found them easily enough. I had to try the combination for my lock three times before it worked, but Nate must have had more luck, since he was standing next to me, waiting patiently when I looked up.

"Where's Leo?" I asked him.

Nate shrugged. "Not sure. Maybe he went to homeroom already."

I sighed. I had a bad feeling about this day and particularly about this Sarah person, who seemed to have spent time with Leo this summer unbeknownst to Nate and me. Once upon a time, Leo would have made fun of a girl like that, but he seemed to like her well enough today.

We threaded our way toward the classrooms. Nate and Leo had the same homeroom, but I was on my own. We caught up with Leo just outside the door to their classroom.

"I wondered where you guys had gone," he said. "I turned around, and I couldn't find you. Did you get your lockers to work?"

I arched my eyebrows. "Yep. You might not have lost us if you hadn't been giggling with your girlfriend."

I expected Leo to laugh at the joke, but instead he frowned at me. "She's not my girlfriend. I just got to know her over the summer. I cut the grass at her house."

"And inspected the sprinklers?"

"I was finishing up one day, and Sarah brought me out a drink. While we were standing there talking, the sprinklers came on, and we both got soaked. That's all there was to it."

I didn't have time to answer. Nate pulled at Leo's arm. "We have to go in, Leo. She's starting to take attendance. See you at lunch, Quinn."

I gave Nate a half-hearted wave and glared at Leo once more before I flounced off to my own homeroom.

★ Five ★

Nate

I WAS TEN WHEN I FIRST OVERHEARD A DOCTOR TALKING about life expectancy. He and my parents had sent me out to get some water in the waiting room while they chatted in his office. I came back quietly enough that none of them heard me, and I realized the doctor was talking about me in a very solemn tone of voice.

"There's every reason to expect that Nathaniel will live well into his early adulthood. We're doing everything we can, and who knows what treatment might be discovered by the time he's eighteen? The important thing is to help him to enjoy every minute. Quality of life, you know, and Nathaniel has that in spades."

My mother sighed, and my father cleared his throat. I stood frozen just outside the doorway.

My dad spoke quietly. "Is there anything else we can do right now? More therapies, other doctors at other hospitals?"

"We're doing everything we can," the doctor repeated, patience in his voice. "I make it a point to keep up with all the articles and papers published on this condition. If I think there's anything that will help him, you know I'll be the first to let you know. Try not to let what might happen in the future rob you of what you have here in the present—a wonderful, loving son."

I couldn't stand it any longer, and I stepped loudly in the hallway before I pushed the door open. My mother turned toward me, her eyes bright and a smile on her lips. She grabbed her purse and patted my father's arm.

"Are we all set then? Ready to go?"

On the drive home, my mom chattered about everything and nothing. My father chimed in only when she specifically addressed him, and I was silent. As soon as the car pulled into the driveway, my mother jumped out and said something about getting dinner in the oven. My father climbed out of the driver's seat more slowly and opened the back door for me.

"Dad?" I said. "Can I ask you something?"

He smiled at me and tousled my hair. "Sure, kiddo. Anything. What's up? Woman trouble?" My father always did that, pretended that we were talking man-to-man and that I might really have some sort of adult problem that we could discuss.

I shook my head. "No. I just wanted to ask you. Am I going to die? I mean, like soon? Like sooner than most people?"

His face fell into the less familiar lines of sadness. He didn't ask me why I wanted to know or pretend that I was posing a silly question. Instead he answered me thoughtfully.

"No one knows the answer to that question, Nate. We're on this earth for a certain span of time, and truthfully, no one can tell us what the future holds. My grandfather lived to be a hundred and two, and my dad is still going strong. But I could walk out to get the paper in the morning and get hit by an out-of-control car. We just don't know. We try our best to stay healthy and safe, but life is a fragile thing sometimes."

"But what about me, about what's wrong with me? It

makes me different from other kids, but is it going to make me die younger, too?"

My father sank onto the bottom step of our front porch. "I don't know. I guess, if everything stayed exactly the same as it is right now, the answer would be yes. The same disease that makes your muscles weak and complicates your breathing sometimes would eventually end your life. But we know that nothing stays the same. There are scientists and doctors working to figure out how to cure you. You're working hard to get better, too. So you see, we could focus on the possibility that's there right at this moment, or we can choose to believe that there's a better future out there."

I thought about what he said, and I nodded to show that I had listened. And I really had. I decided that I was going to do everything I could to live as long as possible, and I was also going to make sure that I lived as fully as I could. I had a good reason to want to live, the best reason in the world, actually.

I was in love.

I don't know when I realized that I was in love with Quinn. I had loved her all my life, that was for sure. Along with Leo, she was my best friend. But Quinn was always more patient with me than even Leo was. She chose me more often than he did. I knew that making choice didn't help her social life, but she did it anyway.

But the summer before we started junior high, something changed. Not Quinn, although she was growing up and getting prettier every day. It was me. That August, when my family was about to go to my grandparents' house in the mountains and Quinn's family was heading to the shore, I was grumpy. I couldn't figure out why; I loved our two weeks in the Poconos. We hiked trails and played in the creek and sat around reading for hours.

Then the night before I left, Quinn came over to say good-bye. She gave me a typical Quinn hug—fierce and tight and full of her particular brand of love—and she said, "I guess I'll see you the first day of school!"

And just like that, I knew. I was in a perpetual bad mood because I was going to have to go two weeks without my best friend, who, as it turned out, was also the love of my life.

I spent most of that night trying to figure out how I could get Quinn to come to the Poconos with us. Or how I could go to the beach with her family. Of course, it wasn't possible. My mom never would let me be away from her for that long; she always worried if I were out of her sight for longer than a typical school day. And Quinn was an only child, like me. Her mom and dad had planned this week at the beach especially for her. They wouldn't let her go with us, and even if they would, how could I explain this sudden need not to be away from her?

So the next morning, I got into the car with my parents, and we drove west. I stared out the window as we crossed the Walt Whitman Bridge into Pennsylvania. My mother was talking about everything she wanted to do on vacation, all the food she'd brought to cook delicious meals. My dad was in a good mood, too. It was his parents we stayed with during these two weeks, and he enjoyed that family time.

We had been the car almost an hour before my mother noticed that I was quiet. I shrugged and told her that I was tired, that I hadn't slept well. A few minutes later, so they wouldn't guess that my sleeplessness was related to my question, I spoke up.

"Mom? Will I be able to get married some day?" I tried to make it a casual question, something that had just randomly gone through my mind.

I caught the quick glance my parents exchanged, and then

my mother turned around in her seat.

"Why do you ask? You planning to propose to someone soon?"

I stifled a sigh. Just once I wished they would take me seriously and give me a straight answer.

"I just wondered, that's all. You know, with me being . . . different and all."

My dad met my eyes in the rearview mirror. "I think it's one of those things we talked about a few years back, bud. Your mom and I hope you can fall in love and get married. But since I'm thinking you're not going to be eloping any time soon, maybe we don't have to worry about it today."

"What made you ask that?" My mother tried to keep her voice light, but I could hear the curiosity and just a tinge of apprehension.

"Oh . . . I don't know. Just wondering about it."

We were all quiet for a while, and then my mother, still keeping her tone deceptively casual, remarked, "Quinn has really grown up this summer, hasn't she?"

I didn't know whether I really blushed, but my face felt hot. "Yeah, I guess," I mumbled.

"Leo is sprouting up, too," my father added. "I guess it shouldn't surprise me. Both his brothers are tall boys. Do you think Leo will play basketball next year?"

"I don't know." I wasn't really worried about Leo's potential in basketball. He was always going to play sports that I wouldn't be able to dream of trying. I was used to it, but since sports didn't interest me anyway, his prowess didn't bother me.

"Hard to believe the three of you are thirteen," my mother mused. "I remember when you were all babies, and Lisa and I used to tease Quinn's mom about one of you boys being her son-in-law one day."

"Seriously, Mom." I rolled my eyes. "We're not babies anymore."

"No, you're not," she agreed. "And things are going to change soon. I hope you and Leo and Quinn will be friends forever. But now that you're getting older, you might find that Quinn wants to start spending more time with other girls. She may begin dating, even."

The idea of Quinn—*my* Quinn—dating someone other than me made me feel like I did when my lungs were tightening. I couldn't take it, and I began rubbing my chest absently, trying to loosen the muscles.

"Nate! Are you okay?" My mom twisted around in her seat, concern all over her face. "Do we need to stop?"

"No, I'm fine," I told her. "Sorry. Just habit, I guess."

She looked both relieved and suspicious, but she nodded. "Okay. Why don't you try to catch some sleep? We've still got another couple of hours."

I closed my eyes and lay my head back against the seat, but in my head, all I could see was Quinn. It had suddenly struck me that having her for my own might not be as easy as I thought. What if she didn't love me?

I made up my mind in that moment. I would make her fall in love with me. That was all there was to it.

★ Six ★

Leo

I KNEW QUINN AND NATE WEREN'T REALLY EXCITED TO begin junior high, but I thought it was going to be great. We'd get to change classes, so I wouldn't be bored sitting in the same classroom with the same teacher for seven hours a day. And we'd get to have real lockers, which sounded pretty cool. Best of all, I'd finally be able to play honest-to-goodness sports, not the baby kind where they never really kept score or told us who won. Our junior high had football, basketball, soccer, baseball and track teams. I wanted to play them all, but my dad said I had to make a choice, or my schoolwork might suffer.

My brothers played basketball, and everyone kind of expected me to do the same. It was the bad thing about being the youngest of three boys; everyone expected me to be just like my brothers. But I really didn't like basketball, not the way I liked football. So I decided that was what I was going to play.

That summer before eighth grade, I spent most of my time mowing lawns. Simon and Danny, my brothers, had started the business when they were my age, and now I was part of it, too.

It was pretty cool to be earning money, even though my mom made me put most of it away for college. She said someday I would thank her. I told her I was going to get a football scholarship and get a free ride to whatever college I chose, but she said it was good to have a back-up plan.

I liked mowing lawns. Pushing the mower or using the trimmer, I had a lot of time to think. I also met new people, and I liked that. Most of them were older, but that was okay. Some of the old ladies would invite me to the porch for lemonade and cookies. The men would inspect my work carefully and nod approvingly, and that was cool. They told my parents that I was really responsible and did a good job, and I know that made my parents happy, too.

Sometimes I met kids, but most of the families who had kids my age didn't hire us to cut the grass; they would just have their own kid do it, which only makes sense. But this one family had all daughters, and I guess they didn't want girls doing yard work. So I did the lawn, and I met their oldest daughter. Her name was Sarah, and she was in the same grade as me. I guess she'd been in school with us for a while, but I'd never noticed her.

When we met, she was wearing a bathing suit and heading out to the family's pool. Now, I'd never noticed girls and what they wore before. I mean, yuck. Quinn never cared about what she had on as long as it didn't get in her way. But seeing Sarah in this bathing suit kind of made me look twice. She was really pretty, in a different way, and she smiled and waved at me.

The next time I was at her house doing the lawn, she came out and brought me a drink. It was really hot, and I was grateful for both the break and the ice water. I stood there gulping it down, trying not to be impolite about it, and she started talking. She told me that she knew me from school.

"You hang out with the girl who has all that curly hair and that kid who—" She stopped, and I knew exactly how she was going to describe Nate. With most people, I'd get mad, but I could tell she didn't mean it in a cruel way.

"Yeah. That's Quinn and Nate. We've been friends as long as I can remember."

"Wow, that's cool. We've only lived here for about a year, so I haven't known anyone that long." Sarah smiled up at me, shading her eyes with her hand. I noticed that her fingers were long and her nails were painted bright pink.

"Where did you live before?"

"Chicago. And before that, California. And before that, Texas. My dad is a project manager, so we move all the time."

"I've never lived anywhere but New Jersey," I admitted. "But I like it here, so that's okay."

"So . . ." Sarah drew out the syllable. She was rubbing her bare foot absently across the newly mown grass, and she kept her eyes on the ground. "Quinn, you said her name was—is she, like, your girlfriend?"

"Quinn?" I was so surprised by the question that I couldn't answer for a minute. "No! No, she's my friend. One of my best friends. I don't have a girlfriend. And Quinn's not like that, anyway. She's not interested in that kind of thing." Even as I said it, I wondered. I hadn't ever asked Quinn anything like that, but she was the least girly-girl I knew. She never said she liked a boy or even paid attention to anyone but Nate and me. None of us was interested in dating or anything. At least, not until now.

"Well, I guess with all of us starting junior high in a few weeks, we're going to get interested in it!" Sarah said brightly. "They have dances and everything . . . I can't wait. I think it'll be fun."

"I guess so." My tone was doubtful. I couldn't imagine what a dance would be like, and trying to picture the people I knew dancing with each other was really kind of funny. I decided it would be safer to change the subject.

"I'm going to play football this fall," I announced. "It's going to be awesome."

"Football? Really?" Sarah's smile widened. "I'm going out for cheerleading. So I guess I'll see you at the games!"

"Yeah, I guess so—" Whatever I might have said next was lost in a torrent of water as the sprinklers under our feet suddenly turned on. Within seconds I was drenched, and Sarah was shrieking and trying to get away from the spray.

"Oh, my gosh!" She was wringing her black hair and giggling. "I thought they only went on at night and in the morning! Something must have messed up the timer." She looked at me, standing there dripping, and her giggles turned to full-blown laughter. "Well, you were pretty hot, weren't you?"

I managed a smile. "Yeah, I guess I'm cooled off now."

Sarah cocked an eyebrow at me. "Want a towel? We've got them around back by the pool."

"Nah. I'll just run home and change." And I would be literally running home; my brother usually picked me up from this job and took me to the next one. Since he could drive and I couldn't, I had to depend on him for the houses where we used our own equipment. But if he saw me soaking wet, I'd never hear the end of it.

"Listen, Sarah, can I push the mower over by your house? I'll just go get changed and come back to finish up. My brother is supposed to take me to the next client in about forty-five minutes. I think I can make it."

Sarah helped me move the mower and then I booked it for home. My mother just shook her head as I grabbed a dry set of clothes and ran back to Sarah's house. I had just finished the last strip of grass when Simon pulled up.

"That one took you long enough," he grumbled after we loaded the equipment. "What happen?"

"Sprinklers turned on," I told him. "Had to wait until they could turn them off until I could finish." I knew my mom wouldn't say anything; she was cool that way. I made it to the next client and got back to work. But I couldn't stop thinking about Sarah and how she had looked when the water had soaked her shorts and T-shirt.

I didn't see her again until the first day of school, when she came over to me in line. Nate and I had been there for a little bit before Quinn got to school. The whole thing was weird. First when Nate got there, he asked right away if I'd seen Quinn. Well, that wasn't weird—Nate always wants to know where she was, but there was something different about it that day. He tried to brush it off and said he hadn't seen her since he got home from vacation and wondered if she'd had a good time at the shore, but I swore he turned red when he said her name.

And then to make things even more bizarre, when Quinn did show up, she was wearing, like, a dress. I hadn't seen Quinn in anything but jeans or shorts since we were in kindergarten, except when her mom made her wear a dress on picture day. I was shocked.

But when I said something to tease her, to make her feel better about having to wear a dress—just so she understood that I knew her mom must've made her wear it—she got mad. She shot me a snappy comeback, but I could tell she was really annoyed. Who knew why? Nate told her looked pretty, and that seemed to make her feel a little better.

And then before I could really check out what was happening, why Nate was acting so off, I saw Sarah. She was wearing some kind of dress, too, but it just kind of floated around her. I couldn't take my eyes off her for a minute, and then Quinn made some kind of snarky comment about Sarah and how she was dressed. I realized as I stood there, too, that Sarah seemed a lot older than Quinn did. I wondered if she thought I looked younger than the boys in our class.

Quinn changed the subject, and she and Nate started talking about their vacations. I kept quiet. My family didn't take the kind of regular vacations Quinn and Nate's family did. My mother said that with three boys who were heading to college, we needed to save everything we could. We mostly took day trips and what my mom called backyard vacations.

And then I heard my name, and when I turned around, Sarah was standing next to me, smiling. I tried to play it cool, be nice without doing anything to make Quinn and Nate suspicious. We were just rehashing the whole sprinkler episode when the bell rang, and the crowd of kids around us surged into the school.

I lost Quinn and Nate, but Sarah stuck with me. I felt bad, because I had promised to help Nate at his locker. But by the time I found them, we were at my homeroom, and Nate was going in the room with me. Quinn made another comment about Sarah and about her being my girlfriend. I didn't like how that made me feel. On one hand, she wasn't my girlfriend. But part of me wouldn't have minded if she was. On the other hand, I didn't want to hurt Quinn's feelings, and I had the sense that inviting any girl into our little circle was going to do just that.

★ Seven ★

Nate

THE TWO WEEKS I SPENT WITH MY PARENTS IN THE
mountains of Pennsylvania were a roller coaster for
me. I would wake up in the morning, bursting with
excitement over my newly-realized love for Quinn. And then by
lunch time, I'd be brooding and depressed— sure that she could
never see me as more than her best friend from childhood. I
spent hours trying to remember whether Quinn had ever acted
interested in any boys in our class, and I spent an equal amount
of time remembering how often she had chosen to be with me
over other people.

By the time we got home, two days before school began, I
was nervous and jumpy. My parents turned to their fall-back
position of worrying that this was some new symptom of my
disease, but I explained that I was just anxious about the new
school. They bought that. My mom told me long stories about
her life as a teenager, and my dad just kept patting my shoulder,
telling me it would all work out.

I didn't call Quinn before school began because we never
did that. If I had called her just to talk, she would have known

something was up. So I suffered in silence by myself until my mother dropped me at school on the morning of the first day.

I scanned the lines of kids milling around in loosely formed lines, but there was no sign of Quinn. After a few minutes, Leo came up behind me and gave me his signature light punch on the arm.

"Hey, Nate. You ready for this?" He spun his finger around in a circle, encompassing the whole school, the kids, everything.

"I think so," I said. "Just another school, right? Hey, have you seen Quinn?"

"I don't think she's here yet. At least I haven't seen her." We both looked around, checking it all out. It was weird to be with older kids, people we hadn't seen since they'd left our elementary school. They looked a lot older than I remembered. Leo eased back until he was leaning against the brick wall of the school, and I moved to stand with him.

A few minutes later, Leo caught my eye and tilted his head. "There's Quinn." I turned and saw her mother's car, and then Quinn coming around from the passenger side. My heart began to pound. This was the first time I'd seen her since I really knew that I loved her, that I was *in* love with her. I couldn't remember how to act, what to say or where to look.

She looked so pretty. She was wearing a skirt that was made out of jeans material, and a pretty blue top. Her hair, always so curly and unruly, was partly pulled back into a clip so that I could see her face, her eyes bright as she caught sight of Leo and me.

She smiled, and my breath caught. She was beautiful. The girl I loved, the girl who would always have my heart, was really and truly beautiful. I wanted to run and jump and shout and do all those things I'd never been able to do, just to show the world how I felt.

I smiled back as she approached us and blurted out the first thing I could think to say. "Hey, Quinn. You look really pretty."

She looked down as if she'd forgotten what she was wearing and ran a hand down the skirt. "Thanks, Nate." For a fleeting moment I had her full attention and her gratitude, and it felt amazing.

And then I saw her glance up at Leo, who was still standing against the wall. Something flickered in her eyes that I didn't quite understand. Leo made some comment about how her mother must have dressed her, and Quinn snapped back. She lost the look of eagerness that I'd seen on her face a few minutes earlier.

I was confused, wondering what had changed. Quinn and Leo had always had that kind of relationship, where he teased her and she shot back at him. I didn't know why his joking would have bothered her now.

Leo looked off over her shoulder, and this time it was his eyes that flared. Obviously he saw someone or something that interested him. Quinn followed his gaze, and her face changed again. It wasn't curiosity so much as it was hurt. I was still confused.

Quinn snapped at Leo again, something about kick ball which I didn't quite understand. And then Leo wisely changed the subject, asking about my vacation. I was eager to tell them both about the canoeing we had done, how excited my dad had been when I could handle a canoe on my own; the idea of going out for something like crew gave me hope that they might be something me, a way to be more in Quinn's eyes.

Before I could tell them too much about it, a girl walked over behind Leo and said hello. Her name was Sarah. I was curious, since I couldn't figure out how Leo would have met her, but he explained that her family was a client in the lawn mowing business. For some reason, it made Quinn really mad. I could tell that.

The bell rang, and everyone surged forward toward the doors. Quinn stayed close to me, and I knew she was making sure I didn't get knocked over by the bigger kids. We found our lockers, and I was able to work mine without any problem. Quinn was grumbling at hers, and then she turned to me.

"Where's Leo?"

I shrugged. We had lost him in the crowd. But since he and I were in the same homeroom, I was pretty sure we'd catch up to him later.

Sure enough, he was just about to go into the classroom when we got there. Quinn snapped at him again, and he seemed embarrassed about the fact that she referred to Sarah as his girlfriend. Before they could get too far into this discussion, I saw that the teacher had risen from her desk and was beginning to take attendance. I pulled Leo into the room with me, and turned just in time to see Quinn wave to me before she shot Leo another dirty look.

Leo and I found two desks next to each other, and he flopped down in the chair. "What's her issue, anyway?" he grumbled.

I shrugged. "I guess maybe she just didn't feel like getting teased today. Maybe she's nervous about the new school." I waited a beat and then went on. "She did look really pretty today, though."

"Yeah," Leo conceded. "But she was acting like—I don't know. Girls are just crazy sometimes, I guess."

I thought about it for a long time as the teacher went through the typical first day of school spiel. Quinn had seemed

all right when she was with me. It was only Leo that was bothering her. And she had clearly been hurt when he didn't compliment her the same way I had.

A new thought dawned in my mind, more troublesome
than I cared to admit. What if Quinn really didn't feel the same
away about me that I did about her? What if she was in love
with someone else? And worst of all, what if that someone else
was Leo?

My palms began to sweat, and my heart pounded again.
These were my two best friends. What would I do if Quinn was
going to break my heart?

★ Eight ★

Quinn

EIGHTH GRADE WAS A SPECIAL KIND OF HELL FOR ME. Things were changing, and I didn't like it.

First there was Leo. He had always been the more popular one of our little group. His looks and his sports ability gave him more of an in with the other kids than Nate and I had. It had never seemed to make a difference between the three of us, but now it did. Suddenly Leo wanted to go to school dances. He wanted to hang out with the other kids, and although he invited Nate and me along, both of us knew that it wouldn't work.

And then there were the girls. It seemed as though Leo was always surrounded with a bunch of giggling, smirking girls who flirted and teased him, wanted him to eat lunch with them, walk home with them . . . it made me insane. Couldn't he see how much this was hurting Nate and me?

Something else was going on with Nate. He had taken to calling me every night, just to talk and check in. The problem was that we spent most of the school day together, and there just wasn't much to talk about at the end of the day. So I dreaded those phone conversations with their long and awkward silences. What was more disconcerting was that I often caught him staring at me the same way that Leo stared at other girls. It made me uncomfortable.

One December day, I came home from school and threw my books on the kitchen table. My mother was standing at the sink, and she turned to give me a look.

"Sorry," I mumbled.

"Tough day?" she inquired, drying her hands as she came to sit next to me.

I sighed. "School was okay. But it's so hard, Mom. Leo is just—he's just weird now. He likes all these girls, and he hangs out with them, and it seems like he just doesn't have time for me and Nate anymore. It's not like it used to be."

My mother reached over and smoothed my hair away from my face. "You're all growing up, sweetie. You can't expect everything to stay the same forever. So Leo is making some new friends. That's okay. You could do that, too."

"I don't *need* new friends," I cried. "I like the ones I have. At least I did when they weren't acting like idiots."

"Why, what's going with Nate? Is he hanging around with other kids, too?"

I shook my head. "No. Nate doesn't hang out with anyone but me. But he's with me all the time, and he looks at me—" I felt my face grow warm. "I just don't like the way he looks at me."

"Ah." My mother smiled and touched my cheek. "So it seems Nate has a crush on you. Well, I can't say I'm surprised. I wondered when one of the boys was going to realize what a beauty they had in their midst."

"Mom!" I groaned, rolling my eyes. "Seriously. We're friends. We've known each other literally forever. How could you say that?"

"What bothers you more, Quinn? The fact that Nate might have feelings for you, or the idea that Leo might not?"

To my utter mortification, tears filled my eyes. I dropped my head onto my folded arms.

"I love Nate, Mom. He's like—I don't know, kind of the brother I never had. And I always thought Leo was the same way. But then this year, when all these girls have been fussing over Leo, I felt—I guess I felt jealous. Jealous that he pays them so much attention and doesn't really seem to care about me anymore."

"I don't blame you, sweetie. But let me ask you this. If it were Nate the girls were fawning over, would that bother you as much?"

"I don't know. I guess so. I just can't imagine it. Nate depends on me for everything. Maybe it might be a relief if he had someone else to count on."

My mom nodded. "Interesting. Well, let me give you some advice. Just ride this out. Keep being Nate's friend, but be Leo's friend, too. Don't let him see that you're bothered by the girls. Pretty soon he'll realize what—or who—he really wants." She stood to give me a hug. "Have I told you lately that I wouldn't be thirteen again for all the money in the world? But don't let it make you sad, love. It'll all come out right in the end."

I tried to smile and believe that she was right. But I had a feeling that eighth grade was going to be a long year.

★ Nine ★

Leo

BY THE TIME WE STARTED OUR JUNIOR YEAR IN HIGH school, I was eating, breathing and sleeping football. And I loved it. I never complained about the day-long practices in a hundred-degree heat or about the games where they had to clear snow from the ground so that we could see the yard markers. As long as I was out on the field, I was in heaven.

The rest of my life wasn't so bad, either. I had a pretty cool group of friends. Most of them were football players, too, because it was easier to hang with guys who knew what I was talking about. And the girls were usually cheerleaders or the girlfriends of the football players. They understood the game and the commitment.

I still saw Nate and Quinn pretty often, although they weren't part of my main crowd. Nate had gotten involved in rowing crew, and he spent long hours down at the river, practicing and competing. It was beginning to show, too. Although he was still smaller than the rest of us and still had that sort of scrawny look to his face, his arms and chest had filled out, and he seemed to have found some kind of quiet confidence that he'd never had before.

Quinn was a different story. She had grown, too, until she was among the tallest girls in our class. She had long legs and arms, but she carried herself with a sort of grace I didn't notice in the other girls. Her face had slimmed and softened, too. The only thing that hadn't really changed was her hair, which was still long and curly and always in her way. I knew that she had made friends with a few girls who worked on the high school newspaper, and when I asked her about it, she went on and on about the joys of writing. I didn't get it myself, but since she helped me sometimes with my essays and term papers, I kept my mouth shut.

Other boys in school had begun to notice Quinn, too. Some of them asked me about her, what she was really like, and I knew a few tried to ask her out. Whenever that happened, my chest got tight, and I wanted to punch something, which I knew made no sense. I didn't want to admit to myself that my feelings toward the girl who'd gone skinny-dipping with me in our baby pool were . . . complicated. Yeah, I dreamed about her sometimes. Yeah, there were times when she turned a certain way, looked at me or smiled when I felt like I couldn't breathe. But she was *Quinn*, the same perfect, innocent girl who'd been almost part of me our whole lives. And I'd made choices that meant I wasn't good for her. Not anymore.

To my secret relief, Quinn never seemed interested in the guys who asked her out. She was always nice enough to everyone, but she just didn't date. I couldn't figure out why. She didn't seem to want the same popularity that I had, and there were times I wondered if she thought less of me because I did want it.

I was doing okay in the girl department. I didn't have

a steady girlfriend, but I dated. I hooked up. I liked to hang around with all of my friends most of the time, but a movie or a dance with a pretty girl was okay, too. Whenever my mom or my brothers teased me about having a date though, I had to remind them that for me, football came first. If a girl didn't get that, she didn't get me.

I asked Nate once if Quinn liked any particular boy. He got the funniest look on his face and shrugged.

"Maybe she just doesn't want to date," he mumbled. "Maybe she doesn't feel like she needs to."

I saw that his face had turned red, and right away I got it. Nate didn't want Quinn to be interested in any boy—not in any boy other than him, that is. I kind of felt sorry for him, because although I knew that Quinn loved Nate as her best friend and would always be loyal to him, I didn't think she cared about him that way. I wondered if Nate realized that.

A few weeks into school that year, I passed Quinn in the hallway right after the last bell. She was clutching a pile of notebooks to her chest and walking with her head down. Behind her a bunch of cheerleaders, dressed for the pep rally that day, were giggling.

Before I could say hello, one of the cheerleaders, Trish, reached deftly around Quinn and knocked a book out of her arms. I started to smile, thinking it was the kind of thing a guy would do to a buddy, but then I saw Quinn's reaction. Her face flushed, and she jerked away before leaning down to retrieve her book.

"What's the matter, queen? Clumsy today?" The girls surrounded her, hemming her in.

Quinn pressed her lips together tightly and didn't answer. She began to stand up, and another cheerleader shoved her back down.

"We didn't like what you wrote about the squad. You need to stop saying stuff like that."

"It's an editorial. Opinion. Look it up. It means I can write what I want."

I winced. That wasn't what these girls wanted to hear. I knew them all from parties and from away games, when we traveled together on the bus, but these three weren't people I generally hung around with. They tended toward meanness, and I didn't have time for that shit.

"Leave her alone." I stepped forward and stood in front of Quinn. "What the hell's wrong with you?"

One of the cheerleaders smirked at me. "This isn't your business, Leo. We've got it. Run along."

"She's a friend of mine, and she didn't do anything to you. So it's my business." I grabbed Quinn's hand and hauled her up. Trish looked as though she wanted to say something else, but one of the other girls snagged her arm and pulled her away. She threw one more poisonous glare over her shoulder as they headed down the hallway.

I glanced down at Quinn. "What was that all about?"

She was standing frozen, and I realized that she was staring at our still-joined hands. I released hers, and she looked away.

"It was nothing," Quinn mumbled. "Stupid cheerleaders."

"What were they talking about? What did you write to set them off?" I persisted.

She looked me full in the face for the first time. "I guess this means you don't make it a priority to read my editorials." There was something in her voice that wasn't quite humor mixed with a little bit of hurt, and guilt made me snap back.

"I don't read anything but school stuff and play books during football season. No time. So what did you do?"

"I didn't *do* anything. I wrote an opinion piece about the special treatment the cheerleaders get, nothing that everyone else in the school isn't thinking. And some of them obviously didn't like it. No big deal."

I gritted my teeth and ran a hand through my hair. "Mia, are you crazy? That's not exactly the way to make friends."

There it was again, that flare of pain in her eyes. "Thanks. I didn't know I needed help making friends. I used to have some really good ones."

I ignored the sarcasm. "I'm still your friend, Quinn, you know that. But couldn't you try a little harder? I mean, with other people?"

"The people I want for friends wouldn't expect me to be a phony. They would accept me for who I am."

"You don't think I do?" That stung, maybe because it felt a little bit true.

"I don't know, Leo. Do you even know who I am anymore?" She jerked her arms away and stalked off down the hall. I didn't try to follow her.

★ Ten ★

Quinn

IF JUNIOR HIGH WAS HELL FOR ME, HIGH SCHOOL WAS EVEN worse. I watched the people around me change and grow, but it felt like I was standing still. And by the autumn of our junior year, I was more than ready for things to change. Not just how my classmates treated me—though that would've been nice, too—but how I saw myself . . . and definitely how Leo saw me.

Nate spent so much of his time on the water once he joined crew that I hardly saw him at all. After school, his mom picked him up and drove him to the river for practice. I went to as many of his races as I could, but even there I didn't see him for long. He told me though that it made him feel stronger when I was there watching.

"When I know you're there, it's like I could row for miles," he said, eyes shining. I smiled, but I couldn't meet his gaze. Nate had been making it abundantly clear that he thought of me as more than a friend, and I walked a very fine line between ignoring it and accidentally encouraging him. I didn't want to lose my friend, but I knew I didn't like him that way. Mostly

I knew that because there *was* someone who made my heart pound.

Leo was all about football these days. He never talked about anything else, and he had a whole new group of friends who spoke the same language. I didn't think he realized that most of these people looked at Nate and me the same way they would a bug on the sidewalk; they would as soon step on us rather than bother to walk around us. I didn't try to point this out to Leo because he was so clearly happy with life the way it was.

But it was killing me. I never missed a football game, but it was pure torture to sit in the stands, watching him play, knowing that it really didn't matter to him whether or not I was there. And more often than not, after the game ended, Leo would be surrounded by cheerleaders and other popular girls. Sometimes, he would be holding the hand of one of them. Most everyone went to the Starlight Diner after football games, and Nate and I went a few times, too. Leo usually managed to wave at us, or even to stop at our table sometimes, but he was always with a girl who was looking up adoringly at him. There was only so much of that I could take.

I went out of my way to support the athletic interests of my best friends, but I couldn't quite say they did the same. Not that I played any sports, of course, and maybe that was the problem. Nate tried to encourage me in my extracurricular activities, but he didn't understand my love for writing or why I loved hanging out in the editorial office. Newspaper was the one bright spot in my entire high school career, and I'd actually made friends with people who worked on the paper with me. They were a mixed bunch, some of them nerdy like me, and a few who were on the edge of the popular crowd.

The teacher who ran the journalism club was cool, too.

Ms. Nelson was young and had lots of energy, and she was always giving us fun assignments. I was on my way to meet with her when I heard the familiar voice behind me.

"*Some* people think they're so much better than the rest of us. So much smarter." *Trish Dawson.* Perfect. Just who I needed to deal with today.

I clenched my jaw and kept walking. I'd learned through painful experience that ignoring girls like Trish was the only way to deal with them. It didn't make them stop, and it definitely didn't make me feel better, but pretending they didn't exist let me hold onto some dignity.

"Hey, queer queen. I'm talking to you." She was closer to me than I'd thought, and so I wasn't ready when she reached around and knocked the notebooks out of my arms.

I felt my face go hot as I stopped to pick up the books. This wasn't the first time I'd been picked on, so I figured they'd laugh and move away. But this time, they didn't. Trish and the other three girls formed a small, tight circle around me, all of them smirking.

"What's the matter, queen? Clumsy today?" Original insults weren't Trish's strong suit. She'd been calling me queen or queer queen since freshman year. I guessed Quinn didn't lend itself to anything more demeaning.

I began to stand up, all of my stuff in one hand, but one of the girls shoved at my shoulder, pushing me back.

"We didn't like what you wrote about the cheer squad. You need to stop saying stuff like that."

"It's an editorial. *My* opinion. I can write what I want."

Trish's face took on an ugly sneer. "No one cares what you think. So maybe you should—"

"Leave her alone." *Leo.* Now my heart was pounding in earnest. He stood on the other side of Trish, his muscled arms folded over his broad chest. "What the hell's wrong with you?"

Kylie, Trish's right-hand minion, glanced at him. "This isn't any of your business, Leo. We've got it. Run along."

"She's a friend of mine, and she didn't do anything to you. So it's my business." He pushed between Trish and Kylie, grabbed my hand and pulled me to my feet. The girls were still surrounding us, but all I could think was *Leo is holding my hand.* His palm was pressed against mine, warm and so full of strength I wanted to cry.

Trish glared at me, one finely-arched eyebrow raised. I knew that look; it meant *we'll finish this later.* Fabulous.

She and her posse turned and stalked away, still giggling. But I didn't even spare them a glance, because I couldn't tear my eyes away from my hand in Leo's. My fingers were completely enveloped in his grasp. He was saying something, but I was too preoccupied by the buzzing in my ears to pay attention.

"Quinn, what was that all about?" He repeated himself, frowning, and let go of my hand. I felt immediately bereft.

"Um, it was nothing." I took a step back away from Leo. "Stupid cheerleaders."

His forehead creased, and I realized I was talking crap about girls who were probably his friends now. Maybe more than friends. God only knew what he'd done with some of them; I'd heard stories about football parties. I only hoped he hadn't hooked up with Trish. I could handle anything but that.

"What were they talking about? What did you write to set them off?"

Now annoyance flared, almost overshadowing the want surging through my veins. It was typical Leo these days; he'd never assume I was blameless. It had to be me who'd written something wrong.

Plus, this confirmed something I'd suspected—that Leo

didn't read my articles. He gave my work at the school paper great lip-service, but now I knew the truth. "Maybe if you read the school newspaper now and then, you'd know. I guess this means you don't make it a priority to read my editorials."

"I don't read anything but school stuff during football season." He shook his head. "No time. So what did you do?"

"I didn't *do* anything." I hissed out the words. Of course, it was my fault that those bitches were threatened by me. Leo would see it that way. Once upon a time he would've stuck up for me no matter what, but those days were in the past. "I wrote an opinion piece about the special treatment the cheerleaders get. It's nothing that everyone else in the school isn't thinking. Guess some of them obviously didn't like it. No biggie."

Leo ran a hand through his hair, his go-to gesture when he was exasperated. "Mia, are you crazy? That's not exactly the way to make friends."

Pain sliced through me. Leo rarely used his special nickname for me anymore, and hearing him say it—his voice husky—reminded me of how far apart we'd drifted. And now he was giving me advice on finding friends? What kind of loser did he think I was?

"Thanks. I didn't know I needed help making friends. I used to have some really good ones." The words were laced with sarcasm.

Leo winced. "I'm still your friend, Quinn, you know that. But couldn't you try a little harder? I mean, with other people?"

The truth was right there in his voice. I was an embarrassment to him. Poor Quinn, the geeky girl who just couldn't seem to find her own circle. The girl who reminded Leo of a part of him he'd turned his back on when football and popularity became more important. The impact of what he was saying hurt, and I lashed out in response.

"The people I'd want for my friends wouldn't expect me to be a phony. They would accept me for who I am." I leaned forward a little, just to make sure he heard me.

"You don't think I do?" Leo looked stricken, as though what I'd said was some huge revelation.

Anger bubbled up inside me. I was sick of the whole thing. Sick of mooning after this boy, sick of the pain of losing my best friend. Sick of him pretending nothing had changed, when everyone else in the world knew that it had. I took another step back and spoke in a low voice.

"I don't know, Leo. Do you even know who I am anymore?"

Before he could respond, I wheeled around and started walking away as fast as I could. I knew he wouldn't follow me, though in my fantasy world, Leo did chase after me, grab me by the arm and push me up against the wall between two sets of lockers. What happened next in my daydreams was something I couldn't bear to think about just now.

I made it to the newspaper office without breaking down into tears, which I considered to be a minor victory. Jake Donavan was sitting at a desk, and he glanced up at me with a smile.

"Hey, Q! We're getting lots of response on your cheerleader editorial. Want to read some of the comments?"

Gritting my teeth, I slid a chair out from beneath the long, cluttered counter that went all the way around the room. "I just got an up-close and personal comment on that piece, thanks."

Jake frowned. "What happened?"

I slumped back in the chair. "I had a run-in with Trish. Let's just say her response was decidedly in the against column. She's not a happy camper."

"Shit." He spun his chair around to face me. "When you say run-in, do you mean she spewed venom at you, or . . . she didn't, like, actually get physical, did she?"

I quirked at eyebrow at him. "Are you worried about me, or are you intrigued by the idea of a chick fight?"

Jake laughed. "Your opinion of the male of the species could use some work, Q. Of course I was just concerned about you." His lips curved up into a wicked smile. "But if you want to tell me how she pushed you down, and then you pulled her hair, please. Feel free."

"Perv." I crumpled up a sheet of newsprint and tossed it at him. "Sorry, but it didn't get that involved. She knocked my books down, and then she and her goonies stood over me while I was trying to pick them up. I guess she might've gone further if—" I stopped abruptly, and Jake waved his hand in a go-on gesture.

"If?"

"If Leo hadn't been there. He stepped in, and they left. Not without a subtle warning that we weren't quite finished, but you know them. There's not much long-term memory there. She'll forget me the next time she has to memorize another cheer routine."

"You're probably not wrong. But still . . . if she gives you trouble, say something to Ms. Nelson. She'll take care of it."

I leaned back in my chair and propped my feet on the counter desk. "She always tells us that genuine journalism can sometimes make people edgy, and we need to be prepared to deal with the fallout. Right?"

"Sure, but Q, this is a high school newspaper, not the *Washington Post*. No one expects you to put your safety on the line for the sake of an editorial."

"Why would you be putting your safety on the line?"

A new voice from the doorway of the newspaper office made both Jake and me jerk our attention in that direction. Nate stood there, leaning against the jamb with what might've looked like casual nonchalance in other guys. But I knew he did that to rest his legs after the long walk down the hallway. Rowing crew had helped Nate improve his strength, no doubt, but it couldn't take away the damage caused by the degenerative muscle disease.

"Hey, Nate." I smiled, craning my head back so I could see him better. "I thought you had practice today."

"Canceled." His eyes flickered over to Jake. "Hey, man."

I motioned him into the room. "Come on in and sit down. Jake and I were just talking about the response to my cheerleader piece."

Nate didn't budge from the door, but he shifted his laser-sharp focus on me. "What happened?"

"Nothing really. Tell you about it later. Are you heading home now?"

"Yeah, I was about to. I wanted to see if you were ready to go, too. It's a nice day for a walk."

I hesitated, for more than one reason. We all lived fairly close to the high school, but what was easy walking distance for me wasn't necessarily the same for Nate. I couldn't bring that up in front of Jake, though. Nate was sensitive enough about how other guys saw him; the last thing I needed to do was coddle him in front of an audience.

I had a more selfish angle, too, though. I'd planned on spending at least another hour here in the newspaper office, maybe brainstorming for my next opinion piece and just hanging out with Jake and anyone else who happened to wander in. These were *my* people, my friends. One of the benefits of Nate getting involved in crew was that it freed me to do my own thing for the first time in . . . well, ever. I didn't have to feel guilty about leaving him out. And I liked that.

Jake must have misinterpreted the reason that I didn't respond immediately to Nate. He gave my rolling chair a little kick, knocking my feet off the desk.

"Nothing's happening here, Q. Go on home for now. Probably better you stay out of Trish's orbit anyway. At least until she cools down."

I heaved a deep sigh. "Fine. But I want a shot at that article on tenure for teachers. I can think of more than a few in this school who're only still here because the union protects them."

"Q, that's going to be straightforward report. No bias allowed. Remember? That's only way Ms. Nelson would okay it."

"Bias? Me?" I stood up and fluttered my eyelids in feigned innocence. "I am all about the journalistic integrity and impartiality. You know that."

Jake rolled his eyes. "Get the hell out of here, would you? I'll make sure you're in the running."

"Fine." I stuck out my tongue at our editor-in-chief as I scooped my books. "See you tomorrow, Jake."

"Later, Q. Bye, Nate."

Nate answered only with a curt nod, letting me pass him through the doorway before he slowly pushed off and walked alongside.

"You need to stop at your locker?" His tone when it was just the two of us was much gentler, less defensive.

"Nope. I'm good."

We walked toward the side doors of the school, both of us silent. I slowed my steps to accommodate Nate's, as I always had. Anyone watching us might think we were a typical couple, taking our time as we meandered down the hall, but I could still see the slight stutter and the occasional jerkiness of Nate's gait.

As soon as we were outside, on the sidewalk, Nate glanced down at me. "Want me to carry your books?"

"No." I brushed up against him, not quite shoving into his side, but almost. "I'm a strong, independent young woman, Nate. I carry my own damn books."

"Nice. I was just offering. Being a gentleman." He grinned, shaking his head.

"Duly noted and appreciated, but no, thanks." I stepped onto a cluster of acorns, relishing the satisfying crunch beneath the rubber sole of my sneaker. "The trees are so pretty, aren't they? If only they could stay like this and not fall. I hate winter, when they all look so dead."

A shadow passed over Nate's face. "Yeah, me too. But then spring comes. You just have to hold on long enough to get through the winter."

"I guess. Still. I'd be okay if we went right from fall to spring, with maybe a little bit of snow just on Christmas day."

"Customized weather, huh? Someone should get working on that." He kicked a pile of dried leaves. "Quinn, what happened with Trish?"

"Oh." A strand of my brown hair fell over my eyes, and I blew up a breath to brush it away. "It really wasn't anything. She didn't like what I wrote, and she tried to intimidate me. That was it."

"She just backed down?" Nate, all too familiar with the ways of bullies, sounded skeptical. "Really?"

"Well . . . no. It might've been worse, but Leo showed up and got her to leave." I tried to keep my own frustration out of my words, but it was impossible, especially when I was with Nate. He was the only other person who truly understood what it was like to see one of our best friends—the third in our Trio—change so much that he was more like a stranger these days.

"What did *Leo* do?"

I didn't miss the heavy irony. Nate's resentment of Leo was even greater than mine; on the rare occasions I was around both of them, I felt like the rope in a game of tug-of-war.

"Oh, he just sort of diffused the situation. Told Trish to cease and desist." I paused, wondering how much more I should share with Nate. "And then he basically told me that I was wrong for having written that op-ed piece."

"So it's your fault that Trish attacked you?" Nate shifted his backpack from one shoulder to the other, and I noticed tiny beads of sweat on his upper lip. I must've been walking too fast without realizing it. I gradually slowed my steps.

"He didn't come out and say that, but that's the way I took it. I might've gotten a little pissy with him. I think I hurt his feelings."

Nate scoffed. "Yeah, I doubt that. I know you try to give him the benefit of the doubt, Quinn, but Leo hasn't had feelings for a long time when it comes to us. He always looks at me like I'm . . . I don't know. The old teddy bear his mom refuses to throw away. Like he's outgrown me."

"I don't think that's true." The mad that had carried me after I'd turned my back on Leo was giving way to hurt. Misery was a band around my heart, squeezing until I felt like I was going to cry. I kept seeing Leo's face when we were arguing in the hallway. His expression had been almost one of . . . pity. Maybe Nate was right. But admitting that to myself was excruciating, since apparently some small part of me had been clinging to the belief that some day, Leo was going to fall in love with me. He was going to see me the same way I saw him, and he would realize that we really were meant to be together.

That faith was beginning to waver, though. It died a little each time I saw Leo walk off the football field with his arm around one cheerleader or another, and when I heard stories passed around school about how Leo the Lion—that was his nickname on the team—was more accurately Leo the Lover.

"You don't want to see it, but that's the way he acts. When you're around, it's not so bad, but when you're not, he ignores me. Or worse."

I wasn't sure I wanted to know what *worse* meant. Fortunately, we'd just reached my house, and I turned down my front walk. "Come on. Let's sit down for a minute."

Kicking the leaves from the brick step at the edge of the porch, I sank down, dropping my books onto the ground next to me. Nate took a minute to hook his backpack on the railing, and I turned my back on him for a moment, pretending to check one of my notebooks, intentionally giving him some privacy as he joined me. Going from standing to sitting and back again was always a little bit of a process for Nate, and I knew it embarrassed him for me to sit gawking while he made it happen.

Once I heard him exhale loudly, I knew it was my cue to shift attention back to him. I picked up the thread of our conversation while delicately skirting what he'd said last. "Nate, I'm not defending Leo. I think the way he treats us is shitty. I'm just saying, I don't think he actually realizes it sometimes. He looked genuinely surprised and hurt today when I said he didn't know me anymore."

"You said that to him?" Nate sounded both surprised and pleased.

"Yep." The errant strand of hair fell into my face again, but before I could blow it out of the way, Nate reached over and gently tucked it behind my ear. He trailed one finger over my jaw, just barely skimming the skin. I froze, painfully aware of how close he was sitting to me and the brush of his breath on my neck.

It was getting more and more difficult to ignore the hints Nate dropped about his feelings toward me. More than once, he'd acted as though we were already a couple. Even this afternoon, when he'd stopped at the newspaper office, there had been an air of possessiveness that transcended our reality— that we were best friends, and nothing else. But until Nate actually made a move, I couldn't very well tell him I didn't feel the same way about him. And I didn't want to hurt him—the very thought of that made my stomach clench and roll.

So I fell back onto my old stand-by: ignore and deflect. With a half-laugh that sounded forced even to my own ears, I ran both hands over the top of my head, pulling back my hair and holding it in ponytail form.

"God, I swear, this hair drives me nuts. I should just cut it all off."

"No way." Nate shifted back, and if there was disappointment on his face, I chose to ignore it. "Your hair is so pretty."

"Oh, you're sweet, Nate." I rolled a hair band off my wrist and secured it over my hair. "Don't worry. I don't think I could ever get rid of it. I just like to complain about how much it bugs me." I tightened the band and then scooted over just a little, so I could swivel and bend up my knee as I faced Nate.

"Listen, I know Leo's said and done some things that hurt you. And me, too. I'm not sticking up for him, but I'm not willing to make him our enemy either. We have too much history, the three of us. When I look at him, I try to see that boy instead of the football star. You know?"

Nate shrugged, but his eyes never left my face. "It always was easier for you to forgive Leo. You've always been willing to think the best of him."

"I'd do the same for you." I covered his hand where it rested on the warm brick of the porch.

"I'd never put you in a position where you'd have to do that." Nate pushed himself to his feet, teetering just slightly. He grabbed his backpack and slung it over his shoulder. "I gotta go. See you tomorrow, Quinn."

I watched him walk down the block with his careful precision, never sparing me a backwards glance. I'd thought I was miserable after my spat with Leo at school—and I had been— but now, with both of them unhappy with me, everything in my world felt wrong.

I buried my face in my hands and wished I could turn back time.

★ Eleven ★

Nate

"NATE. HELLO? EARTH TO NATHANIEL. YOUR mother's been talking to you for the last five minutes."

I glanced up from my plate. "What?"

My parents exchanged a look I was all too familiar with: worry and anxiety thinly veiled with amusement. They were wondering if me being preoccupied meant something was brewing inside me, something that could threaten my health and possibly land me in the hospital for days. And of course, along with that concern came the fear that this could be a symptom that my disease was progressing. I knew it was what they dreaded. Hell, I did, too. I'd been maintaining for so long, rolling along on a careful regiment of meds, monitored exercise and an enforced eight hours of sleep each night. It would be easy to fall into the trap of complacency, but after seventeen plus years of battling this motherfucker, health was nothing I ever took for granted.

"I'm fine." I stressed the two words. "I feel great. Not hiding anything. I'm just in a bad mood. You guys have to remember I'm a teenager. Aren't you, like, supposed to be ready for me being sullen and rude?"

My dad nodded, his expression solemn. "Sher, this is the day we've been waiting for. Get out his baby book. Mark down the day. Our son is being a moody teenager."

"If you think this is a first, you haven't been paying attention." My mother shook her head and resumed eating. "He's been surly and mopey before tonight." She winked at me. "On occasion, of course."

"I must've missed that." My dad took another serving of carrots, but I could feel his eyes on me. "Practice go okay today?"

"It was canceled." I dragged my fork through the white sauce my mom had made for the chicken.

"He walked home." My mom was trying to keep her tone casual, but I detected that underlying curiosity. "With Quinn, right?"

"Yeah." I pushed the plate away from me, my appetite gone. I knew that if I asked to be excused right now, it would only ramp up their worry. Instead, I leaned back in my chair, stretching out my legs beneath the table.

"Hey, Sheri, don't you have your chick meet up tonight? It's almost seven." My dad glanced at the clock on the microwave.

"Crap." My mother slid back her chair and jumped up. "I didn't realize it was so late. Can you guys—"

"We got clean up here. Go on, get going. Don't forget the wine, and tell Lisa and Carrie I said hey."

"You two are my heroes." Mom dropped a quick kiss on my dad's lips, patted my shoulder, snagged a bottle of wine and her keys from the counter and dashed out the back door. My father grinned at me, shaking his head.

"I swear that woman would be late to her own funeral." He

stood up, carrying his plate to the sink. "You cool to scrape and load if I clear and wipe?"

"Sure." That was our normal mode; any time I could stand still to do something, it worked out better for everyone.

We handled the dishes in comfortable silence, until I couldn't take it anymore. "Dad, can I ask you something?"

"Ah, are you finally going to break down and ask me to teach you my killer dance moves?" He executed a spin in the middle of the kitchen floor, complete with jazz hands. It was the kind of stuff that cracked my mom up, and I just shook my head, sighing.

"Sorry, no. How did you know Mom was the one?"

He brought me two empty bowls and leaned a hip against the counter. "The one what?"

"The one. You know. The one you wanted to marry. To love forever. Your soul mate, or whatever." I ran a plate under the water.

"Nate, you know, I'm not sure I believe in that stuff. The one? Like if I hadn't met your mother, I'd never have fallen in love with anyone, ever, and I'd have been alone my whole life? No, I don't buy that." When I shot him an incredulous look, he laughed. "That doesn't mean I don't love your mom. I do. She's awesome, and she's hot."

"Dad. Ew. God, who wants to hear that?"

"You asked, bud. Okay, I'm assuming you mean how did I fall in love with your mom." He crossed his arms over his chest. "It was the way she stood."

That made no sense at all to me. "What do you mean?"

"We were both working on a float for homecoming. My fraternity and her sorority were co-sponsoring it. I walked into this garage, down the college motor pool, and it was crowded with people milling around, drinking beer—hey, it was college."

Dad smirked. "Tons of people there, but I headed for the trailer where they were building the float. They had the chicken wire up already, and all these girls were stuffing it with tissue paper. Some of them were cute, but there was this chick standing off to the side, watching them, and she had her hands in the back pockets of her jeans—" He demonstrated. "And there was just something about the way she stood there. I'm not going to lie about it. A good part of her appeal was physical. I was twenty years old, and my first thought was, *hey, I'd tap that.*"

"Dad, this isn't what I was talking about." I loaded the last glass into the dishwasher and closed the door. "I get that you thought Mom was a total babe. But how did you get the ba— the guts to do something about it?"

"There wasn't any choice. I couldn't *not* walk over to her. I couldn't stop myself from talking to her. It was a while before she took me seriously, but once she did, I was smart enough not to let her go. Not to screw it up, you know?"

"Uh huh."

My father took the dish towel from my hand and folded it, draping the damp cloth over the handle of the dishwasher. "So. Quinn, huh?"

"Hmmm?" I pretended to be occupied with brushing crumbs off the counter. "What about Quinn?"

"Buddy, your mom and I might not be experts in many fields—well, okay, not in any. But we are very proficient in reading our only child. Mom's been a little worried about your feelings for Quinn for quite a while."

My shoulders slumped. "Why?"

Dad sighed and pulled out a chair, spinning it around to sit backward on it. I wondered if he realized how much I wished I could do the same, but I'd end up tangled up when my legs didn't do what I needed them to do. I leaned against the sink instead.

"Nate, like it or not, we're always going to be protective parents. We gave up apologizing for that a long time ago, and we give each other a lot of credit for the areas where we've been able to give you a little latitude. Like crew. But don't fool yourself—it isn't easy. We're always looking ahead to see where there may be danger spots for you. Risks." He took a deep breath and blew it out. "And Quinn is one of those."

When I began to protest, my father held up one hand. "Not on purpose. Your mom and I love that girl like she's our daughter, and we know she loves you, too. But maybe . . . maybe not the same way you love her."

My face was flushed; I could feel the warmth spreading down my neck. "How do you know that? Maybe she does and she just doesn't realize it yet."

"Nate." Dad's eyes locked on me. "Come on, son. One thing we've never done is lie to each other, right? I'm straight with you, and I expect you to be the same with me. It doesn't take a rocket scientist to know that Quinn's got it pretty bad for Leo."

My father was right. This wasn't news to me. I'd realized that Quinn loved Leo when we were in eighth grade, probably even before she knew it herself. Every day since that time, I'd waited for her to figure out that he was never going to return those feelings, but that I did. I held my breath for the moment when she looked at me and saw a guy who was going to love her with all he was for the rest of his life.

But it didn't happen. To Quinn, I was still just Nate, the kid she'd been sticking up for and championing as long as we could both remember. I'd fantasized about just yanking her into my arms and kissing her until she felt the truth. The only thing that stopped me was the fear that she'd kiss me back out of pity. Out of love for a friend, not out of passion.

"He doesn't deserve her." The words, filled with bitterness and yes, jealousy, flew from my mouth. "He's not even a good friend anymore. And he's fucking anything in a skirt." Any other time, I'd have been shocked at dropping the F-bomb in front of my father, but tonight, nothing mattered. What was he going to do? Ground me?

But my dad didn't even blink. He rubbed his forehead, frowning as he looked off into the distance, over my shoulder.

"Leo's feeling his oats, for sure. Lisa and Joe are a little worried about him. He's been partying hard, and his grades are slipping. You know, Simon and Danny were pretty hot on the basketball court, but nothing like what Leo's doing in football. Joe thinks he'll get a full ride at any college he likes—providing he doesn't screw it up."

"Which is just one more reason to keep Quinn away from him. He'd make her miserable."

"Or maybe she'd be the one to help him turn it all around. We don't know. But that's all out of our control, Nate. The only thing I can do in this situation is tell you to be careful. Don't build up your hopes about Quinn, okay, son? You're a terrific guy, and there's a shit-ton of girls who'd love to date someone like you. Don't tell your mom I said that." He grinned, but it began to fade as soon as he realized I wasn't smiling, too. "We don't want to see you waste your high school years pining away after someone who just can't return those feelings. Be Quinn's friend, but please, accept that she's never going to be more than that. Okay?"

He searched my face for acquiescence, and I knew if I didn't give in, he'd keep talking, keep saying the same shit that was tearing at my heart. He was worried, I got that. It was no secret that deep emotion could trigger a flare or make me more vulnerable to getting seriously sick. He and my mom thought that if my heart broke, it would put me at risk.

So I swallowed hard, gave a curt nod and stalked out of the kitchen and down the hall to my bedroom, where I could be alone with my stubbornly-unshattered dreams.

My mood didn't improve the next day. What my father had said lingered in my head, making me both angry and miserable at the same time. I avoided seeing Quinn, which was something I never did, and missing her only made me feel worse.

At lunch, I ignored the cafeteria and instead went outside, planning to spend the forty-five-minute period on one of the more remote benches that were scattered here and there on the school's lawn. I shivered as the autumn wind blew down the collar of my T-shirt and kicked myself for not grabbing my jacket before I left the building.

I'd just spotted an empty seat—and in the sun, no less—when Leo came loping across the grass, heading from the student parking lot toward the side doors of the school. He didn't see me at first; he had his head down and was wearing dark sunglasses. But when he did notice me, his steps slowed, and he paused just short of the sidewalk.

"Hey, Nate. Everything okay?"

"Maybe I should be asking you that. Where were you?" I nodded toward the parking lot. "You're sort of late."

"Yeah, sort of." He laughed once, kind of a harsh bark, and then pinched the bridge of his nose. "Late night, so I slept in a little. I didn't have anything pressing in class this morning, anyway."

I should've kept my mouth shut, but I was so fucking fed

up with him. So angry for reasons that he probably wouldn't begin to understand. "Oh, yeah? Last I heard, all our classes require attendance. That's not optional in high school. At least, it isn't for most of us. Maybe for the great Leo the Lion, the teachers make exceptions." I couldn't keep the snarl from creeping into my tone.

"What's wrong with you? Who pissed in your cereal?" He crossed his arms over his chest and scowled at me. "Did I do something that I don't remember? Did I miss someone's birthday or something? Because you and Quinn have both had bugs up your asses."

"Nice of you to notice, Leo. You must've been a real dick to her yesterday, you know? Quinn was pretty upset after school when I walked her home."

He pulled off the sunglasses, and I could see his bloodshot eyes were narrowed. "I didn't do anything. *She's* the one who's causing all the shit with my friends, and then I stand up for her, and she ends up yelling at me. Saying I don't even know her anymore. I don't know what she expects from me. God, I don't know what either of you want. It's like you want to punish me for having other friends. For playing football. For having a goddamn life."

"You know what, Leo? Keep your fucking friends, your football and your life. Quinn and I don't need you. We have each other."

Leo's lips thinned into a tight line. "You'd like that, wouldn't you? Come to think of it, Nate, maybe you should be thanking me instead of giving me hell. If Quinn's so mad at me, that just makes more room for you, doesn't it? You'll finally have her all to yourself, which is what you've always wanted."

He was so close to the truth, so dangerously near to saying exactly what I was feeling, that my palms began to sweat with both fury and nerves. "At least I'd be smart enough to hold onto her if—if I ever got that chance. I'd never throw away her friendship."

Leo ran a hand through his short hair, making a low noise under his breath. It sounded almost like a growl. "I haven't thrown away anything. I just—it's better for her if I don't spend too much time with her. Quinn's not like the other girls around here, and the chicks who hang around the football team would eat her alive." His lips curled. "If she doesn't stop writing stupid shit about them in the newspaper, that's going to happen anyway. She's making it so the whole school hates her. They all think she's some uptight—" He was going to say something else but broke off. "I just want her to stop and think before she ends up with no friends at all."

"That's not going to happen, because I'll always be there for her. That's what real friends do. So if you can't be that kind of friend, Leo, to both Quinn and me, just stay the hell away from us."

"Are you sure that's what Quinn wants from me?" His jaw tensed. "Because I'd disagree. I think Quinn wants . . . even more than friendship. That's the real issue here, isn't it? It's eating you up because even when we're fighting about something, she still wants me more than she'll ever want you." He leaned closer to me, dropping his voice into an intense whisper. "And even if she did go out with you, you'd never really know if she liked you for real or if was just . . . pity."

My hands curled into fists, and I wanted to hit him. *God,* I wanted to knock him down on his smug ass, but even with my blood boiling, I was smart enough to know that wouldn't end well. I was fairly sure Leo would never hit me back, but I also knew I'd be more likely to hurt myself than him if I threw a punch.

Before I could make up my mind, he jammed the glasses back on his face and stalked away, opening the metal door to the school with so much force that it banged against the brick wall as he disappeared into the building.

I stood still for a moment, still too mad to move. All of the jealousy I'd harbored against Leo—years and years of it—surged through my blood, and *God*, just for one day, I wanted the ability to take off after him, grab him by the arm, spin him around to face me and then pound that arrogant expression off his face. Most of the time, I didn't let what I couldn't do bother me. It was pointless to wish for things that were never going to be. But I'd have given a year of my life to change my body at that moment.

Instead, I did the smarter thing, just like I always did. I found my bench, sat down, and willed my heart to stop pounding. I forced my mind onto something completely unrelated to Leo or Quinn, working out complicated equations in my head. By the time the bell rang, signaling the end of lunch, I didn't feel any better but I was calmer.

I stood up, ignoring the stiffness in my hips, and followed the same path Leo had taken into the school. Both my locker and my first afternoon class were at this end of the building, and I'd learned long ago to plot out any short cuts I could find.

Because I was moving slowly, the hallways were almost empty as I trudged down a short corridor that linked the two wider passages. I'd just turned in front of the steps that led down to the gym when I heard the voice.

"Hey, gimp."

My heart beat sped up. I knew who was talking without even looking up, because it was the same person who'd been torturing me in one way or another since junior high. Brent Collins had taken a special and vicious dislike to me early on, and I wished I could say I had no idea why. But in this case, I'd started it. We'd had math together in eighth grade, and when Brent had made a stupid mistake in front of the whole class, I'd been only too happy to point it out, making him look bad. Those had been the days when I'd channeled all my physical frustration into humiliating my classmates intellectually whenever I could. Unfortunately, some of them hadn't forgotten the embarrassment.

"Running late today? Oh, shit, I forgot, you don't *run* anywhere, do you?" He came at me from the back, but I didn't turn around. Wildly, I tried to figure out the nearest classroom I could duck into.

"'Sup, Collins?"

I risked a glance up, hoping to see someone—anyone—who might distract Brent long enough for me to get away. But of course, I couldn't catch a break—the two guys who'd wandered our way were Brent's buddies, Karl Hays and Tim Stewart. All three of them were linebackers on the football team, big hulking boys who were probably more accurately described as men now.

"Not much." Brent grinned and held out a fist to be pounded. "Gimp here's having trouble keeping up. I was just gonna give him a hand." The glee in his voice was unmistakable, and my earlier mad boiled back to the surface.

"Just leave me the fuck alone."

All three of them hooted with laughter. "Oooooh, gimp's got a gutter mouth now, huh? Dude, we're just trying to give you a hand." Karl shoved at my back, sending me skittering as I tried to keep my balance.

"Yeah. You just stand still, and we'll push you along the floor. Help you get to class on time, huh? You don't want to be late, right? You're a brain, aren't you? Smarter than the rest of us. So you know if I give you a decent kick in that direction, you're gonna end up getting to class faster. Huh?"

"Tim's a decent punter. Did you see the distance he got a few weeks back?"

Karl laughed. "Yeah, he's good. I don't want to see a lot of his work, you know? But nice to know we have him when we're in need, am I right?"

All three of them grunted in what I assumed was agreement, and I took advantage of their distraction. I began to move away slowly, focusing on the closed door across the hallway.

"Hey, gimp, where d'you think you're going? We were talking with you." Tim stood with his hands on hips, blocking my way. "That's rude. You don't just leave when your bros are shootin' the shit with you."

"Hell, yeah. That's rude." Karl echoed the sentiment.

I could feel my face getting redder, and my lungs were tight. Panic was making it harder to breathe. I reeled forward, almost falling into Tim's massive chest.

"Whoa, bud. What's the matter? You wasted or something? You walk like you are. Not cool, man. Personal space and all." Tim gave me a shove, the kind that a normal guy would be able to absorb. But for me, already off-kilter, that kind of force made me stumble backward into Karl.

The good news was that thanks to his tree trunk-like body, I didn't end up on the floor. The bad news was that he didn't exactly catch me so much as he pushed me away, making the situation even worse. I was basically a helpless body in motion, with no way to stop as long as they kept playing with me.

"Dude! Three way. Send him to me." Brent wiggled his fingers as though he was cajoling them into tossing him a ball. Karl chortled, gripped my upper shoulders with his vice-like fingers and threw me toward Brent.

I probably would've been all right. Even at that point, with the three of them playing monkey in the middle and using me a human football, I was pretty sure they'd get bored in a few minutes, or a teacher would hear the commotion and stick his head out the door of a classroom to shout a warning. I just had to get through it.

But just as Karl sent me toward Brent, we all heard a fourth voice come from the other direction, down the hall.

"Hey! What the *fuck*?"

It was Leo, and judging by his tone, he was pissed. Still mad at me? I wasn't sure and frankly didn't care. What did matter to me was the fact that when he yelled, Brent looked up at him, an expression of *oh-shit* on his face, and neatly side-stepped me.

Again, that still wouldn't have been the end of the world. I might've ended up sprawled on the tile floor, my book flying away from my hand, and they probably would've jeered and teased more . . . but that would've been the end of it. Humiliation wasn't fun, but it didn't break bones.

But Brent was standing at the top of the short flight of steps that led down into the gym. I'd hated those steps since we'd started high school, because getting down them was awkward and embarrassing for me. There was a ramp alongside them, but more often than not, people stood there chatting, blocking my way, and having to push past was almost worse than navigating the steps. I was lucky that the rest of the school was on one-level, but still . . . I detested that staircase.

And now I was getting an up-close and personal look at my nemesis as I pitched down them headfirst.

Panic flooded me, even as I flailed my arms to grab for anything that might slow me down. But the fear didn't last long, because the side of my head banged hard into one of the iron posts that supported the middle railing, and after a cruel, sharp knife of pain, everything went dark and silent.

★ Twelve ★

Leo

U P UNTIL JUNIOR YEAR OF HIGH SCHOOL, I'D BEEN
pretty good about limiting my partying to Friday and
Saturday nights. During football season, of course,
Coach was strict about us sticking to a curfew during the
week leading up to a Friday night or Saturday afternoon game.
But there were ways around that, and I'd become an expert in
figuring out those ways.

This week, we were playing on Saturday, which meant no
one was too worried about Thursday night. I used the excuse
of a history group project meeting to convince my parents I
needed to be out. In the interest of maintaining plausibility, I
did go to the meeting, made some contributions . . . and then
when it ended, I headed over to Matt's house.

Matt Lampert and I had been buddies for years. Not close
friends, like Nate and Quinn and me, but more casual—the
way only boys seem to be able to manage. We didn't have deep
conversations, but we played baseball or soccer or football together—pick-up games, usually—and joked around, like pals
do.

When we'd started high school, we'd both made the football team. Matt played quarterback for our freshman squad, and I started out as a halfback, until the end of the year, when Coach noticed my speed and moved me to wide receiver. The varsity quarterback was young, only a year ahead of us, which meant Matt was stuck in JV. On the other hand, they were down receivers, which meant I got bumped up to varsity as a sophomore.

Matt had spent a lot of time grousing about the situation, but we'd worked together, both in regular practice and on our own time, so that when the varsity quarterback, Cole Hampton, was hurt toward the end of the season that year, Matt was able to take over. Since then, we'd been a fairly unstoppable duo, breaking a couple of county records already this year.

Matt was nicknamed Houdini, thanks to his ability to get out of any tight situation on the field, and I'd been labeled the Lion, which I knew came from my name more than any resemblance to that animal. That name had stuck after I'd made my third touchdown in one game and out of pure adrenaline-fueled glee, had let out a primal roar. Now the cheerleaders had made up a special cheer that ended in something like, "We want to hear our lion ROAR!" It was embarrassing as all hell, but then again . . . I wasn't going to complain.

Matter of fact, I really had nothing to complain about. Being one of the school's football stars meant I got away with all kinds of shit and had girls throwing themselves at me every weekend. Matt and I were enjoying ourselves for sure, living the high life, as he put it. And even though we still didn't have deep conversations or anything like that, I definitely considered him more than just a buddy.

We hung out at his house most of the time. Matt had, as my mother wryly put it, a unique family situation. Neither of his parents were in the picture; he'd told me when we were in elementary school that his mom and dad had "checked out" when he was pretty young. I learned later that he'd never really known his dad, and that his mother was a hard-core drug addict. Matt's grandparents had custody of him, which sounded like a good thing—and it was, mostly. They were nice people, but they weren't around much. Matt's grandfather was active in state politics, and his grandmother did a lot of charity work. By the time we were in high school, they were gone more than they were home, which worked out okay for us. Matt had the use of their huge house on the edge of town, with access to a fully-stocked liquor cabinet. There was a housekeeper who lived in, but as long as we didn't get too rowdy, she stayed in her room and let us do what we wanted.

So on that Thursday night after study group ended, I'd texted my mom that I had to review some plays with Matt and then I'd driven over to his house, where we'd played Madden and drunk beer and done shots until after midnight. It was what I'd needed after that afternoon, with Quinn. What she'd said when she'd lashed out . . . it had struck a nerve. Her words had made me think about how I felt about both Nate and her, but mostly about Quinn herself. Part of me had been banking on the belief that I could hold onto her, keep her in reserve, I guessed. I'd been telling myself all along that I didn't want her as anything more than a friend, but now it felt like that was a lie. I wasn't ready to think about that too deeply yet.

Getting drunk with Matt was the perfect way to drive both Quinn and what she'd said out of my brain. But I knew better than to drive home when I was wasted, so I'd walked the couple of miles instead, staggering through the pitch black and cursing myself for forgetting my jacket.

Once I got home, the house was silent, with both my parents asleep. I'd fallen into bed fully dressed, forgetting to set my alarm, which was why I hadn't opened my eyes until ten-thirty this morning. My mom and dad were already at work; being the last kid in the house meant that they had high expectations of my ability to get myself up and out to school every day. I'd jogged back over to Matt's, stopping to toss my cookies along the way, and then driven my car back home before I got ready for school.

I figured I'd slide in at lunch and get through the rest of the afternoon, just hoping that none of my teachers from the morning classes reported my absence to the office—yet. I could deal with a detention or whatever on Monday. Hell, I'd probably be able to talk my mother around to writing me a note of excuse if I explained I'd just overslept. But in order to play in the game the next day, I was required to be in school all day on Friday, unless I had a valid reason for missing.

Nabbing a spot in the front of the lot—most of the juniors and seniors left campus over lunch, making their parking places fair game—I made my way across the grass toward the side doors. I had gym right after lunch, and the way I figured it, I had time to go to my locker, stop at the cafeteria to make an appearance with my friends and still make it back in time for PE.

I was nearly to the building when I caught sight of Nate. He was standing on the walkway, staring at me, and I felt uncomfortable right away. I wondered how much Quinn had said to him about our spat the day before.

I got my answer when he snarled at me, snapping about me being late, and then within a few minutes, he blasted me for being a dick to Quinn, as he put it.

And that was when I lost it. We got into a shouting match, the kind we hadn't had since we were kids. My temper, which always tended to get out of control, got the better of me, and before I knew it, I was jeering at him about his feelings toward Quinn, taunting him that even if she did ever date him, it would only be out of pity.

But it was in course of my outburst that I said something that rattled me. I heard the words come out of my mouth, and they jarred me as much as they did Nate.

"Because I'd disagree. I think Quinn wants . . . even more than friendship. That's the real issue here, isn't it? It's eating you up because even when we're fighting about something, she still wants me more than she'll ever want you."

I hadn't acknowledged that hunch before—the suspicion I had that Quinn was harboring a secret crush on me—and saying it out loud shook me up. I could tell by the look on his face that it didn't come as a surprise to Nate, though. He was livid, and in any other guy, I'd have ducked for the inevitable punch. But Nate was smart. I watched his eyes move from fury to calculating to a sort of flat realization. That was when I put my glasses back on and took off.

I yanked open the doors so hard they banged against the outside of the building, and then I strode blindly through the hallway, heading toward my locker. My little encounter with Nate meant I didn't have time to stop in the cafeteria, but that was okay, because I had a feeling I would've made lousy company. I lingered at my locker for a while, hoping to calm down before it was time to head for the gym.

The bell rang, and I was on my way down the hall when I spotted Quinn coming out of a classroom. She saw me at the same time, and a mix of pain and anger flashed across her face before she shuttered it.

"Quinn." I grabbed for her arm, but she shrugged me off. "Mia, please."

I felt her soften. "What do you want, Leo?"

I ran my hand over my hair. "Look, I'm sorry about yesterday. I don't know what I said that made you so mad, but whatever it was, I'm sorry. Can we just get over this?"

One side of her mouth curled up, but she wasn't smiling, not really. "Sure, Leo. Let's just get over it. Which I guess actually means *I'll* get over it, right? I'll stop being such a pain in your neck and start making friends with the rah-rah squad. Won't that be swell for everyone?"

I clenched my jaw. "I don't get it, Quinn. What do you want from me? What do I need to do?"

The bell rang again, signaling the start of the next period. Quinn glanced down the hall, which was now almost empty, and I knew she was stressing over being late. That was my Quinn, conscientious and responsible.

My Quinn? Where the hell had that come from? I shook my head a little and pushed away the thought as she leaned against the wall of lockers and hugged a book to her chest.

"I don't want anything from you, Leo. I guess I have to accept that things are changing, right?"

"But that doesn't have to mean—" I paused, frowning as I heard something from down the adjacent corridor. When I leaned around the corner, my heart plunged and I groaned. "Shit."

Quinn's forehead wrinkled. "What?"

"Nate—he's—crap." Not waiting to explain any further, I took off toward the gym. "Hey—what the fuck?"

About thirty feet away, in front of the steps that led down to the gym, three of my teammates had formed a sort of triangle. And right in the center of that triangle was Nate. I'd seen Tim shove him toward Karl, and just before I'd yelled, Karl had pushed him to Brent.

But at the sound of my voice, Brent had looked up, a guilty

look on his face, and whether it was out of instinct or deliberate, he took a step to the right, getting out of Nate's way and leaving him hurtling helplessly down the short staircase.

It was like something out of a nightmare. On the football field, I had a reputation for making moves that were so quick and decisive that a few local writers called me the Flash. But here, in a hallway in our school, I couldn't move fast enough to grab Nate before he fell. I was close enough to hear the sickening thud of his head against the iron railing and see his face go slack and blank before his limp body rolled to a halt at the bottom of the steps.

Behind me, Quinn screamed. "*Nate!*" I heard the pounding of her feet, and I turned to catch her before she could trip and fall on top of him. My heart was thudding in dread, but I held it together enough to grip Quinn's upper arms, giving her a little shake.

"Go get help. Do you have your phone? Call 9-1-1, and get—fuck, I don't know—get the school nurse or the principal or someone."

Some of the horror cleared from Quinn's eyes, and she nodded, reaching in her back pocket for her phone even as she took off in the direction of the office. Once I was sure she was on her way, I jogged down the stairs to kneel next to Nate, careful not to jostle him as I tried to remember the little bit of first aid training we'd gotten in health class.

Don't move him, in case his neck is broken. Bile rose in my throat. Nate was lying at an odd angle, but I didn't think he'd fallen far enough to have snapped his neck.

"Taylor, shit, we didn't mean—" Brent was babbling behind me, fear evident in his voice. Son of a bitch was afraid he'd gone too far, and dammit, he should've been scared.

"Shut the fuck up. Just shut the fuck up." I growled the

words. The last thing I needed was to deal with his sniveling right now. I concentrated on Nate again.

Check for breath sounds. His chest was rising and falling— it was almost imperceptible, but there was no doubt that he was breathing. Good. That was good.

Check for bleeding and apply direct pressure. I leaned over him, half-expecting to see a pool of red spilling around his head from where it had hit the railing, but I couldn't find anything. Was that good? I vaguely remembered my mother saying that head wounds always bled a lot, maybe some time when I'd come inside the house, covered with blood. So no bleeding had to be a good thing, I was pretty sure.

"Leo, man, what're you going to say happened?" This time it was Karl talking, anxiety threading his voice. "If we get in trouble for this, we won't play tomorrow. Hell, we'll probably get kicked off the team. Suspended from school."

"Holy fuck, I'm eighteen." Brent sounded like he was on the verge of crying. "I could be prosecuted—"

"Would you shut the fuck up?" I spoke through my teeth, my jaw clenched. "Do you think I fucking care about your problems right now? Nate's unconscious, and he might—shit, do you ever think about anyone other than yourselves? He's sick. Do you fucking understand that? Something like this is a huge deal." I reached for Nate's hand, lying limp alongside his body. The skin was cool, but not cold. That was good, too, wasn't it?

I glanced away from Nate only when I heard the sound of running feet. The school nurse, Mrs. Channing, along with the principal, were following close behind Quinn. I fastened my eyes on her face, needing to make sure she was okay. She was pale, and her eyes looked huge and full of terror, but she wasn't about to pass out or get hysterical. She was holding it together, and I was grateful.

Mrs. Channing knelt on the other side of Nate's body—his body? No, on the other side of Nate. She picked up the hand I wasn't holding, and I realized she was checking his pulse. Her sober gaze met mine.

"What happened?"

It was a loaded question, and of course I knew what she meant, but I chose to focus on the most important information. "He went down the steps, and his head—" Nausea threatened again as I heard the sound in my memory. "He hit his head on the railing. He was unconscious when I got to him. I couldn't get here fast enough to stop him from falling. I went as fast as I could."

"Leo, stop. We'll deal with that later." She touched the side of Nate's head, careful not to move it. "I can't see any bleeding."

"Is that good or bad?" I blurted out the question. "I can't remember. Is it bad when the head doesn't bleed? I didn't move him, and I made sure he was breathing, but I couldn't remember about the head."

"You did just right." Whatever the nurse was going to say next was lost in the noise of a door bursting open as EMTs rushed toward us. I was pushed out of the way as they swarmed Nate. I stood, my body stiff, and moved up the stairs to wait next to Quinn.

Almost as if it was drawn to me like a magnet to steel, the side of her body pressed into mine, and she ducked her head to burrow it in against my chest. My arms went around her, pulling her tight into me, and then I couldn't help lowering my lips to touch the top of her hair. She was trembling, and in that moment, I would've done anything to comfort her. Anything to make it all better for her.

"What happened here, Mr. Taylor?" Mr. Platten, the principal, spoke low.

"I . . ." A lump formed in my throat, and I found it hard to speak. "I'm not really sure, sir. I just came around the corner in time to see Nate falling. I tried to get here to grab him, but I was too far away." I inclined my head toward Quinn. "We were just around the corner, and I heard—something. I ran, but I couldn't get to him in time."

"He tripped." Brent was talking to Mr. Platten, but his eyes were on me. "I guess he was on his way to the gym when I—when we passed him, and the next thing I knew, he was on the ground. It all happened so fast."

Fury burned in my chest, and I wanted to yell, *Liar.* But I kept my mouth shut. Right now, I was only worried about Nate. Later I'd deal with Brent, Karl and Tim.

The EMTs had Nate on a wheeled stretcher, and they moved him fast toward the doors. One lingered to speak to the principal.

"Were his parents notified?" She glanced at Quinn and me. "Are you friends of his?"

"My secretary called his parents right away, but we didn't get through. We'll keep trying." Mr. Platten's lips pressed together. I was sure this was looking like a nightmare to him just about now: a student badly injured on school property, and the only witnesses were four prominent members of the first winning football team the school had known in decades.

"I want to go to the hospital with Nate." Quinn pushed away from me, turning as though to follow the gurney. "He shouldn't be alone."

"You can't ride in the ambulance with him, but you're welcome to meet us there." The EMT's eyes flickered to Mr. Platten. "If that's okay with the school."

"I'll drive her over." I grasped Quinn's hand, holding it

tight. "We—we're like family. We're Nate's best friends, so we should be there until his parents can get to the hospital."

"I agree. Go ahead." Mr. Platten shot me a long and steady look. "Keep me informed, please, Mr. Taylor."

"Will do." I tugged on Quinn's hand. "Let's go."

The ride to the hospital was only about ten minutes, but it felt endless. Quinn had climbed into the front seat of my car without a word, and she didn't speak until we were parked and walking inside.

"Do we go to the emergency room, or . . .?" She flashed wide, confused eyes at me. "I don't know what to do."

"Let's go in here." I led her to the main entrance, through the automatic doors and up to the information desk, where a volunteer sat in front of a computer screen. "Nate Wellman. He was just brought in by ambulance."

The older woman raised one eyebrow. "Family?"

"Yep." I didn't even hesitate.

"Wellman?" She tapped a few keys and scanned the monitor. "He's in the ER, but it looks like he's about to be taken up for a CT scan." She pointed down the hall behind her. "Through those doors, take a left, follow the signs. Ask at the desk there, and they'll tell you where to wait."

We were moving before she'd finished speaking. Quinn stumbled, trying to keep up with me; her legs were long, but I still walked a lot faster. I tightened my grip on her hand.

"You okay?"

She nodded. "I just want to get there. See him."

"I know." We rounded another corner and stopped in

front of another desk. The nurse nodded when I gave her Nate's name.

"The EMTs told me you were coming. He's awake, and you can go back there—but he's about to go up to imaging, so make it fast." She directed us to the right room.

"He's awake. That's good, right?" Quinn looked up at me anxiously.

"I think it's got to be. And they're letting us see him." I halted by the door with a number eight above it. "This is it."

Nate had always looked small to me. Even though he was the oldest of the three of us, as long as I could remember I'd been a good head taller than he was, not to mention just overall sturdier. But when I saw him lying in that hospital bed, he looked . . . weak. Vulnerable. And suddenly I was wracked with guilt for the way I'd let him down over the past few months. Hell, who was I fooling? It had been years since I'd been a friend to either Nate or Quinn. I'd put on a good front, doing the small talk and the waves in the hallway, or stopping when I saw them out and about, but I couldn't remember the last time we'd hung out or had a real conversation.

Beside me, Quinn made a small noise and rushed to the bed. She found Nate's hand and had it pressed between her own before I even took two steps to join her.

"Nate, oh, my God." She gave a half-sob, and tears I guessed she'd been just barely holding back streamed down her face. "How—are you okay? Well, that's stupid, you're laying in a hospital bed, you're clearly not okay."

"I'm going to be fine, Quinn." His voice sounded a little strained and a little slurry. "My head is just killing me right now, but they gave me something for the pain. And I guess I'm going up to get some kind of scan in a few minutes."

"Yeah, that's what the nurse said." Quinn caught my eye

and jerked her head a little, clearly gesturing for me to come stand next to her. I moved into Nate's view, not sure how happy he was going to be to see me there after our last exchange.

"Leo drove me over . . . and he made sure you got help." She was nearly babbling, and I knew she was talking me up to Nate. Trying to patch things between us, just like she'd always done.

"Thanks, Leo." Nate focused on me. "Seriously. Thanks." He paused, his forehead knitting together. "Was that you who yelled right before . . . I went down?"

"Yeah." I crossed my arms over my chest and swallowed hard. "I'm sorry, Nate. Really sorry." I hoped he understood that I meant that apology for more than just failing to rescue him in time.

"There wasn't anything you could've done." He blinked so slowly that I wasn't sure he was going to open his eyes again right away. When he did, I could tell he was having trouble staying awake. "Listen, Leo. What happened with . . . Brent and them?"

I shook my head. "Nothing yet. It wasn't clear exactly what went down, and I was more worried about getting you help. And Brent—he said you tripped." I set my jaw. "But I'll make sure it's straightened out. They were giving you shit, weren't they? Messing with you?"

Nate rocked his head a little, wincing as he did. "No. I mean . . . yeah. They were. But I don't want to get them in trouble. It's kind of my . . .fault, I guess. A little. And I don't want everyone to hate me."

"That's bullshit, Nate." Quinn the avenger was in full protector mode, disbelief painting her face. "They need to be punished. They should get kicked off the football team, and—my God, you could've gotten really hurt. Worse than this."

"No, Quinn." He was adamant. "Don't say anything. I don't want you to do anything, or I'm going to be really pissed, got it?" He shifted his gaze to me. "Go along with whatever Brent says happened, and I will, too. I tripped and fell. That's it." His eyes drifted shut. "Quinn, you got that? Tripped. No one's . . . fault."

And then he was asleep. His mouth opened a little as his breath evened out. Quinn's back bowed, and her inhale was ragged.

"Mia, he's going to be okay." I put a tentative hand on her shoulder, but we were interrupted when the door opened, admitting an orderly.

"We're taking him up to CT right now. You can wait in the family area down the hall." The orderly stood back, waiting for us to pass. I slid my hand down Quinn's back, guiding her into the corridor.

An older man stood just outside, typing into a computer tablet. He glanced up as we emerged.

"You're here for Nate Wellman?" He cocked his head, scrutinizing us. "Family?"

"Yes. We're just waiting for his parents." I lifted my chin, daring the doctor to argue with my claim to be related. "Is he going to be all right?"

The doctor sighed, running his finger down the side of the tablet as he skimmed his notes. "Seems that he is. Now, we won't be sure until we do the scan, but he regained consciousness, and he was completely cognizant. Knows his name, where he is . . . he's fully oriented. Probably a mild concussion, but a little rest and he should be good as new." He drew his brows together something else in the file caught his attention. "He has some ongoing health issues, though, doesn't he? We'll have to run through some extra tests, just to make sure nothing else is going on." Tapping the top of the computer, he turned and walked away from us without saying anything else.

"Let's go find the waiting area." I reached for Quinn's hand, but she jerked away from me, and when she turned to face me, her eyes were stormy.

"How could you agree to that? You didn't mean it, did you? You're not going to let Brent and those other guys get away with what they did to Nate."

I blew out a sigh, slumping against the wall. "Mia, you heard what he said. Nate doesn't want anyone to know what really happened. It's his decision."

"He has a head injury, Leo. I don't think he's in any state of mind to know what's best."

I rolled my eyes. "Did you ever stop to think, Quinn, that maybe it's better for Nate this way? What do you think is going to happen if he points the finger at Brent and the guys? They'll get kicked off the football team, and that's going to piss off the whole school. It's not going to make things any easier for Nate. He'll get picked on even more." I paused. "If that's even possible."

"What's that supposed to mean?" Quinn stood with her hands on her hips, her face stormy as she stared me down.

My blood was beginning to boil just a little. I was getting over the fear that had gripped me since I'd seen Nate at the bottom of those steps, motionless, and now that it looked like he was going to be all right, I had to think about how this was going to play out. Nate's insistence that we protect Brent, Tim and Karl made my job easier. The only obstacle to helping this whole thing go away was standing in front of me, eyes blazing and full lips pushed together.

And I wanted her.

I'd been trying to ignore it and deny it for so long. But looking at Quinn, I couldn't remember anymore why we weren't together. I couldn't remember why I'd been fighting the idea of us. I couldn't pinpoint any of my many reasons—or why I was convinced that I wasn't good for her. That I'd ruin her, dragging her into situations she'd hate.

All I knew was the pounding of my heart, the way my dick was going hard and how much I needed to taste her. I almost reached for her—she was just about an arm's length away, and I knew I could have her body pressed against mine in a matter of seconds. But before I could act on that, she starting talking again.

"You think it's our fault that people—and by people, I'm assuming you mean your new pals, your little football buddies and the groupies—that none of them like Nate and me. All those people who you call friends now—the ones you party with, get drunk with, all the other stupid things you do." She arched one eyebrow, leaving no doubt about where she stood on all those topics. "You think we like being made fun of, being teased—you think we bring it on ourselves. You as much as said that yesterday, didn't you? When you had to pull Trish away right before she started getting rough with me." Something changed in her expression; pain or something like it passed over quickly. "Sorry about that, Leo. Sorry that you had to choose between the person who's known you forever and one of your slut buddies."

Ouch. That one stung. I'd never slept with Trish—hell, I'd never even looked twice at her—but I'd banged my share of cheerleaders. I wasn't proud of it, necessarily, but when a girl threw herself at me, and I was maybe more than a little drunk, it wasn't easy to say no. Not when there wasn't any good reason to deny myself the pleasure they offered.

But that wasn't anything I wanted to discuss with Quinn.

Not when it was *her* my body was burning for right now, not when it was *her* lips I wanted to crush to mine. The sting and the lust were probably why I went the direction I did, lashing out at her without thinking about it first.

"Maybe if you made a little more effort to be nice to people instead of putting them down, and maybe if you gave a shit about how you look, what you wear, you wouldn't have to be jealous of my slut buddies. Maybe then I wouldn't have to make a choice."

Quinn reacted as though I'd slapped her face, jerking back as her mouth fell open. Disbelief and betrayal filled her eyes, and my heart sank. *Shit.* What had I done?

Before I could get another word out or stop her, Quinn turned and sprinted down the hall and out of the hospital.

★ Thirteen ★

Quinn

I FLED DOWN THE HALLWAY OF THE HOSPITAL AND OUT THE automatic doors into the waning afternoon sun. The air was chilly, and I shivered, wrapping my arms around my waist as I leaned against the bumpy stucco wall. My throat was tight with tears, but dammit, I wasn't going to cry. Not here, not where Leo might see me.

I wasn't stupid. I'd known for a long time that this guy who wore my best friend's face and spoke with his voice wasn't the same sweet boy I'd known forever. No matter how much I lied to myself, no matter how many times I searched for any hint that Leo was still in there, it was time to face facts once and for all. Leo wasn't my friend. He wasn't Nate's friend, and even though he'd rescued Nate today, the sooner we accepted that truth, the sooner we could move on. Forget him.

Pain held a vice-grip on my heart. For me, losing Leo meant more than just having one less friend. It also spelled the death of the dream that someday, he might be even more. I couldn't remember a time when I hadn't looked at Leo as the boy I wanted as mine. Even when I hadn't known how to define that feeling, I'd recognized how I felt about him. Leo was like the other piece of my puzzle, the one whose edges complemented my own. Nate was my best friend, too, but there was just something *more* about Leo, and I'd always known it. Maybe that was why I'd tried to compensate all these years, giving Nate more attention and deferring to him; maybe I'd always realized that some day, I'd choose between them. And when that day came, I'd known that I'd choose Leo without hesitation.

"Quinn."

His voice, low and rough, was so close to me that I jumped, sucking a quick breath. "God, you scared the crap out of me. Go away, Leo. Leave me alone."

"Quinn, let me explain." He grabbed my upper arm, and the heat of his hand burned through my sweatshirt. I froze, my heart stuttering.

"You said enough inside." I lifted my hand, trying to ignore how much it was shaking. *From anger*, I told myself. It wasn't because Leo was touching me. Wrenching away from his grip, I began to count off on my fingers. "I'm a loser, because I don't dress like the rah-rah girls and drool over Neanderthal football players. Nate's a wuss because he didn't stand up to three guys who each outweigh him by a good hundred pounds. And you only protected him today because you feel sorry for us. And now, Nate wants me to lie about what really happened, about what those boys tried to do, and you agree with him. You don't want me to rat out your idiot friends or mess up your precious football team. Did I miss anything? Leave out any other truth you feel I need to know?"

Leo's eyebrows drew together, and his gray eyes went thunderous. He bent so that his face was inches from mine.

"I never said that. I never said anything like that, about you being a loser or Nate being a wuss. I was just trying to be a good friend by giving you some advice—"

"I don't need your advice, Leo. I don't need anything from you. Believe me, you've made yourself perfectly clear." I turned away, intent on escape again, but he snagged my arm again before I could get very far.

"Quinn—" He growled out my name, yanking me closer as though he was going to keep yelling at me. I blinked rapidly, breathing hard at his nearness. I could smell that scent that was only Leo, a mix of his shaving cream and some kind of intoxicating musk. It made me want to bury my nose in the crook of his neck, even now when I was angry and hurt. My chest rose and fell so fast, I felt as though I'd just run one of Coach Cramer's laps.

"Quinn." Leo said my name again, this time a little softer, a little less frustrated and a little more desperate. His eyes fastened onto my mouth, and I couldn't help myself; my tongue darted out to run over my lips.

His grip on my arm loosened just a tad, not quite releasing me. Although I could've easily stepped away, I didn't. I stayed close to Leo, the warmth from his body making me forget the cool breeze blowing around us.

Leo didn't draw back, either. His mouth opened a little, and his throat bobbed as he swallowed. A tic jumped in his cheek, distracting me momentarily from staring at his lips. But then his tongue slid out to mimic my earlier move, and all I could think was . . . *please*.

As if he'd heard my silent plea, Leo's hands skimmed slowly down my arms over my ribs to my waist. He drew me closer, lowering his head until I could feel his breath fan my cheek.

But he stopped short of touching my lips. For a moment, time stood still as I watched a silent battle wage in his eyes.

And then his eyelids slid shut. "Fuck it." The words escaped on a sigh that sounded like defeat, but before I could analyze that, his mouth was on mine and everything in the world was new and shiny.

Every girl imagines her first kiss, and I wasn't any different. I'd never pictured sharing that milestone with any boy but Leo, even though that possibility had felt increasingly remote lately. But when it actually happened . . . every preconceived notion I'd had evaporated into nothingness, because reality was better than anything I could have dreamed.

His lips were soft, and they covered mine completely, at first with a tentative touch. I arched my body into his, needing to be closer, and he groaned, opening his mouth and coaxing me to do the same. His tongue teased at the corners of my lips, tracing the seam until I couldn't resist letting them open.

As if he'd been waiting for just that, his hands dropped to my hips, pressing me close to him as his tongue swept into my mouth, tangling with mine and exploring me with such intimacy that my knees went weak. His fingers dug into my back, just above my butt. My hands were linked behind his neck, but I couldn't quite remember how they had gotten there. It didn't matter, because in that minute, close could never be close enough.

"Mia." He broke the kiss just long enough to murmur his endearment against my cheek. I caught one fast breath before he captured my mouth again, this time with more aggression and need. His hands began to move in small circles over my lower back, but it wasn't enough: I wanted everything, and I wanted it now.

I became aware of the hard ridge of his arousal against my stomach, and a thrill of want shot through me. *I did that.* The realization sang into my heart. Leo wanted me. Me. I'd waited so long for this, and I couldn't believe it was finally happening.

I had no idea if I was doing this right, or if there even was a right or wrong way. The part of me that still thought of Leo as my best friend wanted to ask him if he could tell how inexperienced I was. But most of me hoped he didn't notice.

The front of my body was warm as it pressed into him, but the wind was picking up, blowing over my back. I shivered, curling against him.

"You're cold." Leo trailed kisses over my jaw and then drew back, chaffing his hands up and down my arms. "We should probably get inside and check on Nate. See if he's back from the scan yet. And maybe his mom and dad are here. If everything's okay, I'll take you home after that."

I knew that reminder about Nate should've jarred me back to a place where I was worried about my other best friend— and I was concerned about him—but nothing and no one was going to knock me off this high. And the idea of Leo driving me home? Being alone in the car with him? Yeah, that made me want to break out into what the boys and I used to call my joy of silliness dance.

Would he kiss me again when he dropped me off? Would we sit in front of my house, making out until the windows of the car steamed? And what did it mean, exactly, this kiss? I opened my mouth to ask that question at the same time Leo began to speak.

"Quinn, I—"

"Leo, what—"

Whatever Leo was about to say was lost as a woman's voice behind me called out to us. "Leo—Quinn. Thank God. What happened?" Sheri Wellman was sprinting toward us. "We just got your message. I'd had my phone off, until it was closer to time to pick up Nate at the river—damn, that doesn't matter. What happened?"

Leo's eyes darted to mine, pleading. I knew what he was waiting for; he wanted my permission to tell Nate's mother the story the boys had concocted. The lie that was going to let Brent, Karl and Tim get away with what they'd done to Nate. I pressed my lips together, still tasting him there, and although I wasn't at all sure he was right, I gave a little nod.

"It was those steps by the gym. I guess Nate was heading to the locker room, and . . . I don't know, he just fell. I was down the hall and saw him going down, but I couldn't do anything. Couldn't get there in time." Leo rubbed the back of his neck, giving an excellent impression of friend who was suffering from guilt. Or come to think of it, maybe he wasn't acting. "I think he hit his head on the railing. But the doctor said he was going to be okay. They just want to keep an eye on him. We saw him before he went up for a CT scan, and he was awake. He talked to us. They said maybe a mild concussion."

"Oh, my God." Sheri closed her eyes, took a deep breath and then looked at me. "Will you guys take me in to him?"

"Of course." I gave her a quick hug. "He's really going to be fine, Sheri. He talked to us and everything. I bet he's more worried about you and Mark freaking out than anything else."

She gave a semi-hysterical bark of laughter. "He always is. That's Nate. Okay, so you're saying I need to pull myself together, huh?" She managed a smile. "All right. Got it. Oh, and I called your mom and dad, both of you, in case they didn't know where you were. Quinn, your mother's on her way here."

"She is?" It didn't really surprise me. My parents and Leo's all tried to support Sheri and Mark however they could, whether that was bringing meals or sitting in hospital waiting rooms.

"Yes. She said if everything was going well here, she'd drive you home."

Disappointment flooded me. All the anticipation of riding

home with Leo went up in a cloud of smoke. "Oh, well, Leo was going to—"

"I better get going." He tapped his fingers against his jean-covered thigh. "Since Sheri's here with you, and your mom's coming. And Nate's going to be fine." He glanced at me. "If you're doing all right, I'm going to stop in at practice." He cast Sheri an apologetic smile. "Not that I think that's more important than Nate. But if you've got this . . ."

"Sweetie, don't be silly. Nate wouldn't want you to miss football practice, especially not with a big game tomorrow." She patted his shoulder and squeezed. "Not that I keep up with that, but Mark said something about it being an important one."

Leo shrugged. "They're all make-or-break according to Coach. But yeah, it'd be good if I can show my face and explain what's going on." He dropped his gaze to me. "You can tell Nate that I'll see him soon. Explain . . . what's going on and every-thing."

"Oh. Okay." I felt oddly deflated. Leo was backing away from me, both literally and emotionally.

"I'll see you later, Mia. Text me if anything comes up." He reached down to take my hand, squeezing it lightly, and then dropped a quick, friend-zony kiss on my cheek. "Sheri, if you need anything, let me know. I can bring Nate his homework or whatever."

"Thanks, Leo." She managed a smile. "It always makes me feel better to know Nate has the two of you."

Leo winced just a little before he nodded and turned to go. I watched him leave, his long legs striding across the asphalt, and I wondered if he was rushing off because he regretted kiss-ing me. What would he do when we saw each other Monday in school? Or should I go to his game tomorrow and cheer him on? If he saw me there, would he ask me out, and not just as his friend? Or would he pretend the most beautiful moment of my life so far had never happened?

"Quinn? You okay, honey?" Sheri tilted her head at me quizzically.

"Hmmm?" I blinked at her. "Oh, yeah. Come on, I'll take you to Nate."

We went back inside, with me leading Sheri down the same hallway I'd run out a few minutes. She ran her fingers through her hair, wrinkling her nose.

"How many times have I been in one hospital or another with Nate . . . but you know what gets me every time? The smell. That horrible antiseptic slash pine cleaner slash sickness smell. When Nate was little, the first thing I'd do every time we brought him home was wash him with his own sweet baby soap. Or when he got too old for that, make him shower."

I made myself smile at her, although cheery was pretty far from what I felt at the moment. "I get that. Remember when I had to be in here overnight? I had that ear infection that wouldn't go away. The smell still reminds me of that night." I shuddered. "I've always thought Nate was so brave to face everything he does without freaking."

"He's got more than his share of chutzpah." Sheri stopped when I did, by the door to Nate's room. We both leaned inside, but the bed was still empty.

A passing nurse paused. "Imaging's backed up today. You can wait in the room if you want. The waiting area's pretty full."

"Thanks." Sheri dragged a chair from the hallway into the room and then pointed to the other one already there. "Sit down, hon. Your mom'll text me when she gets here."

"Okay." I sank into the ugly brown imitation leather chair. "I'm sorry we couldn't get you sooner. We tried both you and

Mark. And I know the school tried to call, too." I flashed back to that horrible moment when I'd seen Nate lying so still on the steps. "I was so scared."

She nodded, her eyes welling up. "I'll give myself permission to break down a little now, while he's not here. But don't worry. I can man up the minute they wheel him in here."

I reached out to touch her hand. "I said before that Nate's brave, but I kind of think I know where he gets it."

She half-laughed through her tears. "It never gets easier." She laid her other hand over mine, holding it there. "And no matter what, you'll do anything to keep your child from being hurt. In any way." Her eyes searched mine, and I felt my face heat.

"I'm sure it's hard when—well, with Nate sometimes it seems like anything that can go wrong with his health does."

"There's that. And then there's a different kind of hurt." Sheri didn't move, but her fingers tightened, holding me where I was, as though I might try to run. "Quinn, I don't mean to interfere or to pry. But when I walked up, it seemed to me like you and Leo were . . . close. Is there something between you two that I haven't heard about?"

Part of me was thinking, *I wish I knew the answer to that question.* I lifted one shoulder before I spoke. "I don't think so. I was pretty upset about Nate, and so was Leo. He was just . . . hugging me. Trying to make me feel better."

"Hmmm." Sheri raised one eyebrow. "Was that all it was?" Before I could answer, she gave her head a little shake. "Never mind. Forgive me for being nosy. Quinn, I hope you know I love you. I love Leo, too. I want all of you kids to be happy. But Nate's my number one priority. He has to be. And I don't think I'm betraying any secret when I say he thinks he's in love with you."

I opened my mouth, but misery and guilt made it impossible to say anything.

"It's all right, Quinn. It's nothing you've done. You've always been Nate's best friend, and I wouldn't change that for anything in the world. All I'm asking is that you don't abandon him. Whatever happens between you and Leo—or anyone else—please don't forget about Nate."

"I never could." It was my turn to cry, warm tears trickling over my cheeks. "Sheri, Nate's one of the most important people in the world to me. I love him." I swallowed hard. "I wish I could say that I felt the same way. But Nate's always been like my brother. My best friend. I can't imagine not having him in my life. I just don't see him . . ." My gaze slid away from hers. "Any other way."

Sheri sighed. "Believe me, honey, I understand that. I've always been able to see it, but Nate doesn't. Or if he does, he's just too stubborn to admit otherwise. I'm not asking you to lie to him, or to pretend to feel something that you don't. I just want you to keep being the best friend you can. And if—" She broke off as we both heard the sound of wheels at the door. An orderly backed into the room, steering Nate's gurney around the corner.

"Well, if it isn't my daredevil son." Sheri jumped to her feet, her eyes taking in Nate's form under the thin blanket. She set her shoulders and pasted on a smile, and if I hadn't seen her crying a few minutes before, I'd have never believed she had been.

"Hey, Mom." He glanced at me, a small frown on his face. "I guess you heard what happened?" It was more question than statement, and by the way his eyes bored into me, I knew I was the one he was asking. He needed to know if I'd gone along with his story.

"That you tried to take all the steps in one bound? Yeah, I might've heard a rumor about that." She leaned over and kissed his cheek.

"I'm going to be fine, though." His gaze darted between the two of us. "What were you two talking about?"

"Nothing special. Just girl talk." Sheri smiled wider and winked at me. "Right, Quinn?"

"Yup, that's all." I nodded, hoping that neither Nate nor his mother could sense the turmoil and confusion whirling inside me.

I was more than ready for this day to be over.

★ Fourteen ★

Nate

I'D HAD SOME KILLER HEADACHES IN MY DAY, THANKS TO the side effects of medication and other treatments, but this one was a definite contender for the worst one. I lay in my hospital bed, staring at the ceiling tiles and waiting for the dose of painkiller I'd just been given to take effect.

"Nate."

Quinn's voice was soft and questioning; she wasn't sure if I were truly awake or not. I steeled myself against the pain and turned my head just a little to track her movement toward me.

"I'm awake." My voice sounded faraway and kind of slurred. Yeah, maybe those meds were kicking in, after all.

"My mom and I are going to leave in just a minute. Is there anything . . . do you need anything before I go?"

I managed a smile. "Nah, I'm good." My lips felt dry and numb, and I licked them, wondering idly if Quinn might be turned off by dry lips. Should I ask her? No, I decided. I shouldn't point out any of my deficiencies, on the off chance she might not notice.

"Okay. Well . . . I guess I'll see you tomorrow. The doctor

told your mom and dad that you'd probably be released in the afternoon, so if you want to text me when you get home, I'll come by. If you want."

"Of course, I want. I always want you, Quinn. Always. Everrrrrry day." My eyelids had become too heavy to keep open, and I groped blindly for Quinn's hand. When I felt her slim fingers close around mine, I relaxed. "I always wanted to hold your hand. And kiss you. Do you like when lips are dry? I use lip balm sometimes, but I don't have it here."

"Nate, I think you're sleepy." Quinn's tone was strained. "You go to sleep, and I'll see—"

"You didn't tell anyone what really happened today, right? I don't want them to know. 'Spartly my fault, you know. I made 'em mad. I pushed Brent. Teased him."

"No, Nate. That's not true." I recognized that emotion. Quinn was mad. Or frustrated. Which usually meant Leo was involved.

"Where's Leo?" I managed to open one eye a little bit. Quinn looked fuzzy and odd, but I didn't miss the raw hurt on her face when I mentioned his name.

"He went home. Or I guess actually, he went to football practice." Yeah, there was definite bitterness there. "He said he'll see you when you're out of here."

"You're pissed at him." Only my tongue felt a little big in my mouth, and it came out "pithed". I'd never lisped, never had any speech issues, and it made me want to laugh now, hearing myself talk like this.

"Why do you say that? Oh, you mean because you two boys concocted a cover story so that the jerks who let you fall down the steps—or maybe even outright pushed you down— will get away with it? And you expect me to go along with that? Why would that make me mad, Nate?" Quinn was practically hissing. *Shit*, she was really upset.

"Don't be mad, Quinn." My eyes were both closed again. Keeping even one open was too hard. "This is better, this way. Trust me, honey." The endearment slid off my tongue like butter. Some distant part of my brain went into panic mode that I'd said it, but why shouldn't I? I loved Quinn. She was my girl. I should tell her how I feel. Holding back . . . why I had been doing that? I was just wasting time.

"I love you, Quinn."

The meds were pulling me deeper now, dragging me away from Quinn and from this conversation, and that was okay, too. Because the pain was dulled, and I could sleep.

The last thing I heard before I fell deep into the drugged sleep was Quinn's voice. She sounded sad.

"Love you, too, Nate. Sleep well. I'll see you tomorrow."

★ Fifteen ★

Leo

BY THE TIME I MADE IT BACK OVER TO THE HIGH SCHOOL and changed, the afternoon light was gray. Everyone was on the field, running drills, but I stopped on the sidelines where Coach Cramer stood, holding a tablet that looked just like the one the doctor had used at the hospital.

"Taylor." Coach nodded at me. "Mr. Platten filled me in on where you were. What's the news on the kid?"

I shrugged. "Far as I know, doing okay. Doctor said he might have a mild concussion, and they're keeping him overnight, probably." I worked hard to keep the worry out of my voice. This entire afternoon had been a mess, from beginning to end. I wouldn't have minded just forgetting the whole damn day. The image of Quinn's eyes, soft and luminous when she'd looked up at after our kiss, filled my head, reminding me that maybe not *all* of it had been so bad.

But no. Kissing Quinn had been a mistake of monumental proportions, and now I had to figure out an exit strategy. I'd seen the expression on her face just before Sheri had interrupted us. I knew Quinn was reading love, commitment and always into that kiss. All of those things made me panic.

Coach was staring at me, curiosity etched between his eyes. "You okay, boy?" Clearly my thoughts about Quinn must've been playing out across my face. I relaxed my expression into a grin and nodded.

"Sure. I'll get out there and get to work, okay?"

He nodded. "Give me a couple of laps around the field first." When I raised my eyebrows, he shook his head. "Not punishment. Just getting you warmed up so you're ready to run a few plays. Lampert's been throwing to Simmons, so he needs to get in some passes to you before we shut down for the night." He gave me his trademark swat on the ass. "Get moving. Tomorrow's going to be a tough one."

"You got it." I took off down the sidelines, keeping my strides long and my breath even. Matt bellowed out my name as I passed him, but I just gave him a wave and kept going. I spotted Brent, Karl and Tim on the field, too, and I felt their eyes on me. I didn't acknowledge them at all. Let them sweat it out a little longer. I wasn't going to compromise my team—or put Nate in a bad position—by spilling my guts to the principal, but fuck if the three of them were going to get away with this totally.

Guilt trickled down my back, thinking about them. I heard Quinn's voice again, accusing me of valuing the team over my friends. Was she right? I'd told myself I was thinking of Nate, of what he wanted, but then again, I'd lied to the principal about how everything had gone down, and that was before Nate had asked me to cover for the guys.

Truth to tell, I wasn't sure what Quinn would do. She hadn't seen what had happened, but nothing was stopping her from going to Mr. Platten with the suspicions she had. I tried to focus on those worries—what Quinn might decide to do—

rather than let my mind wander to the more dangerous topic: why in the hell had I kissed her?

I hadn't planned on it. I'd followed her outside the hospital just to make sure she understood that I hadn't meant any of those things she'd accused me of saying. Yeah, I'd gone too far when I'd jeered about the way she dressed, but she'd pushed my buttons, too, lashing out about the slut buddies. Where did she even get those terms, anyway? Among the guys, we called the girls who showed up at every game, party and celebration the pussy pack. Crude, yeah, and my mom would've smacked me in the back of the head if she ever heard me use those words, but at the same time, the chicks themselves used the name, too. Most of them were unashamed of their availability, and as long as everyone understood the expectations upfront, I didn't see any problems. I was smart and I played safe, and I never fucked a girl who was so drunk she couldn't say yes, loud and clear.

But all of that was so far removed from Quinn and her standards that I felt a little dirty even thinking of them at the same time. As much distance as I'd had lately from her, I still knew who Quinn was. She was good, and kind, and pure. She hadn't dated anyone as far as I knew. I'd overheard some of the cheerleaders snickering about her being gay, referring to her as queer Quinn, but I was pretty sure that wasn't the case, either.

Okay, if I was going to be honest with myself, I knew it wasn't true. I'd known Quinn had been crushing on me for a while. Deep down, I'd known I felt the same, which was why I'd stayed away. Quinn wasn't the type of girl who'd understand and accept the pussy pack. She'd rail and rant about it and cause trouble, and before we knew it, she'd probably have those girls either hating her or coming around to her way of thinking.

But it was more than that. I couldn't stand the idea that Quinn would see the real me, the guy I'd become. I knew for sure she'd hate this side of me, the one who partied and fucked around and acted like a jerk. The prospect of seeing her face when she realized the truth about me was just something I couldn't handle. I swallowed hard and picked up the pace as I rounded the corner of the field.

Which meant that I was going to have to figure out how to deal with the ramifications of that kiss. I had a sneaking suspicion that it might've been Quinn's first kiss, and that sliced me even deeper. When I'd given in and touched her lips with mine, I hadn't planned on doing anything other than keeping it simple. Testing it out. Tasting her. But the minute our mouths had met, all rational thinking had flown out the door, and every bit of logic had fled. At the same time, all the blood in my body seemed to have surged between my legs, swelling my dick until it pushed against the zipper of my jeans, painfully hard.

I'd wanted to touch her everywhere. I'd wanted to hike her up against that rough stucco wall, fill my hands with her tits and grind into her core. When she made that tiny breathless moan, I knew I wanted to hear that sound again and again, and I wanted to hear her call out my name while I filled her. I wanted to taste the tempting heat between her legs.

I wanted it all, and I wanted it from Quinn.

Only her shivering had pulled me back from the brink. I'd realized that she was cold, out there in the late autumn chill wearing only a thin T-shirt and jeans. And needing to keep her warm and safe had made me pull back long enough for reality to come crashing in on me.

I wasn't sure what I'd planned to say to her when we'd both spoken at the same time. Was I going to pretend it didn't mean anything? Tell her I'd made a mistake? Maybe. That would've been the smart thing to do, but then again, nothing about this day had been smart.

Still, now that I had a little distance, I knew that my only option was making it clear that there could never be anything between us. Nothing but friendship, and fuck if I could handle even that now. I didn't trust myself to be around her at all, not when I knew how she tasted and knew the electricity between us.

Unfortunately, I also knew that maintaining that distance meant hurting Quinn. In the long run, it was better for her, but in the short term, she was probably going to hate me.

But wasn't it better that she hated me like this, as the guy who'd stolen her first kiss and then pretended it didn't mean anything, instead hating what I'd really become? Or maybe it didn't make any difference. Maybe those two were one and the same. But if she was going to end up detesting me, better it should happen now, when she was still only a little hurt, than later, when things could be much, much worse. Right now, she was still the same Quinn. But if I dragged her into my world, she'd be spoiled and ruined. I wasn't going to let that happen.

I finished the last lap, not breaking stride as I jogged onto the field. Matt met me on the thirty-yard line, punching me in the shoulder.

"Heard you had to rescue the gimp, dude. What happened?"

I glanced over his shoulder. Tim stood about ten feet away, frowning in my direction. I narrowed my eyes, giving him a steely glare, and then turned back to Matt. "Tell you later, man. Hey, Coach says you warmed up with Simmons. What the fuck, dude, you cheating on me now?"

Down the line, Dylan Simmons cracked up, shaking his head. "No worries on my part, Taylor. You and Lampert have something special. Something magical. It's a love for the ages, man. I'm not getting in the way of that."

"Damn straight!" Lampert wrapped his arms around my middle and tried to haul me up. "We're like Romeo and fucking Juliet." Without pausing for breath, he added, "Dibs on being Romeo."

"No problem, Houdini. You keep delivering your balls right into my waiting hands, and I'll be your Juliet every time." I batted my eyes at him, and all the guys around us fell apart, hooting and laughing.

"Taylor, what the hell? You get on the field and suddenly no one's taking anything serious?" Coach blew his whistle, and we all snapped to attention. "Get moving on those passes before I come out there and kick your sorry asses. Do I have to remind you that we're playing Franklin Township tomorrow? Those farm boys are going to roll in here and hand you your asses if you don't watch out. Move it. Now!"

I shoved Matt. "Get down there and show me some love, buddy. Make it a good one." I puckered my lips and made a kissy-kissy sound. "Remember, I'm your one and only!"

Matt trotted back across mid-field to his own twenty-yard line, where he scooped up a football. He held it in one hand, and I grinned, watching him go into the zone, where opponents only he could see threatened to sack him. He had the uncanny ability to fake being in a tight situation, even in the middle of the the most laid-back practices. He stuttered forward a few feet, eyes darting downfield to where I waited. Simmons stepped into the role of safety, trying to both distract me and intercept the pass. None of us were wearing pads today, since there wasn't any hitting on the offensive line the day before a game, but I knew Simmons would give snagging the ball his best shot, short of tackling me.

Lampert finally let go the ball, sending it spiraling through the air. I tracked it, falling into that place where nothing else existed but an oblong piece of inflated leather and me. I measured the arc with practiced eyes and stepped backward at the last minute, feeling the rough and welcome texture even before it fell neatly into my waiting hands.

Twisting away from Simmons, I tucked the ball securely against my chest and sprinted toward the goal line, crossing it without even getting winded. Behind me, a few teammates clapped, and I heard some hoots of praise from the sidelines, where the cheerleaders had just finished their own practice. Standing a little apart from the crowd, I recognized one girl by her jet black hair, caught up in a high ponytail. She waved and cupped her hands over her mouth.

"Nice moves, Lion!"

I made a show out of giving her a little bow and went back to my team.

If I'd thought I was going to get off easy by coming in late to practice, I was sorely mistaken. Coach had all of us receivers do a series of route running drills, separation drills and some three hard aways. By the time he finally blew his whistle and sent us into the locker room to shower and change, I was dripping with sweat even though the air had gone from chilled to downright cold.

I was bringing up the rear, dragging my feet, as I tried to figure out how I was going to deal with Brent and his buddies. I'd just cleared the field and was passing the stands when I heard my name.

"Leo. You looked good out there today." Sarah Jenkins stood just on the other side of the low wall that separated the bleachers from the sidelines. She was wearing an oversized hoodie on top of the shorts the cheerleaders all wore for practice, and her hair gleamed in the low lights from the field. Her legs were long, slim and still tanned, probably from being outside for practices. The sweatshirt hid her other assets, but I knew from previous experience that this girl had curves for days.

I'd dated Sarah back in junior high, when dating hadn't really meant much more than a few afternoons at the movies and a stolen kiss or two. Back then, she'd still been thin, and the boobs I hadn't dared to touch were small and perky. We'd enjoyed hanging out together, and when our infatuation had run its course, we'd stayed casual friends. Over the last few years, I'd seen Sarah at parties, where we'd chatted from time to time. She'd blossomed, as my mom would say, and she'd become part of the popular crowd. I knew she'd gone out with a couple of different football players, but as far as I'd heard, she hadn't gotten serious with anyone. Sarah was one of those rare girls who was genuinely nice, yet could hold her own with the bitchier chicks.

"Thanks." I stopped and gripped the metal railing separating us. "What're you doing still here? I thought cheer practice ended an hour ago. At least."

She shrugged. "It did. I wanted to watch you guys." Her eyes searched my face. "I also wanted to ask you how Nate is. I heard talk around school that he was pushed down the steps to the gym."

I frowned. "Where'd you hear that?"

"It's going around. If you're worried about Mr. Platten hearing it, I don't think that's going to happen. No one wants to see the team have to play without Brent tomorrow."

I nodded. "Good. I'm pissed at them. God, I'm more than

pissed, I'm furious. But Nate doesn't want to rat them out, so
I'm doing what he wants." My frustration laced the words.

"Hey." Sarah laid one small hand over mine where it rested on the railing. "If that's what he wants . . . but is he okay?
Someone said he was unconscious when the EMTs took him
out of here."

"He was, but yeah. He's going to be all right, I think. I just
don't get why those jackasses feel like they have to torture him.
We're not in junior high anymore. Nate doesn't bother anyone."

She sighed. "Guys like them don't need reasons to act like
assholes. Just like all the cheerleaders who're bitchy to—to
some of the other girls. My mom calls it stupid high school
crap. She told me she'd like to say it ends after graduation, but
some people just never grow up."

"Great." I groaned, rolling my eyes. "Nice to know I have
more of the same shit to look forward to, huh?"

"Guess so." She lifted her hands from mine and crossed
her arms over her chest. "God, it's cold, isn't it? I'd better get
home. Early night, with the game tomorrow."

"Yeah. I should go get changed. We've got the Twelfth Man
dinner tonight." Every week that we played on Saturday, Coach
organized a team dinner on Friday night, complete with pasta
so we could carb load and a motivational speaker. Some of the
guys groused about having to go—attendance was mandato-
ry—but I secretly loved the dinners. The food was always excellent, the speakers Coach found were interesting, and hanging with the team—there was nothing better than being with
my buds, in a situation where there were no chicks, no booze
and no drugs. No pressure to be anyone but who we were.

But I hesitated before I turned to leave. Something had
been percolating in my brain since I'd spotted Sarah watching
us from the sidelines. It wasn't an idea I was proud of, but I

was pretty certain it would work. "Hey, Sarah, you going to the diner with us tomorrow after the game?"

She tilted her head. "I always do. Maybe you don't notice because you're surrounded by other girls." She sounded teasing, not accusing, and I grinned.

"Hey, I can't help it if they all find me irresistible." I reached out, tugging at a lock of her hair that had escaped from the hairband. "Maybe I need someone to help me fight them off. Want to be my protector?"

Happiness sparkled in her brown eyes, and brand-new guilt stabbed at me. I liked Sarah. I didn't want to use her. But maybe . . . maybe I could give her a good time, too. I didn't need to hurt her. We'd had fun back when we were younger, and there was no reason to think that couldn't happen again.

"Well, I guess if someone has to do it, I might as well volunteer." She lifted her face, her lips curving into a smile. I wondered if she expected me to kiss her then, but I couldn't make myself do it. Not when the memory of Quinn's lips was still so fresh in my mind. Not when I could practically still taste her on my tongue.

Instead, I touched Sarah's cheek with the tip of my finger. "I'll see you after the game then. I better get inside before Coach comes gunning for me."

"Okay." Sarah turned her back to me, bending to pick up her pom-poms and handbag. I eyed her sweet little ass as the material of her shorts stretched tight over it.

Yeah, there wasn't any reason Sarah and I couldn't have fun together again. Maybe even more than that.

The fact that it was going to hurt Quinn wasn't something I wanted to think about. In the long run, she'd be better off. In the long run, the only one who'd end up losing was me.

And I was willing to pay that price.

Speaking of paying for sins, I knew I had to talk to Brent, Tim and Karl, the sooner the better. They had to understand that what they'd done today wasn't cool. Just because I hadn't thrown them under the bus didn't mean I was going to let them get away with it.

The three of them were standing in front of the lockers, eyeing me as I came in. I glanced around, but Coach wasn't anywhere in sight. I stopped behind them, hands on my hips.

"In case you're wondering, Nate's going to be okay. No thanks to the three of you assholes. Are you out of your fucking minds? You could've killed him. And if that doesn't bother you, if you're that damned hard, think about yourselves. You think they'd let three cold-blooded killers play on this team? You think you'd still be in school at all? No way, man. Even now, if it wasn't for Nate, you'd be facing assault charges."

Tim's eyes were wide, and Brent's mouth had dropped open. Karl ran a hand over his face.

"Dude, we were just messing around. If you hadn't yelled—"

"If I hadn't yelled, the whole thing would've escalated and Nate might've been hurt worse. I'm not taking any blame for this, except that I didn't get there faster to stop it. But I want you to know this: Nate's the one who made the call to cover for you. If he hadn't insisted on me keeping my mouth shut, I was planning to come back here and tell Coach the whole story. So you keep that in mind the next time you're tempted to get physical with Nate. Or with anyone else you like to harass. Stay away from him, you got that? Or I swear, I'll make you sorry you didn't."

Brent shuffled his feet and reached for a clean T-shirt. "Loud and clear, Lion." He glanced at Tim and Karl.

Tim cleared his throat. "I'm sorry, man. I didn't . . ." He

shrugged. "I don't know. I don't know why we did it. I guess we just fucked up."

Karl slammed his locker shut. "Yeah, whatever. I'll stay away from the—from him." He turned his back on me and stalked off toward the showers.

The entire locker room had fallen silent, listening to us. I ignored them and went to my own locker, rooting around for my towel and clean clothes. Next to me, Matt was already shrugging into a button-up shirt, his blond hair still damp from the shower.

"You okay, Lion?" He kept his voice low, and his eyes were glued to my face.

"Yeah, guess so. I will be." I exhaled long and deep.

"Hey, man. It's done. Shake it off."

"Yeah." I closed my locker. "That's what I'm going to do. I'm going to shake it all off. Every damn thing." I thought about Quinn again, remembering with a pang the softness of her lips beneath mine and the way her body had molded to me. I closed my eyes and swallowed hard, repeating my last words.

"Every damn thing."

★ Sixteen ★

Quinn

I HADN'T EXPECTED TO HEAR FROM LEO THAT NIGHT AFTER he'd kissed me. Not really. Yes, I'd kept my phone in my pocket and then on my nightstand, and yes, I'd checked the volume and made sure the ringer was turned on about every fifteen minutes or so. But it hadn't surprised me when the phone stayed silent.

It hadn't surprised me, but it had hurt.

I'd already planned to go to the football game the next day. I went to every game, and I knew my parents wouldn't think twice about me heading there today. I'd texted with Sheri that morning and learned that the doctors wanted to keep Nate one more day, because he was still in a great deal of pain. I could almost feel her anxiety through the phone, even though she assured me that it was nothing to worry about.

Go have fun today at the game. Give Leo a hug from me and scream for him like I do, LOL. I'll tell Nate you'll see him later.

It felt weird to climb to the upper bleachers on my own, since usually I stuck to the first row, to make it easier on Nate. Quite a few people stopped me to ask about Nate; I guessed word of his accident had made it around the school. Gia Capri, one of the girls who worked on the paper with me, grabbed my arm as I passed.

"Hey, Quinn. I heard what happened to your friend. What're you going to do?" She glanced down at the field, where the players were just finishing warm-up. "You're not going to let them get away with what they did, are you?"

I hesitated. Clearly the truth about what had happened with Nate wasn't much of a secret around the school. I lowered my voice. "What did you hear, exactly?"

Gia stepped around two of her friends who stood between us, flashing a smile of apology to them. "Sorry, newspaper business!" She dragged me out of the way of the people climbing the steps until we stood against the side railing.

"I thought you were there when it happened."

I shook my head. "No, I got there a few minutes later. After Nate was already at the bottom of the steps."

"Ah, okay." She nodded. "What I heard was that Brent started picking on him, things got out of hand, and Nate ended up falling. But someone else said Tim pushed him."

I closed my eyes. "Shit."

"Yeah, exactly. The kind of bullshit that goes on around here and no one does a damn thing about." She cocked her head. "You should write about it."

"I can't." I sighed. "I promised Nate that I wouldn't. I think he doesn't want to be the one responsible for getting them kicked off the team."

Gia growled and tugged on the ends of her short blonde hair. "I get that. I really do. But how's it going to change if no one talks about it? What happened to fighting the bullies?"

"I don't know. Leo . . . he said he'd take care of it."

She snorted. "Yeah, I'm sure. Leo Taylor's going to stick up for someone like Nate."

"They're friends. We're all three friends. Leo's the one who got to Nate first yesterday, and he drove me to the hospital." *And kissed me until I forgot my own first name.* Yeah, I thought I'd better leave that part out.

"Yeah?" Gia didn't look convinced. "Let's just say he doesn't strike me as someone who's going to stick his neck out for anyone but himself. Or maybe his football buds." She lifted up her hands. "But hey, I've been wrong before." She looked over her shoulder at her friends. "I need to go sit down before I lose my seat."

"Yeah, I need to find one before it's standing room only." I pointed up higher.

"I'd invite you to join us, but it's pretty tight here. But hey, next time, right? My friends and I come to games ironically." She quirked an eyebrow. "Meaning that we make fun of the players, the cheerleaders . . . you know, the whole school spirit deal."

If it wasn't for Leo, I could see myself feeling the same way. "Sounds like fun. Thanks, Gia. See you Monday."

I'd just started to move away when she called my name again. "Hey, Quinn, we're going over to the diner after. If you want to come? I know you usually hang with Nate, so . . ." She let her voice trail off, but somehow, being Gia, she didn't make the invitation sound like a pity offer. I considered for a minute before I nodded.

"That sounds like fun. Meet you there?"

"Yep. We'll save you a seat, and if you get there first, get a booth for four."

I waved and began the climb again. There was a little space at the very top, just below the press box, and I murmured my excuses as I sidled in front of people and sat down.

Franklin Township wasn't exactly Eatonboro's arch rival, but they were a strong opponent, I knew. Township was a regional school, and a lot of the kids came from area farms. They were big guys, probably outweighing our boys by a good forty pounds each. I watched Matt Lampert on the sidelines, bouncing on the balls of his feet, helmet in his hand as he scanned the field where the opposition was taking their warm-up. His face was impassive, and I wondered if he got nervous before games. I knew Leo had a routine he stuck to every time they played. He was definitely superstitious about it.

As if I'd summoned him by my thoughts, Leo wandered into my line of vision, coming up to stand next to Matt. A rush of longing flooded through me, my eyes hungrily taking in his shoulders under the wide pads and the way they accented his narrow hips, his tight rear end . . . God, I wished I'd taken the opportunity to cop a feel of that backside yesterday when I'd had the chance. The pants of his uniform clung to the muscles of his legs, and I remembered the feel of those legs pushing into mine yesterday, the touch of his hands all over me.

"Hey, Q! What're you doing here?"

I swiveled on my seat just as Jake gripped my shoulder and squeezed. He was leaning out of the open window of the press box, grinning at me.

"Hi, Jake." I craned my neck to see him without bothering the men who sat on either side of me. "Oh, I come to all the games. But I usually sit down lower, with Nate."

"Ah, okay. Yeah." Regret filled Jake's eyes. "I heard about his accident. He's okay, though?"

"Yeah, looks that way." I smiled. "Thanks for asking."

"You look like you're pretty crowded there. Why don't you come back here? We've got extra seats in the press box, and you're press, after all."

It took me about two seconds to make the decision. "I'd love to, thanks, Jake." I stood up and stumbled past more knees and glares from people who felt that my nanosecond in front of them was impacting their ability to see the game that hadn't even started yet.

Jake held the door open for me and pointed at a metal folding chair. "It's not exactly luxury, but at least you've got leg room." He gestured to the older man sitting at a mic, wearing headphones. "That's Mr. Ranetti. He announces the games and broadcasts them, too. You know Ken—" He nodded to the skinny kid sitting by the window, who I knew helped to cover sports for the newspaper. "And this is Caren Hopkins. She's the high school sports reporter for the *Lawrence County Journal*. Everyone, this is Quinn Russell. She's our columns and opinions editor at the paper."

There was a low hum as everyone mumbled hellos, but their attention—and mine—snapped back to the field, as the game was about to begin. Mr. Ranetti read off both team rosters, and a kind of contrary pride swelled in my heart when the loudest cheers seemed to come for "Number ten, wide receiver Leo Tayyyyylor!" The cheerleaders launched into the chant they'd written expressly for Leo, and I managed not to roll my eyes. I called that a victory.

The Eatonboro Eagles won the toss and deferred to receive in the second half. Beau Dunton, our kicker, sent the ball flying end over end until it landed around Franklin Township's thirty-yard line, where the kick returner scooped it up and attempted to run downfield. He only got about five yards before the Eagles laid him out.

In the next ten minutes, Township attempted to get past our defense, but the line was strong. Watching Brent plow through the blockers, I felt a twinge of empathy for Leo, realizing why it was so important to him that his linebackers were able to play today. I didn't condone what they'd done, and I still thought Nate was wrong to cover it up, but I understood it just a little more.

Almost the entire first half of the game was essentially a stand-off. The Eagles managed to run for a few first downs, but they weren't able to convert them into any real yardage or a score. Even from up in the press box, I could see the frustration on Leo's face each time Matt was forced to throw the ball away or run with it, rather than pass it to him. Although I knew our blockers were working hard to protect their QB, Matt was finding it nearly impossible to get out of the pocket long enough to execute a decent pass.

"Damn!" I dropped back into my seat, clenching my jaw after Franklin Township actually succeeded in sacking Lampert. "Harris missed that block. He practically invited their DE to stroll in for the sack."

"They're all wearing down." Jake leaned back in his chair, studying me. "You know a lot about the game, don't you? I mean, I don't want to sound sexist, because I'm not. But most girls I've known are proud when they can talk about touchdowns and field goals. They know the basics, but you seem to know what you're doing."

I lifted one shoulder. "Leo's been my best friend since we were born. He started to be obsessed with football when we were about nine, and I had to listen to him jabber on about it all the time. After a while, I figured I might as well pay attention. You know, if you can't beat them, join them. And yeah, I love the game. It's got history, it's got a certain elegance . . ." I smiled and shook my head. "Sorry. Not many people ask me about football. Now you know why."

One side of Jake's mouth curled into a half-smile. "It's just another piece in the mystery that is Quinn Russell. I like finding out about you, a little at a time."

I flushed. "I'm really not that interesting, Jake. Sorry to disappoint you. I'm actually pretty boring."

He laughed. "Q, the last thing I'd ever call you is boring. Matter of fact, I'd say you've brought more excitement to the paper in the time you've been on staff than I can remember us having before you joined."

I smiled and turned away to pay attention to the game, but I could feel Jake's gaze on my back. It made me a little uncomfortable; I liked Jake, and I loved working with him on the school newspaper. We'd developed an easy camaraderie right off the bat, and I relaxed more around him than I did anyone else outside of Leo and Nate. But I wasn't interested in dating him. At least, I was pretty sure I wasn't. If I'd toyed with the idea of going out with other boys before—and I never had, not seriously—the kiss I'd shared with Leo yesterday had cemented in my mind that he was the only one I wanted. If I couldn't have him, there wasn't any point in dating someone else.

My eyes rested on Leo's back as he stood in the huddle just before they broke and lined up for the next play. I focused on him and him alone, sending him vibes of support. As though that made a difference, Matt managed to get free long enough to fire off a spiral. We all held our breath as it soared, arcing down into Leo's waiting arms as though there'd never been any doubt that he was going to catch it.

Unfortunately, even though the completed pass gave the Eagles at first down, they couldn't push forward into the end zone. We all had to settle for the unsatisfactory second-best of field goal, which Beau made with beautiful precision. The half ended just after the ball went through the uprights, and the Eagles ran into the locker room leading three to zip.

"Do you want anything from the concession?" Jake stood up, stretching. I watched him, trying to look at him through eyes that didn't only see Leo. Yeah, Jake was cute, in a geeky, hipster sort of way. His reddish-brown hair was a little longer than I liked on a guy, but his eyes were bright blue and wide. Now they gazed down at me as his question lingered in the air.

"Concession? Oh, food? No, thanks. I'm good." I knew a little something about the cheap brand of hotdogs our school sold at sporting events, and it made me want to gag. As a matter of fact, I'd written an article, exposing the poor quality of the food at games. Needless to say, that piece hadn't gone over well, any more than my cheerleader expo had.

Jake was gone for most of half-time. I watched distractedly as the band marched onto the field and regaled us with their ability to march and play at the same time without running into each other or anything else. I sounded like Gia and her friends, I decided; they'd rather make fun of the game instead of joining in the excitement, and I was mocking people who were talented in areas I'd never even tried to conquer.

Kickoff for the second half was just underway when Jake came back inside, whistling. He dragged his chair over closer to mine and sat down.

"Did I miss anything?" He stretched out his legs and folded his arms over his chest.

"Gus Walker got some decent yardage on the kickoff return. Our rushing game is basically non-existent today, though. They've got to do better than three and done if we're ever going to really score."

"Huh." Jake scanned the field, wincing along with me when Franklin made a tackle that resulted in a loss of yards for us. "Oh, hey, I almost forgot." He twisted his body, digging into his pocket, and pulled out a chocolate bar, tossing it into my lap. "I brought you something."

"Chocolate?" My mouth watered. "But I said I didn't need anything."

"Q, no one *needs* chocolate. But you like it, right? You're always scarfing up the chocolate kisses in the newspaper office. And leaving the foil all over the place."

"I am not!" I defended myself, but I couldn't help a little grin. I was totally guilty of just that. "Okay, well, maybe if I'm really deep in writing a story or working on layout with you, I might have left a wrapper or two."

Jake shrugged. "So I figured you wouldn't say no to— whoa!" He jumped to his feet as the entire stadium came to life. Down on the field, on third and long, Matt had somehow gotten free of the defenders and sent a gorgeous pass downfield where it landed neatly in Leo's hands. And Leo was managing to elude the Franklin cornerback who was pursuing him. Watching him run down the field, neatly sidestepping the other team, was a thing of beauty.

And when he crossed into the end zone, still on his feet, it felt as though the entire place was going to shake apart. The noise was deafening, but even so, I could still hear Leo's trademark roar as he raised the ball high over his head.

"Holy shit, that was beautiful!" Jake turned toward me, scooping me into a quick, tight hug of celebration. I knew it didn't mean anything; like everyone else around us, he was caught up in the moment, and I just happened to be the closest person to him. But still.

It was the second time in less than twenty-four hours that I'd been held close to a boy, and I couldn't help but compare the two. The 'boy' part was where the similarity ended. Jake wasn't as tall as Leo, and where Leo was muscled and hard, Jake was thin and almost bony. His chest was firm, but it wasn't as broad as Leo's.

I felt guilty comparing them. First of all, Jake was my friend. Just a friend. And Leo . . . well, he was my friend, too, but I wanted him to be so much more. Of course, it wasn't like Jake meant anything by this quick hug.

Or did he? He drew back from me slowly, and the smile on his face, along with the subtle question in his eyes, made my heart sink. I liked Jake, but he wasn't Leo, and I had no experience in letting down a guy easy.

I stepped back, intentionally focusing my attention down to the field where the team was lining up to attempt the extra point. "That was beautiful, wasn't it? The catch, I mean. And the run."

"Yeah. Beautiful." Jake's voice sounded odd, but I refused to look back at him. I kept my eyes on Leo. He was standing on the sideline again, and he'd taken off his helmet. I could see the rapid rise and fall of his chest from here; he was still breathing hard from that run. His teammates—at least those who weren't on the field for the field goal—were clustered around him, smacking his butt, slapping him on his back, offering congratulations. Leo turned, his gaze sweeping over the stands, and I wondered who he was hoping to find. Probably his parents and his brothers, I assumed, but God, how I wished it was me he was seeking. I imagined him finding me in the stands and a broad grin spreading over his face when he caught my eye. He wouldn't have to do anything else, but I'd know what he was thinking. I'd know that he was thinking only of me . . .

"Q! Earth to Quinn." Jake kept his tone light and teasing, but a small frown hovered between his eyes. "You okay?"

"Oh." I gave a little laugh. "Yeah. I just, you know, get into the zone. Watching the game." We both watched the ball fly neatly between the goal posts, giving us a lead of ten to zip.

"Sorry about that. What were you saying?"

Jake shook his head. "Nothing important. Nothing that can't keep for later."

The game ended with a win for the Eagles and a final score of ten to six. As the stands began to empty, I folded up my chair and propped it against the wall of the press box.

"Thanks for letting me watch up here. I really appreciate it." I paused. "I'm meeting Gia and her friends over at the diner. Do you . . . would you want to come with us, or do you have other plans?"

Jake's face brightened. "I was going to head over there, too. I'd love to hang with you guys. Or maybe I should say you girls." He winked. "Want a ride?"

I shook my head. "Thanks, but I have my car. Meet you there."

"Okay, sure. See you there."

I stepped out of the box and joined the throngs of people trying to make their way down the bleachers and out of the stadium. Down on the field, most of the team was still milling around, talking to the Franklin Township players or congratulating each other. As usual, the cheerleaders were there, too. A bunch of them surrounded Leo, their hands all over his body. Watching it made my blood boil, even as I tried to rationalize it. He was a football player. He couldn't help what those girls did. He was just being polite. Nice.

But still, I was glad when the people in front of me moved, clearing the way for me to head to my car.

The Starlight Diner was in the middle of town, but it had

the advantage of having a large parking lot. Even so, I nabbed one of the very last spots, since the restaurant was the most popular post-game meeting place. That was abundantly clear when I opened the door and nearly stumbled back at the crescendo of voices that greeted me.

"Hey, Quinn! Over here." Gia waved her arms, and I smiled, winding around the people standing in the aisles to get to the booth where the three girls sat.

"Thanks for saving me a seat." I slid in to sit next to Gia. "I hope it's okay, but I invited Jake. If we don't have room, I'll just go sit with him . . ." I glanced around. "Well, somewhere."

"Nah, that's cool. We love Jake." Gia pushed a glass of water toward me. "We didn't order yet, but the waiter brought us these."

"Thank you." I took a grateful gulp. "Wow, it's crowded in here, isn't it?"

"Yeah." Heather, the girl sitting across from me, didn't bother to try to hide her bitterness. "They rope off a whole section for the football team, so the rest of us little people have to fight for every seat." She glanced over my shoulder. "Speaking of the devils . . . here they are. All hail the conquering heroes."

Suddenly, the diner felt much smaller than it had before, and my heart began to pound. The football team in all its post-victory glory came bursting through the glass doors, raising a cheer and shouts from everyone already sitting down. The defensive line appeared first, and then I saw Matt and Leo, laughing as they came into the restaurant.

"There's our Lion! Hear him ROAR!" The cheerleaders already inside began to chant, and Leo shook his head. I couldn't tell if he was embarrassed or pleased. All I could think about was what would happen when he caught sight of me. Would he stop and say something? Or would he invite me over to sit with the team, the way the players sometimes did? My stomach turned over in anticipation.

Someone yelled out Matt's name, and he stopped, bending over a chair to talk to the guy who was punching him in the arm. Leo turned his head, checking out the rest of the diner.

I knew the minute he spotted me. He froze, and then with deliberate carelessness, gave me a quick wave before he looked away. A group of cheerleaders thronged him, and he relaxed, chatting with them and pretending that they were overwhelming him.

I dropped my gaze to the table and swallowed hard over the lump that had risen in my throat. I hadn't had expectations—not really—but down deep inside, I'd held out a small spark of hope that had just now died a painful death.

"Fucking football players." Gia's voice dripped with contempt. "Look at that. Quinn, you can't tell me it doesn't piss you off. Your friend's hurt, and there's the assholes who caused it, living it up and making out with the fucking rah-rah bitches."

I glanced up automatically, but instead of seeing Brent and the cheerleader who apparently was checking on the status of his tonsils—with her tongue—I saw Leo. He'd found a seat, but he wasn't alone. One cheerleader had pushed through the rest of the crowd and was leaning over him. As I watched in misery, Leo raked his fingers through the girl's shiny black hair and tugged her close for a kiss.

I knew who she was. Sarah Jenkins had been the bane of my existence when we were in junior high; Leo had dated her for a little while, and the entire time, I'd been horribly jealous. What made the situation especially difficult was that Sarah seemed like a really nice girl. She was always friendly to me, and she tried to include Nate and me whenever we were all together. Her only real fault was that Leo liked her.

Seeing them together now felt like a slap in the face. Leo ignoring me was bad enough. Even watching him flirt with cheerleaders was tough, but knowing the connection he'd always had with Sarah made their cozy little scene excruciating. It was almost as if he was trying to hurt me . . . sending me a message that the kiss we'd shared, the one that had meant everything to me, had been utterly forgettable to him.

I pushed myself up to stand. "I'm sorry, I need to—the ladies room." I choked out the words and pushed through the people standing between tables, desperate to get out of the diner. I heard Gia calling me, but I didn't turn around.

The bathrooms at the Starlight were down a long hallway, and I groaned inwardly when I saw the length of the line for the women's room. At least ten girls stood leaning against the wall, waiting, chattering with each other. And at least three of those girls were cheerleaders.

I didn't relish the idea of spending quality time with this group just now, so I kept walking down the hall, passing them with my head down and my eyes on the floor. I knew there was an exit in the back; when I'd done volunteer work with a local food pantry, we'd come to that door to pick up the diner's unsold baked goods every other day. If I could get there and then get out, at least I'd be able to breathe. I'd just tell Gia on Monday . . . well, I'd come up with something plausible by then.

Pushing open the door, I stepped outside into the cold and sucked in a deep breath. The silence in the alley was a welcome relief after the noise level inside, and I leaned against the brick wall, taking a minute to soak it in and let my ears recover.

But my respite was short-lived. The door to the alley opened again, and Leo stepped out. His eyes zeroed in on me right away as the door slammed behind him.

"Quinn, what're you doing out here?" He stood with his

hands on his hips, brows drawn together as he stared me down.

"It was too loud in there. Too many people. I needed to get out."

"But why did you—"

"Leo, go back inside. Go back to your celebration. I don't know why you're even out here. You've made it abundantly clear that you don't care about me. Don't worry, I got the message tonight."

I couldn't miss the shadow of guilt and regret that passed over his face before he got himself under control again. "Mia, I—"

"*Don't call me that.*" I spit out the words. "Don't you dare fucking call me that, pretending that it means anything. It doesn't. Not when you treat me like—like you did. Do you think I'm an idiot, Leo? Do you think I'm not smart enough to know when I'm being used?"

He stepped back as though I'd struck him. "What the hell are you talking about?"

"Yesterday. At the hospital." My mouth was moving faster than my brain, but I didn't stop speaking. "How long do you think it took me to figure out that you—you did what you did just so I'd go along with your stupid plan to protect your precious football players? Did you get a good laugh at my expense, Leo? Poor, pathetic Quinn, too busy mooning over you to realize that it didn't mean a fucking thing. Kiss her, make her feel like you care, and she'll go along with anything. Right? I bet you couldn't wait to tell your good buddies how easy it was to manipulate me."

"I never—" Leo started and then bit off the words, pressing his lips shut. "You know what, Quinn? Fine. Have it your way. You're going to believe the worst about me anyway, aren't you? So go right ahead."

To my absolute disgust, tears had sprung up in my eyes. I wiped them away furiously. "I wouldn't have to believe the worst if you ever did anything to prove me wrong. You're saying you have another excuse for why you—you kissed me? Please. Enlighten me." I crossed my arms over my chest and waited.

Leo glared at me, but he didn't reply.

"Oh, come on, Leo. You're disappointing me. Can't come up with any plausible explanation? You're not going to claim that you were overcome with passion for me?" I stepped closer to him, until we were nearly touching. "You're not going to say you couldn't help yourself?"

"Quinn." Leo grabbed me by the shoulders, and for a heady moment, I thought he was going to pull me against him again. And damn my weak will, I probably would've let him.

But in the end, he carefully set me away from him. "Think whatever you want, but I wasn't trying to manipulate you to go along with me. I was—it was just the heat of the moment. We were both emotional, and things got out of hand." His gaze skittered away from mine. "I felt bad for you. And I let that feeling go too far. It didn't mean anything."

I stared up at him. "It did mean something, actually. It meant you're selfish and—" I couldn't think of a word to describe the way I felt. *A pity kiss.* That was what he was calling it. "Just leave me alone, Leo. Stay away from me. Stay away from Nate. Don't pretend to be our friend." I swiveled on my heel and rounded the corner of the diner, half-running and half-walking toward my car, praying Leo wouldn't follow me and wishing like hell he would.

Blinded with tears, I didn't notice the person in front of me until I'd slammed into him.

"God, I'm sorry, I wasn't paying attention." I made to move around him before I realized it was Jake.

"Q? What's up?" He frowned down at me. "You okay? What happened?"

I shook my head. "Nothing. I don't want to talk about it, if that's okay." I swiped my hand over my face and tried for a watery smile. "I'm so sorry, Jake. I know I said I'd meet you here, but something kind of came up. Gia and the others are inside, though, and you're welcome to take my seat there."

He smiled. "No offense to any of them, but I was coming to be with *you.*"

Of course he was, because now was the perfect time for Jake to begin showing real interest in me. A week ago, I might've been flattered. Hell, I might've even been tempted, since a week ago, it had felt like there wasn't any chance for me with Leo. But all of that had changed yesterday when he'd kissed me, and despite his words moments before, now that I knew what kissing Leo was like . . . I wasn't sure I could accept second-best.

"I'm sorry," I repeated. "But I need to go. It's so crowded in there and . . ." I shrugged. "You know. Football players."

"Oh. Yeah." Jake nodded as though I'd said something that had made sense, which of course I hadn't. "Well, are you all right to drive? You seem kind of shaken up."

"Yep, I'll be fine." I dug into my pocket and pulled out my keys. "I'll see you Monday."

"Hey, Q?"

I stopped and glanced back at Jake, lifting my eyebrows in question.

"Uh, I was thinking, maybe, if you wanted, we could go out. You know. Have dinner." Jake sounded casual, but I noticed that he was shifting his weight from one foot to the other, and his eyes were intent on my face.

I bit the side of my lip. "I'm sorry, Jake. Tonight's not good. I have to go check on Nate, and I'm just tired. It's been a long couple of days." I stretched my neck. None of that was a lie; I was suddenly exhausted.

"Next week, then? How about Friday? I'll pick you up, and we can eat dinner and then maybe, I don't know. See a movie. Play mini golf. Bug the campaign offices of our political opponents."

I smiled for real then. Jake was so dang nice, and it was a welcome change from . . . other people. "It sounds fun, but I don't know."

"What's not to know? I'm not asking you to elope, Q. Just a date. One little date."

When he put it that way, it would've been silly to say no. Besides, why the hell should I say no to a guy I liked, even if it was only as a friend at this point? Maybe once we'd spent time together, I'd realized there was something more. Maybe if Jake kissed me, I'd find that same spark I had with Leo.

And maybe pigs would sprout wings and fly.

But I'd never know if I didn't give it a shot. With that in mind, I finally nodded. "Okay. Dinner on Friday sounds good."

Jake grinned, his whole face lighting up. "Awesome. You just made my whole night." He reached down to take my hand, giving it a quick squeeze before letting it go. "See you Monday, Q."

I watched Jake jog down the sidewalk toward where I assumed his car was parked, surprised despite what he'd said that he wasn't going into the diner if I weren't there. He really was a pretty great person. I owed it to him—and to myself—to give our date a decent shot.

But now, tonight, I just needed to go home, climb into bed and rest my bruised heart.

★ Seventeen ★

Nate

B Y MID-MORNING ON SUNDAY, THE PAIN IN MY HEAD
had subsided enough that it could be controlled with
regular over-the-counter meds, and the doctors agreed
that I could be released. I'd just gotten dressed and was sitting
on the edge of the bed when I heard a noise at the door.

"Knock, knock." Dr. Randall stepped into the room. "I
hear my favorite patient of all time needed a little staycation at
his number one resort this weekend."

I snorted. Dr. Randall had been monitoring me and coor-
dinating all of my care since I was four years old. At this point,
he was almost like family.

Leaning against the door jamb, he skimmed my file on
his ever-present tablet. "So the bad news is, that new protocol
we introduced last summer? Apparently it doesn't give you the
ability to fly."

I rolled my eyes. "It also doesn't make your jokes any fun-
nier, either."

He clutched his chest as though wounded. "Now that one
hurts." He lowered the computer to his side. "Looks like you're

going to be okay. I'm just here to ask you a few questions about how this happened."

"All the other docs already did that." I turned to reach for my phone, hoping he got the hint that this conversation was over.

"Yeah, but none of those bozos—I mean, those esteemed medical personnel—know you the way I do. I know what to ask. What happened in the minute before you fell? Ten minutes before? Did you feel at all off when you woke up that morning?"

"No." I sighed. He wasn't going to drop this, and I knew from experience that it would be better to come clean. "If I give you some insider information about what made me fall, can we put it under the heading of doctor-patient confidentiality?"

"As in, I don't share it with your parents? It's possible, unless it's something medically significant that they need to know."

"It isn't." I scrolled through my phone, checking to see if Quinn had answered my last text. "Truth is, I didn't fall down those steps so much as I was shoved."

Dr. Randall didn't react. It was one reason he was so good at his job; nothing seemed to surprise him. "Okay. And since you haven't given this information to anyone else, I'm assuming you don't want to implicate whoever did the deed."

"Nope."

"May I ask why?"

I trusted Dr. Randall, so I didn't hedge. "The guys who did it are on the football team. They'd get suspended at best, kicked off the team at worst. Everyone at school would hate me. And maybe by not ratting them out, they'll give me a break. For a while, anyway."

"Hmmm. Okay." The doctor pushed off the wall and came

over to me, casually beginning his typical basic exam.

"That's it? Just 'okay'? You don't want to give me some sage advice?"

He shrugged. "Nah. You seem like you've got it under control." He stepped back, grinning at me. "You can't tell because I'm so freaking cool, but I'm actually doing a happy dance inside. I'm sorry you got hurt, but how you're reacting, how you're handling it, is completely age-appropriate. You're normal, kiddo. Or at least in some senses you are. Color me pleased."

"Glad I could help you out. Are we done?"

"Pretty much, but out of professional necessity, I have to ask if you feel like you're being bullied on a regular basis or if you feel unsafe in your current environment." He made a face. "It's a thing. I have to document that I asked you so you don't come back and sue my ass someday."

I barked out a laugh. "I've been bullied as long as I've been in school. Most kids are, and that's the hard truth no one wants to hear. But no, it's not any worse now than it's ever been, and no, I don't feel unsafe." I managed to stand up without swaying. "Thanks for stopping by. See you next month."

"All righty then. Here's my hat, what's my hurry?" Dr. Randall dropped one hand on my shoulder. "You know how to reach me if you need anything, Nate." He paused in the doorway, glancing back over his shoulder. "All joking aside, bud, try to stay away from the physical stuff. You're okay now, but anything like this has the potential for setting you back. Or triggering an advance in the disease. So . . . do your best to stay on your feet."

I humored my mom and stayed home from school on Monday. The truth was, for once I wasn't eager to see Quinn. I had a hazy memory of a conversation we'd had on Friday before she left the hospital, and I was pretty sure I'd said things that I shouldn't have.

Since then, we'd only communicated by text. She hadn't seemed any different, and she'd offered to come over to my house on Sunday afternoon, after my discharge from the hospital. But I'd begged off, saying I was tired and wanted to rest. It was true, but I was also too scared to face Quinn that day. I was afraid that she'd feel compelled to bring up what I'd said, and if she did, I was fairly certain it wouldn't end well for me.

When I got to school on Tuesday, I wasn't sure what to expect. Quinn had texted me that the truth about what had happened was an open secret; everyone seemed to know, but no one was talking about it to the administration. I'd texted her back:

Did Leo say anything to them? To Brent, I mean.

Quinn didn't respond for so long that I was just about to resend mine when she finally answered.

Have no idea. If you want to know, ask him yourself. I'm done with him.

I'd read that line over a few times, frowning. Quinn's patience with both Leo and me was something I took for granted. If she said she was 'done' with Leo, something really serious must've gone down while I was still in the hospital.

Everything began to fall into place after I'd stopped at my locker and turned around. Across the hall, Leo was leaning against the wall, and Sarah Jenkins stood in front of him, her arms around his neck and her lips locked to his. Leo's hands rested on her butt. There was an intimacy between them that didn't leave much to the imagination.

The fact that it was Sarah in the lip lock with Leo must've especially hurt Quinn, I thought. She'd been crushed a few years before, when the two had dated. I'd actually liked Sarah; she was friendly, willing to include us, and never made me feel like I was the 'special' friend. But Quinn seemed to sense something between Sarah and Leo that threatened her, and although she wasn't ever outright mean to her—that wasn't Quinn's way—neither was she especially warm or welcoming.

Quinn herself came around the corner at that moment. If she saw Leo and Sarah out of the corner of her eye, she didn't give any indication. Instead, she greeted me with a bright smile and one of her signature Quinn hugs.

"I'm so glad you're back." She stood back, checking me out with narrowed eyes. "You're feeling better?"

"Hundred percent," I lied. My head was still a little achy, but she didn't need to know that. I hated for Quinn to see me as weak and sickly; there were times when it was unavoidable, but if I could help it, I would. "So you want to fill me in on what's been happening since Friday afternoon?"

She shrugged. "We won the football game. It was the typical scene at the Starlight afterwards. Oh . . ." She lowered her voice. "And Gia thinks I should write a piece for the newspaper about bullying and what happened to you."

"No." I put as emphasis into that one syllable as I could. "I mean it, Quinn. I don't want you to do that. I just need for this to go away. For everyone to forget. You understand?"

Quinn drew back, frowning, a tinge of hurt in her eyes. "Yeah, I understand. You don't have to get all upset about it, Nate. It was just a thought. I didn't even say *I* wanted to do it. It was Gia's idea."

"Okay." I nodded, as the bell rang. "I need to get to class." Still, I didn't move quite yet. Leo and Sarah had separated and were strolling away from us, hand in hand. I waited until they'd passed before I spoke again. "Um, I wanted to say . . . thanks for coming with me to the hospital. I was pretty out of it, you know? But I kind of remember you being there. I hope I didn't say anything . . . you know, crazy."

Pink washed over Quinn's cheeks. *Crap.* She knew exactly what I was getting at. "Of course I was going to be there for you. We actually didn't get to see you that much, though. You talked to Leo and me, and then you were taken up for your scan. By the time you came back down, your mom had arrived. And then my mom did, too, and I went home with her." She lifted one shoulder. "No big deal. I was just glad you were all right."

"Ah, okay. Good, then." I twisted my neck, looking away from Quinn so she couldn't see the disappointment on my face. I hadn't meant to say those things to her at the hospital, but at the same time, part of me wished that she'd acknowledge them. Answer me.

In my perfect fantasy, Quinn would loop her arms around my neck, just as Sarah had with Leo, and she'd say, "You told me you loved me, Nate. Which works out great, because I love you, too."

Only this time, she'd mean it the same way I did. This time when she pulled me tight, it would be to kiss me, with her mouth open and seeking.

I gave a ragged sigh and began to make my way toward class, glad that my T-shirt was long enough to hide the bulge under the fly in my jeans.

★ Eighteen ★

Quinn

I'D PICTURED MY FIRST DATE FOR YEARS, PROBABLY SINCE I was ten or eleven. And ever since that time, every time I'd thought of it, Leo had been the guy across the table from me.

The fact that Jake Donavan was in that seat tonight was more than a little disconcerting. Still, if it had to be anyone but Leo, Jake wasn't a bad second choice. He'd been a good friend of mine since we'd met on the newspaper, and I felt comfortable with him. Maybe a little too comfortable; there wasn't the same delicious tension and heat I felt when Leo was near me. Which was crazy, considering how long and how well I'd known Leo.

I'd been a little nervous before he picked me up—which wasn't helped by my mother, who was playing it casual even while I was pretty sure she was taking notes to document 'Quinn's First Date' in my baby book—but all the anxiety evaporated as we drove to the restaurant. Jake was low-key and friendly; he didn't act any different than he did when we were together in school. I found myself laughing at his jokes and actually enjoying myself.

The pizza place was busy tonight, but not too loud, which I also liked. I'd just finished my second slice, listening to Jake tell me a story about his little brother, when someone called his name.

"Hey! Donavan." The tall blond guy detached himself from the group of people passing us and paused by Jake's chair. "How's it going?"

"Hey, Scott. What's up?" Jake turned a little in his seat, balling up the paper napkin in one fist. Scott Murray covered some sports for the paper, and from what I'd heard, was the best pitcher our baseball team had. He was that rare person who seemed to be able to straddle two worlds; he was well-liked by just about everyone in the school, both athlete and geek. I didn't know him well, since he didn't hang out in the newspaper room very often, but he was a friend of Leo's, so I was aware of him in that way.

Scott noticed me, and his eyebrows rose a fraction. "Hi, Quinn. You guys having a working dinner? Plotting the next issue?"

"Uh—" Jake glanced at me. "Not really. More like a date."

"Oh." Scott sounded so surprised that I wasn't sure whether I should be confused or offended. Was I considered such an odd choice as a date, or was it that he didn't expect to see me with Jake? I couldn't tell. "I didn't know you guys were together."

"Yeah, well . . . you here with the team?" Jake looked over his shoulder at the table Scott's friends had taken over, a not-so-subtle hint, I thought, that the other guy needed to move on.

"Ah, yeah, some of us. We're grabbing something to eat before we go to Anders' party. You going?"

"Mike Anders? I hadn't heard about it."

Scott shrugged. "He found out he got into Penn State, so his parents gave him their credit card and the house for the night." He shook his head. "Crazy, right? Anyway, everyone's invited, so you guys should definitely come over." He knocked on our table. "I'll let you get back to your food. See you over there, maybe."

After Scott had moved away, Jake raised his eyebrows at me. "So. You up for that?"

I frowned. "For what? For Mike Anders' party?" Distaste was clear in my voice. Mike was a football player, one of Leo's buds, but he was also one of the guys who seemed to take great joy in torturing Nate. He was a year ahead of us, but even back in junior high, Mike used to stalk behind Nate, chanting, "Gimp! Gimp! Gimp!" as they walked down the hallway. Nate ignored Mike, the same way he did everyone who teased him, but I knew he detested him. One of his bigger resentments about Leo these days was that he was still friends with Mike.

"I know." Jake sighed. "He's a dick, right? We don't have to go. I just thought maybe you'd like to hang out with everyone."

I hesitated. I didn't really want to go, but at the same time, I didn't want Jake to think I was a loser who couldn't handle a party. We were juniors in high school. Partying was supposed to be part of our lives, wasn't it?

"If you weren't out with me tonight, would you go?" I took a sip of my water and rested my elbow on the table.

He lifted his shoulders, but the expression on his face told me the truth. Of course he would.

I took a deep breath. "Let's go."

Jake's face brightened as though he couldn't help it, but when he spoke, his voice was cautious. "Are you sure? We really don't have to. We can . . . I don't know, go get ice cream or something. Just hang."

"Full disclosure: I've never been to a party. I mean, not one like this. So this is my chance to experience a high school rite of passage, isn't it? If I'm going to be a journalist, I have to learn to broaden my horizons. I want to go. Really."

Five minutes inside Mike Anders' front door, I wasn't so sure I was ready for this, after all.

The wide foyer opened into a great room, which was wall-to-wall people and blaring music. The door had been propped open when we approached, and the front porch was crowded, too. A couple of guys had greeted Jake with typical shoulder punches and fist bumps, and someone had what had appeared to be a short conversation with him, pointing in a few different directions. Maybe explaining where to find drinks? Food? A reliable fire exit? I wasn't sure, since whatever he said was lost in the thump-thump-thump of the bass.

"Are you okay?" Jake touched my shoulder and leaned down to speak right into my ear, which was the only way I was going to hear him. "Someone said they've got a fire going in the backyard. It'll be quieter out there."

I hugged my arms around my ribs. "Yes, please!" I had to yell to be heard.

Jake nodded, jerked his head toward the kitchen and offered me his hand. I hesitated only a second before I took it. When his fingers closed around mine, I waited to feel the same zing I'd experienced when Leo touched me, but it didn't happen. Jake's hand was warm, and his grip was firm, but it only felt . . . friendly. Comfortable. Like when Nate held my hand.

But still and all, I was grateful for someone to hold onto as we pushed through the throngs of people in the kitchen. Near the table, a group was chanting something as a girl who stood on a chair chugged a bottle of . . . was that whiskey? The label looked familiar. The girl, not so much. I wondered if she was from another school.

We finally made it to the back door, and Jake managed to get us both through it. When he closed it again, I heaved a sigh of relief at the relative silence.

Small clumps of people stood on the deck. Some were smoking, and I was pretty sure not all of the cigarettes were straight tobacco. A few of them were making out, although it might've been more accurate to say they were hooking up. One girl's shirt was hiked up so high that it looked more like a scarf. She was wearing a silky purple bra, and I thought distractedly that it was pretty. Another girl was perched on the deck railing while the guy she was kissing stood between her spread legs.

I felt like a voyeur. Jake glanced back at me over his shoulder, raised his eyebrows and shook his head, and gratification filled me. I was so glad he didn't expect me to join in on the porn fest out here. I couldn't remember when I'd been more uncomfortable.

We made our way to the steps that led off the deck down to the yard. It was dark, but the fire in the pit a few feet away lent enough light so that I didn't trip as we walked across the grass. There were some chairs around the fire; most of them were empty, but someone was sitting with his back toward us. When we got a little closer, my heart sank. It was Leo slumped in the Adirondack chair, and Sarah Jenkins was on his lap. No, correction: she was actually sitting on the chair, between Leo's legs, sprawled back over his chest.

I wanted to turn around and run away. I wanted to erase the sight of them from my memory. But mostly, I just wanted this to not be happening.

Fleetingly, I considered tugging Jake's hand and pulling him away. I could always use the excuse that I thought Leo and Sarah probably wanted privacy. But before I could put that plan into action, Leo saw us. I knew the minute it happened: he did one of those double-takes, like people do in comedies. And then he straightened up, pushing Sarah up a little so he could move.

"Hey, man." Jake held out a fist, and after a moment's hesitation, Leo pounded it. His eyes fastened on my hand in Jake's, and a muscle in his jaw quivered.

"Donavan." He muttered the word and then turned his head to look at me. "Quinn. I didn't know you were coming tonight."

"It was kind of . . . last-minute." I forced a smile, though I wanted to add, *And since when do you care where I go or what I do?* "Jake and I were out eating, and we ran into Scott Murray. He told us about the party, so . . ." I shrugged. "Here we are."

"Hmmm." Leo didn't say anything more than that, but he didn't look away from me, either.

"Mind if we join you here?" Jake led me toward a chair. For a second, I thought he might expect me to sit with him the same way Sarah was with Leo, but after I sank down, he dragged another chair over and sat down near me. "It was loud as hell in the house. And crowded."

Leo shrugged, and in doing so, he seemed to remember the girl sitting on him. Rubbing a hand down her back, he let his eyes drift back to the fire. "You guys know Sarah, right? Sarah, that's Jake Donavan and you remember Quinn, I guess."

"Sure." Sarah smiled at us. "Jake, we were in Spanish together freshman year, I think."

Jake grinned. "Yeah, that's right. Good old Señorita Tomosa. Did you keep up with it?"

"Are you freaking kidding me?" Sarah rolled her eyes. "No way. I only needed one year, because I took a college-level American Sign Language course over the summer. I hated Spanish."

"Lucky you. I'm in Spanish Three now, but fortunately, I had Señor Aikens last year and this year."

"Oh, yeah. Well, that's good, I guess."

We fell silent after that scintillating exchange of conversation. Leo dropped his arm to the ground on the side of the chair away from me and brought it back up holding a bottle. He lifted it to his lips and took a long swig. I thought it was beer. I hoped it was beer, and not something stronger.

He caught me watching him, and one side of his mouth quirked up. "Want some, Mia? You know I don't have cooties."

I was glad the dark hid my flushed face. "No, thanks."

"Ah, yeah. That's right. I forgot you're too good to drink with us, huh?" He tipped the bottle back again and then held it out to Sarah, who took a pull without hesitation. "So why'd you bother coming tonight if you're not really going to enjoy yourself?"

"I . . . I thought it would be fun. And Jake wanted to come." I shifted in my seat. "I can have a good time without getting drunk. Or high. Or . . ." I looked up at the deck, where the grope-fest continued. "Um, without doing . . . things."

Leo smirked. "Cool. Good for you. But if you're going to sit around and judge everyone who does want to do . . . things, maybe you should just go the fuck home."

"Hey." Jake's tone wasn't aggressive, just chiding. "Chill, Taylor."

A tic jumped in Leo's cheek, and his eyes narrowed. "What's the matter, Donavan? You want to be her big bodyguard? Her boyfriend? Believe me, dude. I'm the last guy you need to protect her from." His gaze slid back to me. "Or am I?" He took another drink, and it occurred to me that he'd probably had quite a few.

My stomach clenched at Leo's random aggression. This was the first time we'd been together or spoken since I'd left him in the alley outside the diner. Clearly neither of us had forgotten that. The tension in the air fairly crackled, and I wasn't sure who was going to break the awkward silence.

"Why do you call her Mia?" It was Sarah who spoke. She only sounded curious, not at all defensive or suspicious. I was pathetically grateful to her for shifting the focus as I held my breath, waiting to see if Leo would answer. "Is it Spanish?"

I saw his throat bob as he swallowed before he spoke. "No. Her name—her real name—is Amelia Quinn. After her great-grandmother. When we were little, sometimes her mom would call her that—Amelia Quinn. I wanted to say it, too, but I couldn't pronounce Amelia. So I called her Mia. Mia Quinn."

His voice was husky and sent a thrill down my spine. When I glanced up, his eyes were on my face again, boring into me until I couldn't breathe. I shivered and then without thinking about it, I licked my lips.

Instantly Leo's stare was fastened on my mouth. His own lips parted, and his chest seemed to rise and fall a little faster. I was dizzy with wanting him, and at the same time, I felt like an idiot. Here I was with another guy—while he was sitting with another girl. And yet the pull between us was undeniable. I was dying to crawl over to him, slither up his body, press my boobs into his chest and kiss him until we forgot our own names. I'd never known want that way—real, tangible need—and I fought back tears, because Leo had made it abundantly clear that he didn't want me the same way.

"I didn't know Quinn wasn't your first name." Jake smiled at me. "You don't seem like an Amelia. Whoever decided to call you Quinn was smart, Q. It suits you."

"Thanks." I studied Jake, with his casually messy hair and his black-rimmed glasses, and wished I could lust after him the way I did after Leo. What was wrong with me? I was seriously screwed up. Jake was kind, fun and smart. We had so much more in common than Leo and I did. And yet I didn't feel anything more for him than friendship. I wasn't sitting here, wishing he hadn't let go of my hand.

"Lion! Dude. Miller's got the new Combat Apocalypse. We're gonna play it in his theater." Kent Pulchaski stomped down the steps from the deck and called toward us. Both of the guys looked up.

"The one that doesn't release for another month? No way, man." Leo turned in his chair, easing Sarah away from his body.

"Yeah, his uncle's part of the development team and got it for him early. You in?"

"You know it." This time, he boosted Sarah to stand and stretched, getting to his feet. "It was getting a little, uh, quiet out here anyway. I was about to nod off."

I wanted to roll my eyes at the obvious put-down, but I chose to ignore it instead. Leo started to follow Kent and then paused, glancing back at Jake. "Donavan, you play?"

Jake fidgeted in his chair. "Uh, yeah. I mean, I played the first two."

"C'mon, then." Leo gestured with one hand. "Let's see what you got."

"Um, I don't know." Jake inched toward the edge of his seat, his eyes flickering toward me. "I promised Q we wouldn't stay too long."

I appreciated Jake's loyalty and consideration, but it was

clear that he wanted to go play video games with the rest of the big kids. I gave him a big sunny smile and shook my head.

"I'm good here. Go ahead and play. If I get too cold, I'll go stake out a spot on a couch and lay low until you're finished. Okay?"

Jake stood up, but he didn't walk away yet. "You sure?"

I nudged his leg with my foot. "Of course I'm sure. I think I can handle being on my own for a little bit, Jake. I promise, I won't do anything drastic. Like attack poor defenseless cheerleaders or something."

Jake snickered, and then with a quick wave in my direction, took off after Leo and Kent. I heaved a deep sigh and leaned back again. Sarah sat down in the chair Leo had just abandoned.

"Boys, huh? I don't understand the whole deal with video games. I mean . . . I just get bored. Leo was playing this zombie game the other night, and I fell asleep. Just conked right out on the sofa."

Another hot bolt of jealousy flared inside me at the idea of Sarah sleeping on the couch next to Leo, but I tamped it down. "Yeah, he's always been a sucker for war games, especially. When we were in elementary school, he and Nate got obsessed with this one—I can't remember what it was called, but there were guns and bombs." I mimed an explosion with both my hands. "They played it together practically every day for two months. At first, they tried to get me interested, too, but every time it was my turn, one of them ended up yanking the controller out of my hands to, uh, 'help' me." I made the air quotes. "So pretty soon I'd just wait until they were absorbed in the game, and then I'd sneak upstairs and hang out with Nate's mom."

"I have to admit, I'm really envious of you." Sarah drew

her legs up onto the chairs and shifted to face me more fully. "Growing up in one place, I mean, with friends you've had your whole life. We moved every few years when I was younger, so until we moved here, I didn't have any idea what it was like to know people for more than a year or two."

I remembered, vaguely, that Sarah had moved to Eaton-boro right before junior high. Still, she hadn't seemed to have had trouble fitting in here. She'd slid right into the popular crowd without an issue. I tried not to resent that.

"I guess there're pros and cons to everything." I shrugged. "When you've spent your life with one group of people, it's hard for them to see you as anything other than who they decided you were years ago." I smiled, thinking of one of my classmates. "For instance, one guy in our class couldn't tie his shoes on the first day of kindergarten, and he cried. He still gets teased about that, even now. Crazy, huh?"

Sarah giggled. "Not anyone we both know, is it?"

"Oh, no. Leo was the first of us to learn how to tie. He used to do my laces, and Nate's, too. Since he was the only one of us with older siblings, he had the leg up. Simon and Danny would've tormented him if he couldn't tie his shoes."

"See, that's what I mean. You all have so much history. I've only known Leo since eighth grade. I met his brother Danny, but I don't know the oldest one."

"Simon's awesome. He comes off like this big tough guy, but he's really a teddy bear. Both of Leo's brothers were always great to Nate and me. They kind of adopted us as theirs, too."

Sarah sighed and hugged her knees tighter to her chest. "Can I tell you something? Please don't laugh. I've been a little . . . threatened by you since I've known Leo. Even before we started dating. He always talks about you like you're this per-fect, amazing person. It's very intimidating."

I was silent for a minute, surprised. "Me? He talks about me like that?"

She nodded. "Oh, yeah. I don't think he even realizes it. But when he mentions your name, something in his voice—it changes. Gets softer." She paused, biting her bottom lip. "I've liked Leo for a long time. Not because of who he is, either. You know, all the cheerleaders . . . they look at him like a prize. A status symbol, almost. There's even—" She flashed me an apologetic glance. "Kind of a title. They talk about bagging the Lion, you know, because of his football nickname?"

I wrinkled my nose. "Ewww."

"Right?" Sarah shook her head. "But that's not why I wanted to go out with him. I've liked Leo since we met the summer before junior high. He was always nice to me, and we kind of dated a couple of times back then, but you know what that was like. No one was really serious. But now . . . it feels more important, you know? He's so nice, and I'm sure it sounds like what every girl would say, but I really like him for *him*. I'd date him even if he were, like, on the newspaper or something."

I saw the moment Sarah realized what she'd said. Her eyes got wide, and a flush stained her cheeks. "Oh, God, I'm sorry. I didn't mean that like it sounded. I just meant—"

"I know what you meant. Don't worry. I get it." I flipped around in the uncomfortable chair so that my legs hung over the armrest. "You're not dating him for his popularity or his mad skills on the football field. I'm glad."

Sarah felt around near the side of the chair and brought up Leo's half-empty bottle of beer. She was about to take a sip, then paused and held it out to me. "Want some? It's probably warm and flat."

I hated the taste of beer, but I liked the smell, since it reminded me of being at baseball games with my dad. I was about to tell her no, thanks, when I thought, *why not?* I was thirsty, and I wasn't driving tonight. There wasn't any good reason to say no, now that Leo wasn't using the beer to taunt me.

"Sure, if you don't mind." I leaned up, tilted the bottle into my mouth and then screwed up my face. "Yeah, it's pretty flat. Ugh." I shuddered and handed her back the beer. "Thanks, though."

"I really am sorry about what I said. I honestly don't care about who's popular or who isn't. Jake seems like a really great guy. He's funny, too."

"Yeah." I watched Sarah take a long swig, and this time I didn't even hesitate when she passed the bottle back to me. "He is. We're just friends, though. I came with him tonight because . . ." *Because your boyfriend kissed me senseless a few weeks back, and since then, I've been going crazy.* "I needed distraction." I finished my sentence lamely. "And uh, I haven't really dated. Like, at all. Anyone. So he asked me and, I guess, I figured, why not?"

"You've never dated? Why?" She seemed genuinely curious, not at all as though she was about to make fun of me.

"I don't know." I let my head thump onto the other armrest. "Or maybe I do. No one ever asked me before. At least, no one I would seriously want to be with."

"No way." Sarah held up the beer bottle. "Finish it up, why don't you."

I discovered that the third time was the charm when it came to beer, because I actually kind of liked it this time. I killed the bottle and dropped it onto the grass.

"So do you like Jake? I mean, he's cute. You two make a nice couple."

I lifted one shoulder. "I'm not sure. He's funny, and he's sweet, and he's a good friend. But I don't think he looks at me as anything other than that."

"Ah, you're wrong about that. I was picking up a definite vibe. I think he's hot for you."

I giggled. "Oh, I highly doubt—" I felt a buzzing in the back pocket of my jeans. "Hold on a second." Pulling it out, I squinted at the screen, frowning when I saw Nate's name. "Um, Sarah, I kind of have to answer this. I'll be right back." I struggled to hit answer on the phone at the same time that I tried to sit up.

"Stay there." Sarah stood, waving a hand at me. "I need to go pee anyway."

I relaxed back into the chair and held the phone to my ear. "Nate? What's up?"

"Where are you?" He sounded strained and anxious.

"I'm . . . out. Why? What's wrong?"

"I went over to your house to see if you wanted to come to the head races tomorrow. My dad's driving me over early, but Mom's coming separately, and she said you could ride with her if you want."

Closing my eyes, I suppressed a sigh. The last thing I wanted to do on my Saturday was stand alongside a river while Nate's boat club went through their races. I loved my friend, and I tried to support him as often as I could, but everything to do with crew rowing was long and drawn-out. It wasn't like going to one of Leo's football games, with a prescribed four quarters of action, where I could sit in the bleachers in relative comfort. Being there for Nate meant hours of monotony at the river and a few minutes of intense cheering.

Still . . . loyalty and guilt mixed together and made me answer in the affirmative. "Sure. What time is she leaving?"

I could almost hear the relief in Nate's voice. "Ten. Do you want her to pick you up?"

"No, that's okay. I'll just walk over there."

"Okay." There was silence on the line, which was not unusual when it came to my conversations with Nate. He never felt the need to fill the gaps that made me uncomfortable.

"So I'll see you . . . well, I guess after you're done." I wanted to wrap this up before Jake came back, and now that Sarah had mentioned it, I realized I needed to go to the bathroom, too.

"Where are you, Quinn?" Nate's voice took on a tone I'd never heard from him before. It was a mix between concern and . . . was that anger?

"I'm at a party. Why?" Yes, I sounded defensive. There was that guilt again, the same feeling I'd been struggling with for as long as I could remember when it came to Nate. When we were very young, I'd stayed inside with him if he wasn't feeling well enough to go out and play, because I felt bad for him. It was the same reason I'd avoided playing kickball the year we were in fifth grade and instead hung out on the swings with Nate. And now, I was almost afraid to tell him I'd gone out tonight, since he hadn't.

"Whose party?"

"Um, Mike Anders." I didn't say anything more, but I felt even worse, knowing the history between Mike and Nate.

This time, the silence was heavier. I was about to try to explain, to justify why I was here, when Nate spoke again.

"Who are you there with?"

I switched the phone to my other ear. "Jake. He, um . . . we were out eating, and someone invited us here, and it sounded fun . . ." Oh, *that* didn't come across too lame. "It's not like you're thinking, Nate. I haven't even seen Mike since I've been here. Jake and I were just sitting outside with Leo—"

"You're with Leo?" Now he was really mad. Hurt. I hadn't thought of how that might come across—that the two of us were together and hadn't included him.

"No. I didn't know he was coming. He didn't know I was here. But I meant that you don't have to worry about me, because Leo's here."

Nate mumbled something I didn't catch. "I'm sorry, what did you say?"

"Nothing. I'll see you tomorrow, Quinn. Have fun tonight." There was a click on the other end of the line, and when I checked the screen, CALL ENDED flashed.

I couldn't remember Nate ever hanging up on me. I sat staring down at the phone, frowning, until I felt a hand on my shoulder.

"Hey." Jake stood next to me, smiling down. "Are you ready to head out? Pretty sure things are only going to get wilder, and I'd rather not be here when it goes south."

"Yeah, I'm ready to leave." I stood up and gave a quick look around the backyard, but neither Leo nor Sarah were anywhere in sight. I tried not to think about where they might be as I followed Jake through the side yard.

"So how was the game?" I picked my way through the dark until we reached the sidewalk. "Did you kill a lot of . . . whatever you were hunting?"

Jake chuckled. "I got a little bit of play time, but most of the guys were pretty wasted. It wasn't much fun." He held the passenger door open for me, and I slid into the seat, nerves suddenly dancing in my stomach. This was the part of the night I'd worried about most. Did Jake expect me to kiss him? Or sit in his car in my driveway and make out with him? I felt stupid and naïve, a seventeen-year old girl who'd never had to deal with this up until now.

Making it worse, of course, was the niggling knowledge that if Leo were the one driving me home right now, I'd be wishing and hoping for him to kiss me. I'd be plotting how to make sure that happened.

We pulled into my driveway, and I was relieved when Jake immediately opened his door and hopped out, jogging around to my side to get my door for me. He walked me up to the front door, where I turned with a smile. I hoped he couldn't tell how forced it was.

"Well, thanks for a fun night." *God.* I sounded insipid even to my own ears. "I really enjoyed the pizza, and . . . just hanging out with you. Thanks for asking me."

"You're welcome." Jake laid a tentative hand on my upper arm and slid it lower to link his fingers with mine. "Would it be okay if I kissed you?"

If I'd thought things were awkward before, now they were a hundred times worse. If he'd just leaned in for the kiss, I would've dealt with it. Now there was the whole issue of giving him permission and then . . . what?

"Um, sure." Oh, *feel* the excitement I was exhibiting.

Jake grinned, and without further ado or time for me to worry about which way I should tilt my head, he tugged me closer and pressed his lips to mine.

I waited for the spark. I waited to feel the same thing I had when Leo had kissed me outside the hospital. But it never came. Kissing Jake was . . . pleasant. His lips were soft, his breath wasn't bad, and he never moved his hand from where it was linked with mine. He didn't open his mouth or stick his tongue down my throat.

But I was able to think about all of this as he kissed me. I wasn't lost in the sensation or overwhelmed with desire. I analyzed it as though I were watching the two of us from a distance. My heart didn't speed up, and my pulse didn't race.

After a minute, Jake stepped back, smiling at me, and

touched my cheek. "Thank you, Quinn. I had fun tonight. Maybe we can do it again?"

"Um, sure." Apparently those were the only words I could handle at this point. I disentangled my hand from his and reached for the doorknob. "I better get inside, though. Thanks again, Jake. See you on Monday."

I didn't wait for him to answer or watch him leave. I managed one more pseudo-smile and slipped inside, closing the door behind me.

When I used to picture my first date, I thought I'd come back home dancing on clouds, just like the girls in romance novels. Or in the movies. But all I wanted to do right now was throw myself across my bed and cry.

★ Nineteen ★

Leo

"LION!

Matt Lampert pounded up behind me in the locker room and gave me a friendly punch in the side. "Dude, you rocked today. We're gonna crush them on Friday night."

"Yeah." I pulled my practice jersey off over my head. "I guess."

"What's the matter?" Matt opened his own locker and began to undress. "You should be flying high. Coach even said something good about you. That almost never happens."

"That's true." I sat down on the bench. "I'm just tired. It's been a long week." It had actually been more like a long month since our game against Franklin Township. We'd ended up playing some of the toughest teams in our conference over the past four weeks, and all those stressful, important games were beginning to take their toll on me. My grades had taken an unusual dip, I'd lost weight, and I wasn't sleeping well.

"We got a couple of days before the game. Let's chill tonight. Come on over, and we'll eat pizza, slay some zombies and knock back some brews."

I rubbed my hand over my face. "I'm supposed to do something with Sarah tonight. I haven't taken her out in like, a week."

"Is she complaining?" Matt grabbed his towel.

"Nah. I just feel bad." Guilty was a more accurate description of how I felt. I hadn't intended to start anything serious with Sarah; she was supposed to be a temporary distraction for me and diversion tactic for Quinn. I'd figured we'd have some fun, and then it would sizzle out, like things always did. We'd part friends again, and I'd be off the hook.

But for some reason, that hadn't happened. One date had led into another, and before I knew it, people in school were referring to us as a couple. Like it was official or something. Sarah, to her credit, never put any pressure on me. If I didn't call her, she didn't give me shit. She didn't insist on hanging all over me in school, the way some girls did with their boyfriends.

And if she'd noticed that I got more interested and affectionate whenever I'd seen Quinn hanging with Jake Donavan, she didn't mention it.

I wasn't sure what was going on between Quinn and Jake. They hung out at school, but I couldn't say for sure if that was happening more than it had before or not. I didn't know anyone who was friends with them, so I couldn't just casually ask. I thought about checking with Nate, but he ignored me whenever we passed in the hall. If Quinn really was dating Donavan, I couldn't imagine Nate was any happier than I was.

Not that I had any right to care. I'd had a chance with Quinn, and I'd thrown it away, on purpose. I'd chosen the way that was better for her. I was sure Jake Donavan was just her type; as a senior and editor of the paper, everyone liked him, even though I didn't think he was a big partier. I'd seen the way his eyes followed Quinn, and I'd sure as hell picked up on how he looked at her that night at Anders' party. He liked her.

I followed Matt into the showers, moving on automatic pilot and not paying any attention to the guys' typical yelling and teasing. Everyone was a little punchy today, after the last few weeks. Even Coach seemed a little worn out, a little more laidback. Still, I was having a hard time getting into the groove. I nodded when someone shouted out to me, I smiled when I realized they expected it, but inside I was brooding.

I pulled on jeans and a Henley after my shower, stuffed my dirty clothes into a duffle bag and headed out of the locker room. Matt hollered after me.

"Taylor, don't forget. Tonight. You bring the pizza, and I'll supply the rest."

I paused. "Yeah, I'll see what's going on, man. I'll text you."

Opening the door of the locker room, I stepped into the silent school hallway. A few feet away, leaning against the wall, Sarah sat on the floor, her phone in her hand as she read something on the screen. She looked up at the sound of the door closing behind me.

"Hey." Pushing against the wall, she rose to her feet in one languid movement. I studied her for a moment, taking in the whole Sarah Jenkins package: the beautiful hair, spilling down around her shoulders, the dark eyes, slender legs encased in her skinny jeans. The shirt she wore had some kind of rounded neckline that hugged her ample tits and dipped just low enough to give me a tantalizing peek. There wasn't any doubt that this chick was sexy. Any sane man would be turned on, hot for her luscious bod and ready to go as far as she'd let him.

But for some reason, my own body, usually so ready to rock and roll, wasn't playing along tonight. If dicks could sigh, mine would have been doing just that.

As if she could sense my feelings, Sarah hesitated. "We were meeting here, right? I thought . . ." Her voice trailed off.

"Yeah, sure." I rubbed my jaw. "Sorry. I'm just tired." I repeated the same excuse I'd given Matt. "Matt invited us over, so maybe we can pick up some pizza and take it over there."

"Oh. Okay." The hint of disappointment in her voice was unmistakable, and unreasonable as it was, this only irked me. And then of course *that* made me feel guiltier.

"Look, do you want to skip tonight? I won't be very good company. I just want to lay around and maybe watch a movie. Play a little *Zombie Chase*. That's not going to be very much fun for you."

Sarah nodded slowly. "Okay. That's fine." She bent over to pick up her bag, and I averted my eyes from her ass. Straightening, she glanced over her shoulder at me. "Maybe tomorrow night we could see a movie or something."

"Can't. Tomorrow's Thursday, and this week we play Friday night, so we have curfew." As a cheerleader, she knew that.

"Oh, right. I forgot. Well, there's always Saturday."

"Yeah."

Neither of us moved. Sarah's face was carefully neutral, giving no hint about how she was really feeling other than where she'd caught her lip between her teeth. I waited, unsure of what to say next.

The painful silence was broken by the buzzing of my phone. I stretched back, reaching into my pocket to dig it out, frowning as I scanned the text. "Hey, I need to go. That was my mom, and she, uh . . . she asked when I was coming home. I guess my brothers are both in town unexpectedly."

"Everything okay?" Sarah tilted her head, studying me.

"I guess. I don't know. It's just weird because they don't come home very often." I typed a quick reply to my mother, telling her I was on my way, and tucked my phone back in my pants. "I'll see you later."

"Leo." Sarah called me just before I rounded the corner. "I . . . can I ask you something real quick before you go?"

My shoulders tensed. "Sure. What's up?"

"Do you even want to date me? I mean, what are we doing here? If you just want to walk away, please just tell me. I don't want you to feel like you're obligated to me in any way. Okay? Seriously." She pressed her lips together before she went on. "I like you, Leo. I have since we met . . . remember the sprinklers that summer?"

I smiled. "Yeah. I remember."

"But I understand that this might not be the right time for us. It's fine. I'd rather you tell me the truth than let me look pathetic, trying to hang on when maybe you never even meant for us to be anything more than—just friends."

"Sarah." I sucked in a deep breath. "I like you, too. You're probably the coolest girl in this school, you know? You're kind to everyone, you're gorgeous . . . but I've got a lot of shit going on in my head right now. It's not you, it's got nothing to do with you, but pretending we could be anything long-term wouldn't be fair. To either of us."

"I understand. Thanks for saying that." Those pretty dark eyes filled with tears, but she managed a smile. "Now you better go home and see your brothers before your mom calls out the National Guard."

I turned to leave again, pausing just before I opened the door. "Sarah? I meant what I said. You really are the coolest girl I know."

She laughed, even as a single tear spilled down her cheek. "Oh, get out of here, you big flirt."

I felt nothing but relief as I jogged down the school steps

and across the lawn toward the parking lot. Mine was one of the few cars still there, but I did spot the ancient Ford Quinn sometimes drove. I assumed she was there late working on the paper. Jake was probably with her, and an image of the two of them, making out in the newspaper office, sent a stab of pain through my heart.

But if Jake Donavan made her happy, I'd take that pain. And maybe someday we'd find our way back to being friends. That was as much as I could hope for at this point.

Simon and Danny's cars were parked along the curb when I got home. Seeing them there gave me an odd feeling. My brothers usually made it back here for holidays, but we didn't see them often other than. Danny was in the last year of his undergrad degree at Rutgers, and Simon had a job at a marketing company in Baltimore. They called often, and Danny came down sometimes if I had a big game, but they had their own lives.

Which was why both of them being back home on a weeknight made me nervous.

I pulled into the driveway, grabbed my bag and walked slowly into the house. The front door was unlocked, and I dropped the duffel just inside, yelling to my mother as I toed off my shoes.

"Yo, Mom! I'm home. What's up? Is this a surprise party deal? Did you all forget my birthday was a month ago?"

It was quiet for a minute, and then my mother's voice floated in from the kitchen. "We're in here, Leo. Come on in."

I swallowed hard and padded down the short hallway in my socks. "Hey, what's going on?"

My parents were sitting close to each other at the kitchen table. Simon and Danny were across from them in the same seats they'd occupied throughout our childhood. Danny's eyes were suspiciously red.

My mother pointed to the empty chair that was my spot. "Sit down, sweetie. We need to talk."

★ Twenty ★

Quinn

"Let's move Lisa's article to the page two, and then stick the picture from the band competition on the front page." Jake leaned back in his chair, dropped his head and looked at me upside down. "Slow news week."

I laughed, and turning back to the computer, focused on dragging the photo onto the right spot on the front page. "Don't worry. If the football team makes it into the playoff games, we'll have pictures and stories for weeks."

"Yeah, it's looking good for them." Jake sat up and spun the chair around to face me. "Okay, that's the front page. I think we're just about done. I'll do one final check and send it over to the printer."

I sighed and crooked my neck, working out the kinks. "Great. I'll upload it to the email service." We were slowly moving the school newspaper over to a completely paperless format, but in the interim, we released it in both paper and ecopy.

"Perfect." Jake stood up, stretching his arms over his head. He leaned over the back of my chair, caging me in with his arms on either side. "Maybe we should celebrate. Ice cream or coffee?"

I tried to stop myself from tensing. Jake and I had fallen into a comfortable relationship over the last month. We hadn't made any formal declarations; he hadn't asked me to be his girlfriend, and I wasn't sure if that made a difference to anyone but me. We hung out in the newspaper office, as we always had, but more often than not, he suggested that we do something together afterwards. He held my hand when we sat in the movie theater and kissed me goodnight when he dropped me off. But he hadn't pushed anything. We didn't make out in his car, and he hadn't even tried to French kiss me.

I'd hoped that if we spent more time together, that missing spark might show up. But so far, it remained MIA. I was comfortable with Jake. We had a wonderful time together. But he didn't make me melt in my chair when he gazed into my eyes.

Apparently, though, Sarah wasn't having any problem finding the passion with Leo. It felt like every time I turned around, there they were, attached at the lips, with Leo's hands all over her perfect curvy body. I found it harder to hate Sarah after we'd talked at Mike Anders' party, but it wasn't so much of a stretch to dislike her when her fingers were tucked into the back pocket of Leo's jeans.

"I don't know about tonight, Jake. I think I might just head home." I smiled, hoping it looked genuine. "After we put the paper to bed, the only thing I want to do is put *me* to bed."

"Oh. Okay." Jake stood up, watching in silence as I gave the file one more go-over. "Q, can I talk to you about something?"

My stomach turned over. Nothing good ever came after those words. "Sure."

"Do you like me?"

I spun my chair around. "Of course I like you, Jake. How

could I help it? You're a great guy."

He sighed. "A great guy. Yeah, that's what I thought."

I quirked one eyebrow. "You'd rather I said you weren't a great guy?"

"No, I'd rather you say . . ." He rolled his eyes up. "I don't know. That I'm exciting. Unpredictable. Maybe even a little dangerous. But that's what keeps you coming back for more."

I couldn't help it. I burst out laughing. "I'm sorry, Jake. I think you're one of the funniest people I know, but you're still a great guy. I always have a wonderful time with you."

"Yeah, that was what I was afraid of." He dropped into his chair and gazed at me glumly. "We have fun, but you're not dying to rip these chinos off me and have your way with my rockin' bod?"

This time I managed to swallow my laughter. "I'm sure it's not you. It's me. I'm just . . . slow. Backward, probably. I know none of the other girls in the school have a problem with, um, getting physical, but it's just not me."

"Or maybe it's just not me who turns you on."

I flushed, thinking of how ready and willing I'd been to let Leo do anything he wanted to me. "I'm really sorry, Jake. I like you. I love spending time with you. Maybe if we just hang out a little bit more . . ."

He shook his head. "If I thought that was likely, I'd spend as much time with you as you wanted. But I don't think it's going to happen. I think—"

"Hey, bitches." Gia cruised into the room, interrupting whatever Jake had been about to say. "Did I miss the big layout party? Sorry, I got held up with this damn group project." She hopped up to sit on the counter, swinging her legs.

Jake closed his eyes for a minute and then turned to face her. "Yeah, we're done." His gaze met mine, and I knew he was talking about more than the paper.

"Aw, well, next week." Gia didn't appear to be too broken up about the whole situation. "But hey, listen. I got the scoop on some juicy gossip, fresh and hot."

"We're serious journalists, Gia. We're not interested in tabloid shit." Jake pretended to look lofty.

"Oh, yeah? So no one's interested in the fact that I just overheard Leo Taylor breaking up with his cheerbitch?"

My head turned toward Gia so fast, I got dizzy. "What? How do you know?"

Gia smiled smugly. "I told you, I overheard it. I was just coming in, and they were the only two in the hallway just outside the locker room. It echoes there. When I realized they were having, like, a serious convo, I stopped walking so I didn't interrupt. And I just happened to hear every word."

My heart sped up. I knew that it was stupid, but somehow this news made me believe I might have another chance with Leo. "Did you . . . could you hear who was breaking up with who?" That was important. I couldn't imagine Sarah not wanting to be with Leo, but stranger things and all that.

"It actually sounded mutual. I mean, I think the cheerleader's still hot for him, but she was really kind of cool about the whole thing. It was the most civilized breakup I've ever heard of between two kids in high school."

"Huh." I went back to the computer screen and hit send on the file, but I really wasn't seeing the page. Suddenly all I wanted to do was to get out of the newspaper office. I didn't know where I wanted to go, but I knew it wasn't here.

"Q." Jake spoke quietly, ignoring Gia, who was still chattering away to us as she flipped through the hard mock-up of the paper. "I get it."

"What?" I was flustered. "What do you get?"

"I saw your face when Gia mentioned Leo. I can't say I'm entirely surprised. That night, at Anders' party, it felt like there was something between you two." He smiled a little sadly. "No dude is that hostile over a girl he doesn't care about."

"But he doesn't." I shook my head. "It's all messy and complicated and . . . I don't know. But I need to work that stuff out, Jake. It doesn't have anything to do with you."

He shrugged. "Whatever you say. But don't sweat it. I promise, I'll nurse my broken heart in private. We can hold onto our working relationship."

"That's a relief." I stood up and gave him a hug, and for the first time since our date, it felt relaxed and spontaneous. "Who else is going to be Woodward to my Bernstein?"

"Hey, wait a minute. I thought *I* was Bernstein."

"No way." I feigned horror. "I'm the only one who could pull off being married to Nora Ephron."

Jake spread his hands. "You got me there."

I picked up my books and paused by the door. "Thanks for being so cool about this, Jake. You really are a great guy."

He made a face, but I could tell he was joking. "Yeah, yeah, yeah. Get out of here. Go home and think about what you just threw away."

"I'm sure I won't be able to sleep tonight, thinking about it."

"Oh, hey, you're going now?" Gia suddenly seemed to realize she'd been missing something. "Don't worry, I'll help Jake close up. See you around, Quinn."

"Yep." Jake winked at me. "See you around, Q."

"Hey, I'm home." I slammed the front door behind me and hung my bag on the newel post.

My dad was coming down the steps. "Hey, kiddo. Long day at the salt mines?"

"Yeah, you know how Wednesdays are, getting the paper wrapped up. Who made dinner, you or Mom?"

He smirked. "You're in luck tonight. Yours truly was the chef du jour. The pharmacist of the house sat there and drank wine the whole time I cooked." He pointed toward the kitchen. "There's a covered plate for you in the oven. Beef bourguignon."

"Have I told you that you're my favorite father?" I stood on my toes to kiss his cheek and followed him into the kitchen.

"What a coincidence. You're my favorite daughter."

"That would mean a lot more if I had any siblings." I picked up a potholder, opened the oven door and reached in to retrieve my plate. "Where's Mom?"

My father's face got a little red, and he cast his eyes up to the ceiling. "Ah, she's upstairs. I was helping her with . . ." His voice trailed off. "Um, something in the bedroom."

"Ewww." I clapped my hands over my ears. "Just stop. Yuck, yuck, yuck. Don't you two realize you've been married, like, forever? And you have an impressionable daughter?"

Dad raised one eyebrow at me. "What can I say, sweetie? I still got it. And I did tell you Mom was drinking wine, right? Oh, and she thinks my cooking is totally sexy."

I pushed the plate back. "Okay, I've officially lost my appetite."

"Seriously?" My father reached for my food, and I curled my body around it.

"No. That was just for effect. Don't touch this. It's delicious."

I had just taken my last bite of beef—and it really was

amazing, tender and bursting with flavor—when my phone buzzed.

"Hot date with the newspaper guy?" My dad slid me a sideways glance. He and my mother had been quietly jubilant the last few weeks; they were relieved, I thought, that their daughter was finally doing something other teenage girls did. They'd met Jake before, of course, and they liked him.

"Uh, actually no." I frowned, trying to stay cool, even while my heart began to pound. "It's Leo."

The text was short and more than a little cryptic.

Meet me at the old playground. Please. I need you.

"Everything okay?" My father was watching me carefully over his tablet, where he'd been skimming an on-line newspaper.

"I don't know." I stared at the screen of the phone, as though an explanation might appear there. "He wants me to meet him at the playground." I lifted my eyes to meet my dad's. "It sounds serious. I think I'll walk over there, okay?"

My father studied me in silence for a few seconds. "Sure. Take your phone, and don't go by the shortcut—stay on the main sidewalk. And text me when you get there."

"Daddy, you do realize I go places all the time? By myself? I'm seventeen. I've been walking to that playground since I was nine."

"Yeah, but it's dark. You always made that walk during the day. So humor your old man, and promise you'll text, or I'll be forced to drive the streets of our neighborhood, slowly, yelling your name out my open car windows. Your full name."

He'd do it, too. I shuddered at the thought.

"All right, all right. I promise. I'll send you a text the moment I'm there safely with Leo."

"Hmm." He still didn't look convinced. "I'm not sure I like

you hanging out at an empty park late at night with a boy."

"Dad, come on. It's not that late. I'm not roaming the streets at midnight. And this is Leo. You've known him longer than you've known me. Twenty-one days longer, to be exact."

"He's still a boy."

"Oh, Bill, let her be." My mother had come downstairs and into the kitchen without either of us hearing her. She was wearing yoga pants and a thin long-sleeved T-shirt . . . inside out. Her hair was a mess, and her cheeks were ruddy. I decided not to think about it.

"But Carrie—"

"It's Leo." My mom's eyes met mine, and in them I read her understanding. "She'll be fine. He'll probably even walk her back here after. Let her go so she can get back at a decent time." She sidled up to my dad, wrapping her arms around his waist and nuzzling his neck. "I could probably have second helpings of that beef, now that I worked off the first round."

"Aaaaand on that note, I'm out of here." I stamped into the foyer where I stopped to slip on a jacket from the front closet. "You two . . . behave yourselves. Watch TV and ignore each other, like other parents."

I went through the door, shutting it behind me and pausing just outside to answer Leo's text.

On my way.

★ Twenty-One ★

Leo

I HADN'T BEEN TO THIS PLAYGROUND SINCE MIDDLE SCHOOL, but when I needed a place to meet Quinn, somewhere quiet and private, that was the first spot that came to mind. I got there first and dropped onto one of the rubber swings, wincing a little when my weight forced the sides into my hips.

"Want a push?"

I hadn't heard Quinn approach; she must've walked to the park. I twisted in the swing to look at her. She stood behind me, her fingers shoved into the back pockets of her faded jeans, and her face was inscrutable. Her hair was pulled up into a messy pony tail, the kind she wore when she was at home in her room, doing homework or reading. She must've dropped whatever she was up to as soon as I'd texted. Something small and pleased stirred in me, a little bit of bright in the sea of downright shitty.

"I'd say sure, but I think I've outgrown the swing. Damn chains are biting into me." I grasped the links and pulled myself to my feet. "You came."

She lifted one shoulder. "You asked me to come."

I leaned against the thick pole that held up the swing set and the attached slide. "After . . . the way things have been, I wasn't sure. I've been a real asshole. I wouldn't blame you if you ignored me."

Her gaze flickered up, sweeping over my face. "You're my friend, Leo. My *best* friend. I'd never ignore you when you asked me to do something." She took the swing I'd just vacated. "What's up?"

Swallowing hard against the gigantic lump in my throat, I stared across the empty blacktop into the dark. "Remember when we were little, and we'd lay out on a blanket in Nate's backyard, looking up at the stars? You used to try to tell us that you could count them."

A small smile curved her lips. "Are you saying I was lying?"

I dropped my head back against the iron pole, closing my eyes. "You were always so sure about everything, Quinn. What was right, what was wrong. You acted like it was easy to know."

Silence stretched between us, broken only by the soft drag of her sneaker on the pavement as the swing moved. When she spoke again, her voice was tinged with sadness. "I was a kid. It's not so hard when you're little. Life gets complicated the older you get."

"No shit." I laughed without humor. I stretched my neck, looking up into the clear night sky. "God, Mia. It's all so fucked up now. Things were better then."

She sighed. "Maybe." The chains on the swing creaked, and I could feel their movement through the frame of the structure. "Leo, why did you ask me to meet you tonight? I'm guessing it wasn't to talk philosophy." The pole behind me shifted; she was swinging a little higher now, and everything moved in concert. "And if you brought me out here to—to tell me again how much you regret kissing me, you can go to hell. You're just—"

"My mother has leukemia."

Everything came to a screeching halt. The pole I was leaning on jerked as Quinn brought the swing to a stop. She stood for a minute, her fingers still wrapped around the chains, the seat resting against her upper thighs. When I let myself meet her eyes, they were round, filled with stricken shock.

And then she was moving, barreling toward me in typical Quinn speed. Before I could take another breath, her arms were around me, pulling me close, offering me the comfort I'd been craving. I let her give it to me, taking for just a few minutes the love she poured over me. She didn't take away the pain, but her nearness dulled it a little. Or maybe it was more of a shifting of weight, moving the fear and uncertainty from where it had rested on my shoulders to be borne by Quinn and me, together. I remembered something my grandmother used to say, about a burden shared being a grief halved.

She leaned back after a moment and gazed up into my face. "Tell me. When . . . and is she okay? What's going to happen?"

I fastened my eyes on a spot of white paint on the ground behind her. "They told us tonight. I guess something weird came up in her blood work, during her regular physical. They ran tests, and . . . yeah." I gritted my teeth together to fight back the tears that wanted to fill my eyes. "Um, I guess they have a plan. She said something about chemo and a bone marrow transplant and needing to find a donor. But honestly, I don't remember. I kind of checked out after they said the word leukemia."

My chest shook as the terror there threatened to rip its way out. I wasn't a mama's boy, not by a long shot. Not with two older brothers who were more than happy to point out any time I might veer into that dangerous territory. But still, I was the youngest. Simon and Danny had already been in school when I was born, so I'd had Mom all to myself, and we'd been buddies. She wasn't too girly to teach me how to toss a baseball, how to hold a bat or how to catch a football. And even though baseball was her first love, when I chose to play football instead, she'd never missed a game.

"Leo, it's okay. This—it sucks. Your mom is one of the best people I know, and I hate that this is happening, but she's strong, too. It's going to be hard, and it's going to be scary, but I know she's going to make it." Quinn rubbed my upper arms with her hands, smiling up at me, through the tears that were streaking silently down her cheeks. "What can I do? Do you want to talk, or do you want me not to talk about it?"

That was my Quinn. My Mia. I'd been fucking shitty to her for weeks—longer than that—but the minute I needed her, that didn't matter. She was here for me, just like she'd always been.

I brushed a few tear drops from her face with my thumbs. "I had to see you. As soon as they were done talking, telling us, and Simon—he was acting all take-charge, trying to figure out how to be here around his work schedule, and Danny just got silent. Like, he didn't say a word. He shut down. But all I wanted was to get to you. I don't know how I can get through this, Mia. I can't do it alone."

"You won't have to." She hugged me tight again and then stepped back, holding onto my hands. "I'll be here for you whenever you want me, and Nate, too—I know he'll do anything he can."

I nodded, but I knew I didn't need Nate. Not like I needed Quinn. Everything I'd been holding at bay for months, every frustrated desire I'd been fighting back, all the deep, messed-up and undeniable feelings I had for Quinn came roaring back until they were about to eat me alive. I couldn't think about anything else but the girl standing in front of me, her fingers warm as they gripped mine. All the reasons I'd had to push her away and to pretend I didn't want her—they all seemed stupid. Idiotic. I'd been wasting my time when I could've had Quinn in my arms.

Her green eyes were shining as she looked up at me. There was concern in them, yes, and sympathy, but something else. Something that made the bottom drop out of my stomach and had me leaning over her, sealing my lips on her soft mouth.

She responded at first, lifting on her toes to meet me better, angling her head to fit us together. The rightness of us— Quinn and me, the way we were meant to be—surged over my body and soul.

And then she tore away from me, pressing her fingers to her lips as more tears welled up in her eyes. "Leo—what're you doing?" She took a step backward, away from me.

"I thought I was kissing you." I advanced on her, but she ducked away from me.

"But why? Why are you kissing me, Leo? Because you're sad about your mom? Because you and Sarah broke up and you need a handy substitute? Or because you're grateful that I came when you called? Or is it—what did you say the other day? That you feel *sorry* for me? Is this just another pity kiss that you're going to pretend didn't happen tomorrow? Poor Quinn, who can't get a boyfriend on her own, doesn't have anyone to kiss her—but it's okay, because Leo the big football star's going to spare me a kiss. Thanks, Leo. I really appreciate it. You're a pal." She wheeled around, turning her back to me.

"*Fuck it!*" Out of desperation, I punched at the nearest target, which happened to be the slide. Pain reverberated up my arm, but it was nothing compared to the anguish I was feeling inside. "Fuck it all. I've been trying to stay away from you, Quinn. Trying to do any goddamn thing to stay out of your path and keep you away from me, too."

"But why?" She was crying now in earnest, not the wimpy tears some girls used to manipulate guys, but real, honest-to-goodness ugly crying, sobs wrenching from her chest and shaking her whole body. "Why do you want to stay away from me? You're my best friend. Or you were."

"Because I'm not that guy anymore. I'm not the Leo who always did the right thing. I'm not the Leo who stood up to bullies with you. I'm a different person now, Mia. I'm not good for you. I'm a fucking mess. And every time I look at you, all I can think of is how goddamn much I want to kiss you. More than that. I don't want to stop at just kissing you, Mia. I want my hands all over you. Right now, standing here, I want to bend you over this bench, strip you down—" I broke off, snarling a curse. "I'd ruin you. I'd make you different, and that would kill me."

"But Leo—" She grabbed for my arm, her grip stronger than I expected. "You wouldn't. You couldn't change me if I don't want you to. I'm not some little girl you can corrupt, you know? I'm only three touchdowns younger than you."

I half-groaned, half-laughed at our old joke about the twenty-one days that separated our birth dates. "You think I don't know that? You think I haven't noticed that you're grown up?" With just the tip of my index finger, I traced the line of her cheekbone. Her eyelids fell shut and she shivered, and God, I wanted to make her look like that again. And again. My dick was so hard under the zipper of my jeans that it ached.

"Leo." She breathed out my name, opening her eyes just a little as she drew closer to me. Her tits pushed against my chest, softness sinking into my hard planes, and instinctively my arms went around her. I angled my body so that my pulsing erection lined up to the heat between her legs. I expected her to pull back, but she didn't. If anything, she plastered herself closer to me.

Looking down into her face, where I expected to see doubt and fear and confusion, I only saw trust and eagerness and desire. Her lips parted slightly, and I couldn't help myself. I dipped my mouth down, taking once again what had been tempting me for weeks.

Quinn opened for me right away, and then my tongue was in her mouth, exploring, teasing and tasting. She was an intoxicating mix of mint and pure Quinn, and I wanted to lap her up. She moaned deep in her throat, and some frantic, insane part of my mind began scrambling, trying to come up with an idea of where we could go. A place where no one would find us and I could keep touching her, possibly forever.

"Mia." I slid my fingers through her hair. "God, you're so beautiful. I've been dying to touch you." I ran my hands down her back, gripping her firm, round ass. She made a small noise of surprise, but she didn't squirm away, so I lifted her up. Her legs wound around me, and she rested her arms on my shoulders, never breaking her mouth away from mine. I realized with surprise that she'd taken control of the kiss. Her tongue stroked the inside of my cheek before circling my tongue, sparring with me in an erotic dance I never dreamed she knew.

I moved my hips against her, and she arched her back, grinding into me. I wondered if she knew quite what she was doing. Maybe she didn't; maybe she was just as innocent as I suspected, but damn if her body didn't know what it wanted. And it wanted me. I thought about breaking away from the kiss, just to watch her face, but I was afraid that might distract her. That wouldn't be a good thing, because when she moved, her center was stroking against my dick, and holy fuck, it felt good.

Growling low, I dug my fingers into her ass, just as Quinn canted her hips, changing her position enough that I was pretty sure the head of my cock, straining against denim, was hitting her clit through her jeans. She sucked in a breath, ripped her mouth away from me, and dropped her head back, pushing into me with everything she had.

"Leeeeo." My name was almost a wail on her lips, and then her mouth dropped open and she panted. Her hands were vices on my arms, but I didn't care if I ended up with ten bruises in the shape of Quinn's fingers. I'd happily carry those marks, because as I watched her expression morph from surprise to absolute, mind-blown pleasure, it was the sexiest, most beautiful thing I'd ever seen. I wanted to make her come every day for the rest of our lives, just to see her face when it happened.

Eventually she sagged against me, her breathing still fast, and I held her tight.

"Mia." I covered her cheeks with kisses. "God, Mia. That was the most incredible thing."

She dropped her forehead onto my shoulder, burying her face into the crook of my neck. Her breath fanned over my damp skin. "I can't believe—oh, my God, Leo. I'm so embarrassed."

"Why would you be embarrassed?" I pulled back, gently nudging her head up. "Mia, I'm not kidding. I am so fucking turned on right now." I managed a laugh. "Well, I was turned on before, but damn, that was hot." I brushed her hair back so I could see her eyes. "Hey. Mia, it's just us. You and me. When have you ever worried about doing something in front of me?"

She flushed pink, and I cupped her face in my hand. "No matter what, this is you and me, and I don't want you to ever be embarrassed. Okay? Having you rub against me and find out what feels good was like . . ." I cast my eyes up to the black and starry sky. "I don't know the words to tell you. Better than anything I ever dreamed." I kissed her, fast and hard, and then murmured against her lips. "And believe me, Mia, I've had plenty of dreams about you." I glanced around us. "Only they don't happen outside on a playground."

She swallowed hard, blinking. "Oh, really? So where do we . . . in your dreams, where are we?"

I pretended to think, though I knew the answers right away. "In one we were on the beach, and you were wearing that bathing suit—the one with the fringe on the boobs?"

A smile curved her lips, although I knew she was fighting it. "God, Leo. It was like two years ago when I wore that one."

I managed a shrug. "Well, it was so sexy, it stuck in my subconscious. It tied in the back with strings, and I wanted to untie them. In my dream, I did."

"I can't believe you really dreamed about us on the beach." She shook her head.

"And in my bed. The ones in my bed, those were fucking hot." My dick swelled a little more, reminding me that even though Quinn had come, I hadn't. If she'd been any other girl, I might've been tempted to ask her to give me a hand there— literally—but I had a feeling that suggesting she help me to orgasm here at the playground might be a little too much for tonight. I did my best to focus on something else.

"If you were dreaming about me . . . why didn't you do anything about it? Why didn't you *tell* me, Leo?"

I blew out a sigh and loosened my hold on her, letting her body slide down mine until her feet hit the soft ground below. "Mia, I was trying to protect you. What I said before . . . it's still true. I *am* a mess. I'm not who I used to be, and I'm scared shitless of disappointing you. Again."

"Again?" Her eyebrows knit together.

"Every time I don't stand up for Nate, every time you see me hanging out with the guys on the football team, every time I flirt with a cheerleader, it's so clear I'm disappointing you. It's like you have this giant set of expectations for me, and when I let you down, it kills me a little. I couldn't stand the thought of letting you get close enough to see what a fuck-up I really am."

"You're not." Her voice was fierce, a patented Quinn-the-protector tone. "Leo, you just—you're popular. I get that. And when you play football, it's amazing what you do out there. It's only natural that you'd be friends with all the football team and the—the cheerleaders." She barely managed to eek out the word without making a face, and I bit back a grin. "That doesn't make you a mess."

"You don't know everything about me, Mia." I thought of the nights I'd drunk myself to oblivion and the nameless girls I'd hooked up with, not to mention the times I'd stood by, silent, when the other guys had ganged up on the less-popular, the weaker links. She wouldn't like that. "What if you hate who I am? What if I can't be good enough for you?"

"Why would you think you couldn't? I've always loved you for who you are, Leo." She framed my face. "Don't you trust me?"

"With everything I have." I skimmed my hands up her back, loving the solid warmth of her. "But I don't know what I'd do if I let you down."

"You won't." She kissed my jaw and then ran her lips down my throat. I bent my face over her and growled.

"Keep that up, and I'm going to drag you under the slide and act out some of those dreams. God, you drive me crazy." I let my hands venture up her sides, my thumbs teasing the soft undersides of her tits. The curve there made my mouth water.

"Are we horrible people, Leo? Making out on the playground right after—you know. Your mom." She searched my eyes. "And am I even worse, because I'm happier right now than I've ever been?"

I sucked in a breath. "I don't think we're horrible. I think I'm the moron who's been fighting what I feel until now. So no. On both fronts. No one's going to be more excited to hear that we're together than my mom, believe me. It'll probably be good for her. Give her something positive to think about."

Quinn raised one eyebrow. "Are we together? Like, out in the open together?"

"Did you think I was going to say we should hide? Sneak around?" I snaked my hands around to her back and cupped that firm ass again. "Nope. Sorry, babe. You're stuck with me now, and I want—" An unexpected lump rose in my throat, and I swallowed it down. "I want everyone to know it."

She smiled and then right before my eyes, the glow on her face began to fade a little. "But you know, Leo, there's going to be a ton of people who won't understand why you'd want to be with me. What if the guys on the team give you a hard time?"

A twinge of unease strummed through my chest, but I ignored it. "Won't happen. We support each other. Anyway, if they did, it wouldn't matter to me. They don't control my life. I'm the one who gets to decide who I date." I snugged her close to me again, just to watch her eyes go soft and hazy. "Who I kiss." I touched my lips to hers. "And I'm finally getting smart and kissing the one I want. Nothing and no one's going to change that." I opened my mouth a little over hers before I came up for air, pressing my forehead against Quinn's.

"You're mine. And I don't want anyone to doubt that. Least of all you."

She sighed and laid her head against my chest. "If I'm dreaming right now, don't wake me up. I like this dream. I could live here."

"Maybe real life is going to be better than dreams now." I threaded my fingers through her thick hair. I was such a confusing mix of emotion right now. Worry about my mother battled with a heady kind of relief that I'd finally come clean with Quinn, that she was wholly and unequivocally mine. The only ripple interrupting my smooth sea of happy was the worry that I'd somehow fuck it up. But I wasn't going to give up a chance to be with this girl because I was scared. I'd never been afraid to take chances in any other part of my life. Why should I let fear stop me now? Fuck that shit.

"Leo . . ." The timber of her voice vibrated over my chest. "We have to talk to Nate."

"Yeah." I rubbed her back. "Should we do it together?"

Her forehead wrinkled, and she bit her lip. "Maybe I should talk to him first. He's—he might be a little upset."

I gave a short laugh. "You think? The last conversation we had before he got hurt wasn't exactly friendly. And . . ." I wasn't sure if I should point this out or not. "He's kind of got a thing for you, Mia."

She groaned. "I know. It's just because we've been friends so long, and he feels like I'm . . . I don't know. Safe? I think he's talked himself into believing he wants me to be his girlfriend."

"Oh, baby, I think it's more than that. He's in love with you. This isn't going to be easy for him."

"Thanks for pointing that out." She pushed her hair out of her face. "Maybe it would be a good idea for me to tell him by myself. I can break it to him gently."

"Well, tell him fast." I pulled her up for another kiss. "Because otherwise he's going to figure it out when he sees you with me in school tomorrow. I don't plan on a hands-off policy when it comes to you."

"How about I drive Nate to school tomorrow? I'll text him tonight, and then I'll pick him up in the morning and tell him on the way." She was grim, as though talking about her own execution.

"Hey, Mia." I tilted up her chin. "It's going to be okay. Nate might be unhappy at first, but he'll come around. Come on, how could he not? Even though things have been a little rough lately, we're still the trio, right? We can make this work."

"I hope so." She blinked, sniffing. "I don't want to lose my friends. Either of you."

"Baby, you're not." I spoke with more conviction than I felt. "Nate might need some time to get used to the idea, but you're not going to lose him. And me—I'm not going anywhere." I held her face between my hands and leaned down to kiss her lightly.

"From now on, it's you and me. Us."

★ Twenty-Two ★

Nate

I KNEW SOMETHING WAS WRONG THE MINUTE I OPENED MY
eyes that Friday morning.

Hot. Hurting. Can't breathe.

My eyes wouldn't stay open, no matter how hard I fought.
I'd just let them drift shut again when I heard my mother's voice,
coming as though she was a long way away. She was saying my
name, the worry in her voice growing each time she spoke.

*Nate. Nate, come on, it's time to . . . Nate? Baby? Oh, God
. . . Nate, come on, honey, wake up.*

Just before I slid into oblivion, I remembered that I was
supposed to ride to school with Quinn today. She'd texted me
late last night, saying she had the car and asking if I wanted a
lift.

Quinn. Yes, I want . . . Quinn.

The tightness in my chest was getting too much to bear,
and I let go of my tentative grip on awareness. The last thread of
consciousness that slipped through my fingers was her name.

Quinn.

★ Twenty-Three ★

Quinn

"WELL, SOMEONE LOOKS BRIGHT-EYED THIS morning." My mother poured her coffee and smiled at me. "I heard you come in last night. And thanks for texting us that you were okay." She took a sip and hummed in appreciation. "So what was going on with Leo?"

"Oh." I lost my walking-on-air smile for a minute. "Oh, God, Mom. I can't believe I almost forgot. It's Lisa. She has leukemia."

"What?" Mom sank down into a kitchen chair. "What're you talking about, Quinn?"

"That's why Leo asked me to meet him last night. I guess they told the boys, and Leo . . . he was pretty upset."

"Oh, my God. I need to call her." My mother pulled out her phone. "Sheri texted. I wonder if she . . . oh, no." I watched her eyes move down the screen. "Nate's in the hospital. Again. Sheri said he had a high temp this morning, and then she couldn't wake him up."

My heart sank. "I was supposed to pick him up for school

today." Which reminded me of why I'd set that up. "Um, Mom, I needed to talk to him because . . . Leo and I are together. Last night, he—" I could feel my face getting red. "Well, we talked."

"Together?" She blinked. "Like . . . you're dating? What about Jake?"

"Yeah, like we're dating." I didn't know why it was so embarrassing to have this conversation with my mother. "Jake and I are just friends, Mom. We'd figured that out before I saw Leo last night."

She gave her head a little shake. "This is a lot of information to take in all at once, sweetie. Lisa's sick. Nate's in the hospital. And you and Leo are now an item."

I managed a wry smile. "I hope that last part is good news. But I guess it's not that important, with everything else going on." I stood up. "Should we go to the hospital?"

"Sheri says not yet. They're running tests, but Nate's in the ICU and they're limiting visitors until they know more." She rubbed her forehead, as though a headache was brewing beneath. "They'll keep us in the loop. I'm going to assume she doesn't know about Lisa yet, and now's not the time to share that news. But I think I'll call Lisa and see if we can get together."

"Okay. I guess I should head out to school." I hooked my bag over one shoulder, hesitating. "Mom, even with everything else, I'm still really happy about Leo and me. You think it's okay, right? I mean, Nate'll be all right with it, won't he?"

Uncertainty filled her eyes. "I want to say yes, Quinn. I've known how you feel about Leo for a long time, and I've just been waiting for the day he realizes how much you mean to him. But at the same time, I've worried—because you and Leo being together is going to change your dynamic. Even if you don't mean it to, it will. Nate's going to feel left out, no matter how hard you try to include him. And sweetie, although I know you wouldn't intentionally hurt Nate for anything, your relationship with Leo is going to break Nate's heart. He loves you. So while I'm so happy for you, honey, I'm a little worried, too. For a lot of different reasons, which we can talk about later. For now, you better scoot. I'll see you tonight?"

I nodded. "And you'll text me if you hear anything about Nate?"

My mom hugged me. "Of course I will. Try not to worry."

My stomach turned over as I drove into the school parking lot. Being alone with Leo last night, kissing him, being held by him, what he did to me . . . my whole body heated up, remembering. It was like I was a different person when he touched me. When his hands were on me, I couldn't be close enough to him.

But the thought of walking into the school as part of a couple was making me quake. I was still a little terrified that Leo had changed his mind overnight, that I'd see him today and he'd ignore me. But another part of me was just as nervous about what would happen if he didn't ignore me. What were people going to say? I was sure most of Leo's friends wouldn't understand why he'd be with someone like me when he could have any girl in school.

My phone vibrated, and I checked it quickly, thinking of Nate. But it wasn't my mother or Sheri; Leo's name was on the readout.

I see you, Mia. Are you hiding? Where's Nate?

Craning my neck to see through the windshield, I spotted Leo a few rows in front of me, leaning against his car. His feet were crossed on the gravel, and his arms were folded over his chest.

And his eyes, those gray and stormy eyes . . . they were on me.

Slowly, I climbed out of the car, slamming the door behind me. As though Leo was a magnet and I was a helpless shard of iron, I moved toward him, my heart beating faster.

When I was about a foot away, he smiled and reached out to pull me close. He didn't kiss me at first, just stood with me in the circle of his arms.

"Good morning, Mia." He bent his head and brushed his lips over mine.

"Hey." I breathed the word, leaning into him. "Mmmmm, you smell good."

He chuckled. "Guess it's better than the alternative." He glanced over my shoulder. "What happened with Nate? Didn't you drive him today?"

I dropped my forehead onto Leo's shoulder. "No. Sheri texted my mom this morning. Nate's back in the hospital with a fever. They don't know what's wrong."

"Shit." Leo rubbed his hands up and down my back, absently.

"Yeah. I know." I slid my arms around his waist, my hands traveling over the muscles beneath his snug T-shirt. "Leo, we can't let him find out about us until he's feeling better."

"No, I get that. But we don't have to hide. No one's going to go running off to the hospital to tattle on us."

"Yeah, you're probably right." I rested my head on his chest, listening to the reassuring thump of his heart.

"Hey. You still . . . you're sure, right?" He sounded tentative, like he was afraid of what I might say.

I tilted my head back to see him better. "Me? Of course I

am. I was kind of scared this morning that you might have, um, regrets."

"Not one." He kissed me firmly, and giving a little growl, teased my closed lips with his tongue until I opened for him. He explored me lazily, setting my blood on fire. I moved closer, standing between the solid columns of his legs. My boobs were crushed against his chest, and my nipples hardened.

"God, Mia. I'm not going to be able to walk into class." Leo groaned and dropped his head into the crook of my neck. "I just want to drag you into my car, drive out . . . I don't know, somewhere we could be alone."

"Me, too." I laughed a little. "But I've got a math quiz this morning, and I have a sneaking suspicion that 'hot for my boyfriend's rocking body' isn't going to cut it as an excused absence." *Boyfriend.* I loved to say that word. I loved it even more that I was talking about Leo when I said it.

"Probably not." He smoothed my hair back from my face. "Okay. I guess I have to let you go to class. I've got English and study hall this morning. But I'll see you at lunch, right? And then maybe we could both go over to the hospital after school and check on Nate. I've got practice, but it's a short one, since tomorrow's game day."

"That works. If I hear anything before then, I'll let you know." I took a step back, feeling instantly colder. I wasn't sure if Leo wanted me to walk in before him, but my question was answered when he took hold of my hand firmly and began to stroll across the school lawn.

"Taylor! Hey, asshole." Matt Lampert jogged up beside us, smacking Leo on the back of the head. "You never texted me last night. I was waiting for you to come over."

"Yeah, sorry." Leo sounded anything but. "Something came up at home."

Matt frowned. "Okay. Everything . . ." He stopped, both talking and walking. And he stared at our joined hands. "Anything you need to tell me, Lion? Something new?"

"Something right." Leo eyed his friend, as though he were daring him to say anything. "Something finally right. Quinn and I are together."

"Oooookay." Matt glanced from my face to Leo's. "Um, congratulations?"

"Thanks." Leo's tone was wry. "Hey, man. I'm sorry about last night. It was a family thing. But I didn't mean to leave you hanging."

"Yeah, no problem." He gestured toward the door of the building. "You coming to English?"

"Yep. Be right there." Leo tossed him a look, and Matt laughed.

"I get you. See you inside."

I glanced up at Leo. "What was that all about?"

"That was about me wanting to kiss my girl before we have to go into class." He combed his fingers into my hair, holding my head still, and slanted his open mouth over mine, kissing me thoroughly. "There. That should hold me a few hours." He dropped one quick kiss on my forehead. "See you at lunch."

By lunch time, apparently word about Leo and me had swept over the campus. I might not have noticed if it hadn't been for the cheerleaders being more hostile toward me than usual and more than a few curious looks from other students. Still, nothing really bothered me until we were in the cafeteria.

Leo met me at my locker, coming up from behind and startling me with a kiss on my neck as his arms circled my waist.

"Hi." He released me, grinning. "Did you have a good morning? How was the math quiz?"

I smiled back. "Morning was good, quiz was so-so. I hate math so hard."

Leo laughed. "Some things never change, huh?" He slid his hand down my arm to link our fingers. "C'mon, let's eat. I'm starved."

"Some things never change," I teased back. "Are you still the guy who's going to take my slice of pizza when my back's turned?"

"No." He touched the tip of my nose with his index finger. "I'm the guy who's going to buy us each an extra slice so I can eat them." He patted his flat stomach. "Gotta keep up the energy. Big game tomorrow."

"That's right. This one determines whether or not you guys make round one of the playoffs, doesn't it?"

"Yeah, but I'm trying not to think of that." Leo led me into the cafeteria, and we joined the food line. "Coach says a game's a game. We play them all hard."

We didn't talk much in line; it was loud and difficult to hear. Leo was good to his word, loading up both of our trays with pizza. After we'd paid, I hesitated.

"What's wrong?" Leo balanced his tray on one hand and glanced back at me.

"Are you sure it's okay for me to sit with you?" I could see the table Leo and his friends usually occupied, and it looked full. Maybe just room enough for one more, and for sure that one more wasn't the girl who wrote newspaper columns.

"Of course it is. Come on." He grasped my hand again and tugged me over to the table, dropping his own tray first and then taking mine from my arms to set down next to it. "Hey,

guys. Make room." He slung one leg over the bench and gave
the guy next to him a little shove. "Move over, Simpson. My
girl doesn't need much space, but you take up half the bench."

"Nice, Taylor." Dylan glanced back at me and then did a
double-take. "Oh. Hi."

"Hi." I felt tremendously self-conscious as the group fell
silent. Keeping my head down, I mimicked Leo's moves and
climbed over the bench, trying to make myself as small as possible as I sat down.

"Oh, hell no, Leo. Hell no." Trish Dawson slammed down
her can of diet soda. "No way. I'm not eating with her."

Down the table, Matt sighed. "Trish, c'mon—"

"Matt, you might be the quarterback, but you're not going
to win this one." She pointed at me. "She hates us. Have you
read what she writes in that stupid school newspaper?"

"Trish, sit down and shut the hell up." Leo didn't raise his
voice, but Trish's eyes rounded in surprise. "Quinn's with me.
If you have something to say to her, discuss it like a normal
person and stop screaming like a banshee."

"Hey, speaking of banshees, you know who's hot?" One of
the other guys leaned up, smirking. "That chick who plays the
banshee on *Teen Wolf*. Am I right? Smokin'."

And just like that, the conversation shifted—now *there*
was a pun—to which female on that television show was the
sexiest. Trish sat down across from me, glaring, and I knew this
was far from over.

And that was just the beginning. By the end of the day, I'd been
shoved from behind by a group of cheerleaders, jeered at by

two girls . . . and then I stopped at the newspaper office. Gia looked at me and shook her head.

"Quinn. I thought you had more smarts than this."

I pasted on a smile. "What do you mean?"

"Leo Taylor? Really? I get that he's built like a freaking god, and his face sure is pretty to look at, but God, seriously. A football player? You're better than that."

I rolled my eyes. "You know, I expected to get shit from the cheerleaders and all their buddies, but I figured my own friends might actually have my back."

Gia sighed. "But . . . but Quinn. It's like you're defecting to the other side. How can I bitch about the football team when you're hooking up with their chief?" She dropped her voice. "Is it just the sex? Because I can get behind that. If you're just using him for his body, I mean."

"Oookay then. And this conversation is over." I turned to leave, but she snagged the handle of my bag.

"I'm sorry, I'm sorry. I know. On principle, as a feminist, I need to support your choice to be with whoever you want. And I'll admit, hearing you bagged the Lion right from under a cheerleader's nose gave me a little happy." She held up her right hand. "I promise, I'll be good. I respect your right to choose."

I shook my head. "I didn't bag anyone, Gia. Leo's been my best friend forever. It's just that now we know there's a little something more between us."

Her smile turned wicked. "I hope it's not just a *little* something, babe. Looking at that guy, I'd lay a bet nothing on him is little."

Great. I could tell my face was flaming. "Anyway, I didn't steal him from Sarah. They were just seeing each other casually, and he'd ended it before—well, before."

"Well, that's less satisfying but more honorable." She folded her arms on the counter and leaned her chin on top. "I gotta give you credit, though. Dating a guy like Leo Taylor would be too much for me to handle. I heard his friends were talking shit already. And Trish Dawson says there's no way you'll ever hang with the team and their girlfriends. You two are like the fucking Romeo and Juliet of Eatonboro High."

I dropped my head back and blew out a long breath. "I know. But it'll settle down. They just aren't used to the idea."

"If you say so." Gia wheeled her chair around and picked up a pile of paper. "Hey, you here to work? Want to help me fold papers?"

"Sure." I took my share and began folding. "I'm waiting for Leo to finish practice, then we're going to the hospital to see Nate. He's pretty sick." I felt a stab of guilt; how could I worry about my own petty crap when my friend was fighting to recover? "My mother just texted that he's awake, so we can see him for a few minutes."

"God, I'm sorry, Quinn." She was quiet for a minute, folding. "He's always been kind of sickly, right? I remember that from grade school."

I nodded. "He was born prematurely, and he has a degenerative muscle disease that has lots of complications with it. It affects his lungs, and it makes him vulnerable to all kinds of viruses and infections." I fought back the gripping fear that always niggled in my heart whenever Nate was sick. "He's been doing pretty well the last few years. Sometimes I forget how sick he can get—and how fast it happens."

We'd just finished the papers when Leo appeared in the doorway of the office. He filled the space, taking my breath away as he leaned on the jamb, grinning. His hair was still damp, and the long-sleeved thermal shirt hugged the roped muscles on his arms. Faded jeans stretched over his long legs.

My mouth went dry and all I could think was . . . *damn.*

Next to me Gia sniffed, but I didn't miss the gleam of appreciation in her eye. I gave her shoulder a little nudge. "Behave yourself."

Turning to Leo, I smiled. "Hey. I'm ready to go. Just let me grab my bag."

He was too fast for me. "I got it." He slung the canvas carryall over his back. I thought he'd just head for the door, but he stopped, offering his hand to Gia. "I'm Leo Taylor. Nice to meet you."

Her mouth dropped open a little. "Uh, Gia. Gia Capri. Yeah, nice to meet you, too." She took his hand, and I was fairly certainly there was a little bit of swooning going on. I tried hard not to giggle.

"When Gia lets go of your hand, we should leave. If we get over to the hospital in the next hour, we can see Nate for a few minutes."

Leo nodded. "I talked to Coach, and he said as long as I was home by nine tonight, I'm cool for curfew. Let's go." He winked at Gia as he freed his hand. "See you around."

I glanced back at Gia as we left. She gave me wide eyes, fanned herself and mouthed, "WOW."

Clearly even feminist journalists were not immune to the charms of the Lion.

★ Twenty-Four ★

Leo

I HATED THIS FUCKING HOSPITAL. WE'D BEEN COMING TO IT
for way too many years, almost always to see Nate; although
I'd had my share of broken bones and mild concussions,
none of them had called for a hospital stay.

"I hate this place," I muttered to Quinn. "It smells funny
and people die here." As soon as I said the words, I could've
bitten off my tongue. I knew how worried she was about Nate.

But to my relief she only smiled and shook her head. "Tell
you what. If you're a good boy, I'll give you a treat when we're
finished here." The sideways glance she shot me gave a hint
about what that treat might be. *Oh, baby.*

The ICU was on the fifth floor. We were silent in the elevator, although Quinn gripped my hand a little tighter the closer
we got to that floor. I could practically feel her nerves.

"Baby, remember, I need to use this hand for catching the
football tomorrow night. Don't break my fingers, okay?"

"I'm sorry." She tried to tug her hand free, but I wouldn't
let her go.

"I didn't mean I don't want to hold your hand. Just let the

blood get through."

She sighed out a breath between clenched teeth. "I hate hospitals, too. And every time Nate's here, I'm afraid."

"I get that." I wrapped my arm around her just as the elevator doors opened, and we stepped out into a small waiting alcove. I was surprised to see my mom there, along with Quinn's. Sheri and Mark were sitting close together, their hands gripped tightly. I couldn't miss the way Sheri's eyes darted to my arm around Quinn's shoulder.

"How's he doing?" Quinn glanced around the room. I felt her body tense.

"Better than this morning. Oh, my God, I was terrified. I couldn't wake him up." Sheri pressed her face into her husband's chest. "He's at least conscious now. He caught some kind of virus, and then there's an infection . . . they're treating him with IV antibiotics and fluids."

"Can we see him? Just for a minute?"

Sheri nodded. "But one at a time, and . . ." Her eyes flickered to me.

As if she'd read her mind, Quinn nodded. "Don't worry. We're not going to say anything."

I took one step back, shoving my hands into my back pockets. "Go ahead. I'll wait for you here."

She glanced back at me as Mark stood up. "I'll show you where to go." The two of them headed down the hall, and I was left alone with the three mothers. I dropped into one of molded plastic chairs and sighed.

When I was a little kid, these three women had been almost interchangeable in my mind as authority figures. I'd obeyed Sheri and Carrie as fast as I did my own mom. And now, sitting among them, I waited for the onslaught.

I didn't have to wait long.

"I hear there was news I missed out on last night." My mother was the first to speak. "Luckily I have friends who tell me things."

"Hey, you were asleep when I got home, and I didn't see you this morning, either. I would've told you." I glanced at Sheri, but she had her head leaned against the back of the chair, with her eyes closed.

"Hmm." Mom didn't say anything else, but her eyes rested on me for a long while. And Carrie leaned over to pat my knee.

"You know we're here for you, no matter what." She whispered the words, and I wondered if they hadn't told Sheri yet about my mother's diagnosis. It would make sense; she had enough on her plate just now.

We sat without speaking for the next ten minutes. I stared up at the tabloid-style talk show that was playing on the television, idly watching as two men argued over who *wasn't* the father of the baby held by the woman between them.

When Quinn came back into the waiting area, she was blinking rapidly and sniffling. Mark beckoned to Sheri.

"The doctor wants to give us an update. Come on down and you can sit with Nate for a while, too."

Quinn inclined her head, motioning for me to follow her. I stood up, and we moved a little way down the hall, into a shadowed doorway. She leaned against the wall and exhaled loudly.

"I've never seen him this sick, Leo. Or not in a long time." She cast her eyes up, and I could tell she was trying not to cry. "He held my hand and kept thanking me for coming to see him. God, it about broke my heart." She twisted her mouth. "I'm sorry you didn't get to see him, but they didn't want him upset right now."

I drew her close to me. "It's okay, Mia. Nate's getting the medicine he needs, and you know how these things go. In a day or two, he'll be better. And then I'll see him, and I promise—I'm going to make things right between us."

"I hope so." Her voice was muffled against me. We stayed that way for a few minutes, breathing in each other's strength.

I almost turned when I heard Mark's voice, but when I realized that neither he nor Sheri had seen us, I stood still, not wanting to interrupt.

"It's going to be okay, Sher. The meds are doing their job, and Dr. Randall's on the case. He's never let us down yet."

"Yet being the operative word." Sheri's voice was a cry of anguish. "Every time this happens, it breaks off another piece of my heart. I think, is this the time we're going to lose him? We don't know how long we're going to have him here, Mark. Nothing's guaranteed to us."

"You could say that about anyone, babe. You know that. We've been climbing this mountain for almost eighteen years. Nate's beat the odds every time. Just hold onto that."

Quinn raised her face to me, her expression bleak. I stared down into her eyes until I was sure Nate's parents had moved away, and then I led her back down the hall.

My mother was kneeling next to Sheri, whose face was buried in her hands. Carrie sat on Sheri's other side, rubbing her back.

I cleared my throat. "If it's okay, I'll take Quinn home. I'm supposed to be at home by nine, so Coach doesn't freak." It sounded so silly, so frivolous, to be talking football when Nate's life was teetering on the brink. I added, "But if you need us to stay, we will. Curfew be damned."

Sheri lifted her face and shook her head. "No, honey, you go home and get some rest. Both of you. Nate would want that." She ran one hand through her hair. "And he's going to be fine." She gave us a watery smile. "And once he's all better, I'm sure he's going to be happy for both of you. You've always been such good friends to him."

Quinn bent to give Sheri a quick hug. "We love him, you know that. Just let me know if you need anything."

We took the elevator back downstairs, where I forced myself to walk slowly, even though I wanted to sprint out of that place. Quinn squeezed my hand.

"Thanks for coming with me, Leo. I know it wasn't easy."

"Hey." I stopped just outside the doors, gripped Quinn by her shoulders and brought her in front of me. "I would do anything for you, Mia. Anything. This was nothing."

She gave me a faint smile. "If you say so."

"I do, and I mean it." I linked our hands again as we walked to the car. It was dark, even though it wasn't quite eight yet, and I paid close attention to the road. "I wish I could take you out eat, but Coach is serious about the curfew. I have to check in that I'm home by nine, and even though we're on the honor code—there aren't any second chances."

"I understand. And honestly, I'm too tired to think about going anywhere." She reached over the gear shift to touch my knee, and my body jumped at the feel of her hand. "But I did promise you a treat, didn't I? If you were a good boy at the hospital."

"And I was a very good boy." I gave her wide eyes and a nod. "Very good."

"Hmm. What kind of treat do you think you deserve?"

"Well . . ." I turned my car into Quinn's driveway and clicked off the headlights. "I'd start with your lips." I pointed at my mouth. "Right here."

She smiled. "We've been together almost twenty-four hours now. Aren't you tired of kissing me yet?"

I shook my head. "Mia, the day I tell you I'm tired of your

kisses will be the last day of my life." I skimmed one hand over her hair. "And even then, your mouth on mine will be what I want as I open up the pearly gates."

Quinn's eyes glistened again, but this time, the tears weren't sad ones. "You say the most wonderful things. How can you be so sure now, when last week you were pretending I didn't exist?"

"Because I finally gave in." I laughed. "I thought I didn't deserve you, Mia. And I was right, I don't. But I got tired of fighting how much I need you, and even though I know I'm not good enough for you, I'm never going to stop trying to be better."

"Okay." Before I knew what was happening, Quinn had flung one leg over my lap, straddling me, her back against the steering wheel.

"Whoa." I caught her by the hips. "What're you doing, babe?"

"Giving you your treat." She leaned down, touching her lips to mine. "This is where you wanted me to start, right?"

"Uh, yeah." I tilted my head up to give her better access.

"Mmmmm." Quinn hummed, as though my mouth was the best thing she'd ever tasted. "Can I ask you something, Leo?"

"Baby, when you're sitting on me like this, you can ask me for the world, and I'd give it to you. What do you want to ask?"

She sighed a little, and her breath fanned over my cheek. "Can you tell . . . how inexperienced I am? I don't want to be boring for you."

"Boring is the last thing you are. And I'm going to be a total male chauvinist pig and say I love the fact that you haven't been with anybody else." I ran my hands up her sides. "When I kissed you outside the hospital last month, was that your first kiss?"

Eyes averted, Quinn nodded.

"Mia, that kiss . . . it's been tormenting me ever since that night. So if that's you being inexperienced and boring, bring it on, baby."

She laughed, and the way her body moved over me ignited a deeper need. I tugged her head down to me and took her mouth, thrusting my tongue between her lips. Quinn moaned, snaking her hands around me neck and threading her fingers through my hair.

I moved my hands back to her hips, centering the heat between her legs over my aching dick. She arched her back, and I couldn't help skimming my fingers under her shirt, desperate to touch warm, smooth skin. Boldly, I cupped her tits, only more eager when I realized that her bra cups were lace. I traced my thumbs around her hardened nipples and was rewarded by her throaty noise of approval.

Encouraged, I lowered my mouth to take one of those tempting peaks into my mouth, wetting the cotton of her shirt. Quinn pushed the back of my head closer, as though she was afraid I'd pull away too soon.

I'd just moved my mouth to her other nipple when the alarm on my telephone began to beep. With a groan of frustration, I let my head drop back.

"Fuck." My cock was pulsing beneath Quinn's core, and I would've given anything in the universe to strip off the clothes between us and thrust up into her. But the part of my brain still capable of rational thought remembered that I had to be home in ten minutes . . . and that Quinn was a virgin. I didn't have any doubt that we'd get there one day, but I knew I had to take care of her. Her first time wasn't going to be some quick screw in my car. It had to be perfect. Special.

"Babe, I have to go." I kissed her one more time. "I don't want to, believe me, but I have to."

"I know." Quinn kissed my jaw, my neck . . . if she kept it up, there was no way I'd be able to leave.

"You're going to come to my game tomorrow night, right?"

"I always do."

"I'd come pick you up in the morning, but I won't be going home after school. We'll just stay there, getting ready for the game."

"Okay." Sighing, she swung back over to her own seat. "Be careful driving to your house. I know you need to be there on time, but don't speed or coast the stop signs."

"Will do, babe." I chucked her under the chin. "Same old Mia Quinn, taking care of me."

"Always will, Leo." She kissed my cheek, smiled and climbed out of the car. "Play a good game tomorrow night." She closed the door and started up the driveway.

I rolled down my window and leaned out. "Quinn!"

She glanced back, still smiling.

"Come down to the field tomorrow night after my game, okay?"

Quinn hesitated, and I could see indecision warring on her face. Finally, she nodded.

"I'll be there."

★ Twenty-Five ★

Quinn

NIGHTTIME FOOTBALL GAMES HAD A SPECIAL KIND OF magic to them, and tonight, the energy was heightened: this was an important game, one that would determine whether or not the Eatonboro Eagles would advance to Round Two of the conference playoffs. We were underdogs, for sure; Gatbury was one of the best teams in our area.

Gia had saved me a seat, so I sat on the bleachers about halfway up from the field, mashed between two girls. I wasn't complaining; it was especially chilly tonight, and I was glad for the extra body heat.

"So how does it feel to know it's your *boyfriend* playing out there tonight?" Gia grinned and poked me. "Pretty exciting, huh? Are we going to see some spontaneous cheers about the Lion roaring?"

I rolled my eyes. "Don't hold your breath. I might be dating one of the team's stars, but I'm here for the game, not just to moon over the players."

"Oh, check her out. It's all business. That's our Quinn—

she's a tough cookie." Gia laughed. "Give her a few weeks, and she'll have the cheerleaders coming around to her way of thinking."

"That's not exactly my top priority." I gazed down onto the field where I saw Sarah chatting with another girl. "And not all of the cheerleaders are so bad. Sarah, for instance. I like her." I shot Gia a quelling look. "And if we generalize about the cheerleaders, how are we any better than they are?"

She sighed. "You're determined to take away all my fun, aren't you? Fine. Whatever you say. I promise I'll try to be more open-minded." She paused as a group of people scooted in front of us, trying to get to the last few open seats down the bench. "What's the word on Nate, by the way? Is he doing any better?"

I bit the side of my lip. "A little. His mom texted today that his temperature was down a bit this afternoon. But he's still pretty sick."

"Aw, I'm sorry. Hope he feels better."

"Thanks."

Conversation was interrupted at that point as the announcer invited us all to rise for the singing of the National Anthem. I rested my eyes on Leo, standing in the row with the rest of his team, helmet in one hand. I could see his profile, the set of his mouth and the eager look of determination in his eyes. We hadn't had much time during the day today, just a few stolen kisses this morning and a little chatting at lunch. I hadn't felt any more welcome at his table, and I wondered if I'd be able to convince him to eat outside with me at least now and then. Sitting across the table from Trish was giving me indigestion.

The Eagles lost the coin toss this week, and since Gatbury elected to defer, we got the ball first. Our receiver caught it on kickoff and ran for a twenty-yard return, giving us decent field position. I clapped with the rest of the stadium as Leo and the other offensive players trotted onto the field.

But they weren't there for long. On second and five, Matt Lampert threw one of his rare interceptions, and the Gatbury defensive back who'd caught the pass intended for Leo made it all the way to the end zone for the touchdown. When Matt reached the sidelines, he tossed down his helmet in frustration. Leo grabbed his arm, speaking to him with their heads close together.

The Eagles didn't do anything with their next two possessions, but luckily, neither did Gatbury. Reminiscent of the Franklin Township game, just before the end of the half, Eatonboro got within field goal distance, and Beau Dunton kicked one between the uprights. Our boys trotted off the field at halftime trailing seven to three.

"It's not looking good, girls." I wrapped my arms around my middle. "They need to pull their shit together, or our season is over."

"That might work out for you," Gia observed. "Just think of all the time Leo would have to spend with you if he's not worried about practices or games."

I groaned. "Gia, what kind of girlfriend would I be if I wanted that? We haven't had a real shot at the playoffs for years. I want our boys to go all the way."

"You're just taking this whole unselfish crap a little too far." She shifted on the bleacher. "Is it just me, or is it getting even colder?"

"I heard we might get snow this weekend." One of the other girls spoke with the glee only associated with the very first snowstorm of the year. "Sure feels like it."

It did, too. I pulled my scarf a little tighter around my neck, shivering. Someone tugged at it, making me gag a little as it stretched over my throat.

"Jake, if you strangle Quinn, who else is going to put up with you on the newspaper? You know she's the only one who can get anything done." Gia winked at our editor.

"You're not wrong, Gia. And hey, look at this. In appreciation of all of the hard work my wonderful team does, I brought you hot chocolate." Jake passed the cardboard tray down the bench, and we all ooohed appreciatively.

"I take back every nasty thing I've ever said about you. Thanks for this." Gia lifted the cup and took a sip.

"You're welcome." He patted my shoulder. "Everything going okay with you, Q?"

I smiled. "I'd be happier if the score were reversed, but otherwise no complaints."

"Cool. I need to talk with you about our op/ed page for next week. Think you can hang out Monday after school?"

"I'm sure I can."

"Maybe you should check with your boy toy first," Gia teased. "He might have plans for you."

"I don't need to check with anybody about anything." I stuck out my tongue at Gia and then turned back to Jake. "Thanks again for the cocoa. See you Monday."

The second half began with Gatbury possessing the ball. They came close to scoring, but happily, our defensive line held strong, and their kicker even missed the attempted field goal.

Still, we didn't seem to be able to move very far, either. Gatbury shut down our running game pretty effectively, and Matt was sacked twice. When he did manage to get off a pass, it always went wide, at one point just missing another interception.

I wasn't one to give up hope easily—clearly, since I'd been in love with the same boy for nine years before he finally admitted he felt the same way—but I was nearly resigned to the fact that we were going to lose this one. There were thirty-eight seconds left on the clock, and Gatbury had the ball on our twenty-six-yard line. Glumly, I just hoped we could keep them from scoring again.

The Gatbury QB fired off a forward pass toward the end zone, intending it for his favorite receiver, but by some miracle, it was our linebacker there instead. He caught the ball as neatly as if it were intended for him all along, looked down at it like he had no idea how it had gotten there, and then took off down the field.

In one of those inspirational football movies, he would've run it all the way back, or at least gotten it across the fifty-yard line. But he didn't. He got to about our own thirty where he was taken down by Gatbury's left tackle, a mountain of a guy.

The clock now stood at twenty-four seconds. Our offense, most of whom had assumed the game, if not the season, was over for us, hustled back onto the field and lined up. There wasn't time for a huddle. The boys were going to have to wing it.

On the first play, Matt tried to run the ball. When he was tackled immediately, I cursed at him as though he could hear me.

"What the fuck, dude? The damn running game hasn't worked all night. Why the hell would you think it's good idea now?"

Gia exchanged a glance with the girl sitting next to me. "Simmer down, Quinn. You're about to bust a vein or something."

My heart was pounding in excitement. This was football. This was why I loved the game. It was second and nine, but since there were only fourteen seconds on the clock, this was likely the last play, unless Matt threw an incomplete pass or the receiver ran out of bounds. The Eagles fans in the stadium held their collective breath as the ball was snapped, flying into Matt's hands. He stagger-stepped backwards, and I could feel his tension as his eyes scanned downfield, looking for Leo or Dylan to break free. Finally, in desperation, he drew back his arm and threw one of the most beautiful forward passes I'd ever seen in high school football.

The ball soared through the night sky, spiraling down. Out of nowhere, Leo came barreling across the field, a Gatbury linebacker close on his heels. He leaped into the air and snagged the ball with one hand, tucking it against his chest. With precision that took my breath away, he spun on one foot and took off.

Leo had always been fast, but tonight, he was a gazelle. His legs moved so fast they were almost invisible, but it didn't matter, because we could all see him step nimbly into the end zone.

The entire stadium erupted into joyful cheers. The place was shaking. I was both laughing and almost crying in relief as I watched the rest of the team descend on Matt and Leo. Brent lifted Leo in a massive hug, spinning him around.

Over the loudspeaker, the announcer pronounced the end of the game, with a final score Eatonboro nine and Gatbury seven.

"Okay. I'm finding it hard to maintain my air of disdainful indifference." Gia laughed, hugging my arm. "That was pretty incredible. And shit, girl! That was your boyfriend who made that catch."

"Yeah, I kind of noticed that." I tugged on my gloves. "I need to get down to the field. I promised Leo."

"Of course you did." Gia winked at me. "Hey, give him an extra smooch from me. You know, just as a fan of the game."

"You got it. See you later!"

It took me a solid ten minutes to push through the milling people in the stand and get to the break in the railing. I managed to side-step a cluster of teachers, avoid the cheerleaders, and make it down the sideline. I caught sight of Leo and began heading his way.

Before I reached him, though, Mr. Ranetti, the announcer, stepped in front of Leo and Matt, holding out a microphone. I couldn't hear the first couple of questions, but as I drew closer, I managed to pick up the last one.

"Leo, that was one of the most amazing catches this reporter has seen in his thirty years of announcing high school games. Can you tell us what was going through your mind as you made that leap for the ball?"

As though he could sense me, Leo turned his head, locking eyes with me. A slow smile spread over his face.

"Well, sir, honestly, I wasn't sure I could make that catch. But I figured I needed to try, so what I was thinking was . . . go big, or go home."

Around us, the crowds began to cheer again. Mr. Ranetti patted Leo's back, apparently congratulating him again. He smiled politely, but the moment the announcer had turned away, Leo took off toward me. He reached me in a few steps, scooped me into his arms and kissed me, holding me against him.

"Mia—babe. Did you see it? God. What a game."

"You were magnificent." I slicked back his sweaty hair from his forehead. "That was the most amazing thing I've ever seen. Congratulations!"

He slid his hands down to my ass and bent his head over to murmur in my ear. "I have to think that kind of play deserves a treat, right? I mean, I was a very good boy. Again. Two nights in a row."

I giggled, held his face in mine and kissed his lips. "I'm sure we can figure out something that works for both of us. Maybe pick up where we left off last night."

Desire flared in Leo's eyes. "Oh, baby. I like how your mind works."

★ Twenty-Six ★

Nate

MY RECOVERY FROM THE VIRUS THAT WOULDN'T quit was slow. I was in the ICU for nearly a week, and then spent another five days in a regular room, arguing with whoever would listen that I wanted to go home.

And even once I was released and got home, I was still so weak that I couldn't go back to school right away. It was frustrating as hell.

The only bright spot during the whole time was that Quinn came to visit me every day. She didn't stay long, but she was always there, entertaining me with stories and making me laugh. I was glad to see that she seemed to have gotten over the whole deal with Leo and Sarah Jenkins. As a bonus, she rarely mentioned Jake Donavan, which I hoped meant she'd stopped dating him. I hadn't been sure what was going on between the two of them, but more competition was not something I needed.

There was something different about Quinn, though. She was somehow softer, and there was a glow in her eyes that I'd never seen before. I was afraid to even think it, but I wondered if maybe my near-death brush had opened up her eyes to her true feelings for me. I thought about how long I should wait until I declared myself and admitted how I felt.

I'd been out of the hospital for about two weeks and was getting antsy to go back to school when Quinn stopped by one afternoon. We were getting closer to Thanksgiving, and my mother had been trying to talk me into staying at home through the holidays and returning after the new year.

But I was ready to be back in school. I felt stronger, and I wanted to spend more time with Quinn. I didn't want to lose another minute together with the girl I'd loved for so long. Who could blame me for that?

"But are you sure you can handle school yet, Nate?" Quinn frowned, and I felt unreasonably annoyed. She was acting like my mother, and that was the last thing I wanted from her.

"Yes, I'm sure. God, you guys all act like I'll be running a marathon when I go back. I'll go to classes and come home. No big deal."

Quinn glanced over my shoulder, and I was sure she was looking at my mom, silently communicating with her. They did that sometimes, like I was a kid who didn't know when people were talking about him.

"Well, I'll let you two visit." My mother stood up, her lips pressed together. "Call me if you need anything."

When the sound of her clicking heels had disappeared, Quinn looked up at me, worry and trepidation in her eyes. "Nate, I need to talk to you about something."

Warning bells went off in my head, but I ignored them. "Okay. I actually want to talk to you about something, too. But it can wait. What's up?"

She took a deep breath. "Nate, you know I love you, right? You know you're my best friend. You always have been. I was so scared when you were sick. I couldn't stand the idea of losing you."

I reached over to squeeze her hand. "You're my best friend and more, Quinn. I love you, too." I hoped she heard the extra emphasis I put on the words.

"But . . ."

God, how I hated that word. It always meant something shitty was about to go down.

We understand how much rowing crew means to you, Nate, but after this illness, we all agree it's best that you step away from that for a time.

You're absolutely normal, Nate, but you have a disease . . .

"But you know, too, that Leo's also my best friend. I love you both." Tears welled up in her eyes. "And I wish there was an easier way to say this, Nate, some way that wouldn't hurt you or make you mad at me, but I don't think there is. The truth is, how I love Leo is a little different than how I love you. I've known that for a long time. And we've been, um . . . we've been together for a little over a month now."

I blinked. *Together?* What the hell did that mean?

"You . . . you're dating Leo? Like . . . he's your boyfriend?" I was amazed at how calm my voice sounded.

Quinn nodded. "Yes. We're dating. We—it's been going so well, Nate. Leo's like a new person. Or an old person, because he's like he used to be. He's been wanting to come to see you since you got sick, but he didn't want to upset you, either. But if you say it's okay, he'd like to come over today."

A red tint began to color my vision. I knew what it meant; I was getting too upset, and I needed to calm down, before my breathing went to hell and I had to have a treatment.

But damn it all to hell, this couldn't be happening. Quinn was mine. She didn't belong with Leo, and I thought I'd finally convinced her of that before I'd gotten sick. I'd felt bad for her, of course, but in the long run, I was better for her than Leo was. I was certain of that.

"Are you out of your mind? After everything that Leo did to us? How he treated us? How did this happen?"

Quinn wiped at her cheeks, biting down on her bottom lip. "It doesn't really matter how. The fact is, we're together. And we want you to be happy for us. But Nate, whether you are or not, whether you approve or not, nothing's going to change. I love Leo. I've wanted this for a long time. Please, be glad for me. Be my friend, and tell me you're okay with it."

I opened my mouth to say something socially appropriate, something about being surprised, but I was still on a lot of medication, and sometimes I said unpredictable things.

"Are you sleeping with him?"

"Nate!" Shock threaded through her voice. "First of all, that's none of your business. Second of all . . . no." She folded her arms over her chest. "Not yet."

Not yet. So it was going to happen, but it hadn't yet. I was honestly surprised, because I would've thought Leo would've nailed her first thing.

"You're an idiot if you think this is going to end well, Quinn. Leo doesn't do girlfriends. Don't you remember all the girls we saw him, ah, date over the last few years? Is that what you want, to become another in a long list of his conquests? You want to be another notch on his bedpost?"

"Oh, for crying out loud, Nate. Just stop it. You're being rude and you're being offensive." She jumped to her feet. "And if this is how you're going to talk to me, I'm leaving. I don't need to listen to this."

Panic seeped into my chest. I couldn't let her leave. I was furious, but if Quinn walked out that door, I didn't know what it would take to get her to come back.

This thing with Leo—whatever it was—would run its course. And when it was over and her heart was broken, Quinn would need me, her best friend, to help her heal. To pick up the pieces.

"Quinn, no. Don't leave. Please. I'm sorry. I was just—surprised. And I'm still on those steroids. They make me a little insane, remember."

She hesitated. "I'm not going to stay if you're going to give me a hard time about Leo. But if you can talk to me like a rational person, I won't leave yet."

I nodded. "I'll be good. I promise."

"All right." She pulled out her phone and checked the time. "I can stay about another ten minutes, and then I need to head out. I'm having dinner with Leo, and he has curfew tonight, since they're playing tomorrow."

"Yeah, I heard about that, about the team being the playoffs. Pretty amazing, huh?"

Quinn's smile lit up her whole face. "It really is. If you could see how Leo's playing . . . it's incredible. Coach said he thinks Leo is going to be able to write his own ticket when it comes to college."

"Good for him." I wasn't going to say anything mean and risk Quinn running away, but damned if I had to pretend to be his best friend. "How's everything going at the newspaper? You write anything interesting lately?"

"Oh, this and that. I did a column about student safety, and I'm working on a piece that talks about bullying on campus." She held up one hand. "No mention of you or of what happened with you. Nothing about the football team, even. Just some facts and some recommendations from the experts on how to defuse bullying in schools."

"You told me you weren't going to write about that."

"No, I told you I wouldn't write about you. I'm not. I haven't mentioned Brent or anyone else." She paused. "But speaking of Brent, you might be interested to know that he pulled me aside in the hall one day while you were in the hospital. He asked me if your fall had anything to do with this illness. And he told me that he was very sorry about what had gone down, and that he'd like a chance to talk to you in person and apologize."

"That's big of him."

"He's trying to be nice, Nate. Trying to be a better person, maybe. You could at least give him a chance."

"Yeah, well, we'll see." I twisted my fingers. "So now you're buddies with all the football players, too? What's next, Quinn? Gonna try out for cheerleading?"

"No, but I don't think it's fair to label all of them just because we've met some who are . . . less than decent. Some of the cheerleaders are really nice."

"Huh." I kicked at a seam in the carpet where it was beginning to pull up. "Did my mom tell you I had to quit crew?"

"Yeah." Quinn rested her hand on my arm. "I'm so sorry, Nate. I know you're going to miss it."

"Yep." I stared at the floor, my mind whirling. "Listen, Quinn, I'm getting tired. I think I'll grab a nap. But if Leo wants to come over later . . . then yeah, I guess I'll see him. I can't promise I'll be friendly, but I'll listen."

"That's all we ask." Quinn smiled, relief evident. "Okay. I'll text Leo, and then you boys can talk."

As it turned out, Leo came over that evening, after he'd dropped

Quinn at her own house. I hadn't seen him in weeks, and I couldn't remember the last time he'd actually been at my house. He looked bigger than ever when he appeared in the living room where I was sitting, and that irritated me. Leo had a way of making me painfully aware that although I was technically older than him, I looked younger. I always felt immature and behind the curve when he was around.

"Nate." He hesitated in the doorway, as though he was afraid I wouldn't let him come all the way in. "You look good."

"Thanks." I motioned to the sofa. "You can sit down if you want."

He sank into the couch, right in the center, spreading out in that way he had. He just sort of sprawled, then sat forward with his elbows resting on his knees.

"I'm glad you're better. You scared the shit out of all of us."

I shrugged. "It's all part of the disease." I was echoing what I'd been hearing the doctors say for the last month. "Ups and downs. We control what we can. Deal with what we can't."

Leo nodded. "So I wanted to tell you . . . I'm sorry for what happened the day you were hurt. I never got a chance to say that. I mean, before it happened. I said shit I didn't mean. I was—uh, well, to be honest, I was hung over, and I didn't mean any of it."

"Yeah." If he expected me to apologize, too, he was going to be waiting a long time. And I wasn't going to say I'd spoken in anger—I'd meant every single word.

Something flickered in Leo's eyes. "I also wanted you to know, I talked to Brent and Karl and Tim. They . . . I know it doesn't change anything, but they were sorry, too. They're stupid, and they acted like idiots, but I think they know better now. I'm keeping my eye on them. The whole team is. We don't like that shit."

"Big of you." I spit out the words.

Leo frowned. "Nate, I'm trying here. I know I've been a crappy friend, but I'm trying to make it better. Be different."

"Yeah? So what do you want from me? You want me to hug it out and say it's all okay, everything's forgiven? Bullshit. You're only here because Quinn pushed the issue. She made you come."

Now I'd done it. I'd named the elephant in the room, and all bets were off.

Leo's jaw clenched. "That's not true. I wanted to come see you. It has nothing to do with Quinn."

"That's crap. And while we're on the subject, you dating her? That's crap, too. What the hell are you thinking?"

Leo stood up, hands on his hips. "This is probably something we don't want to talk about, Nate. We're not going to agree on this one. Quinn and I are together. Period. It's not going to change."

"That's what you say now, but let's be honest about this. We both know you can't stick with one girl. You're going to play with her for as long as it takes, and then once you've fucked her, that'll be it. You'll lose interest. And guess who'll be around to pick up the pieces? Me. I'll be the one who sticks when you've decided you're bored. When you've moved on to the next girl. Keep that in mind."

"I know how I've been in the past, but those girls weren't Mia. She's different. *We're* different, together. I'm not just in this to get into her pants, Nate, no matter what you think. I . . ." He exhaled, raking his hand through his hair. "I love her, Nate. I always have. And now it's even more."

"You had a funny way of showing it the last few years. You know, when you were screwing your way through the cheerleaders and—well, just about any girl who wasn't Quinn. Do you know how much that hurt her?"

"I was scared. I was afraid I'd let her down, and I couldn't deal with it."

"Ah, poor Leo. Having to dull the pain of not being good enough for the one girl he could love . . . by fucking all the other girls. You really are a tortured hero, aren't you?"

Leo spoke through gritted teeth. "I'm not doing this, Nate. I'm not going to argue with you. I know you're only talking like this because you're hurt, and you're afraid you're going to lose Quinn. But I don't want to take her away from you. Why can't we be like we used to? When we were kids, we all got along. We could be friends again."

I'd thought this through this afternoon, after Quinn had left. I wasn't going to lose her over this, even if it meant putting up with Leo and putting a happy face on a situation I hated.

But I wasn't going to let that happen without making myself very clear.

"We can be friends, Leo. Sure. But never forget that I know the truth. I know what's going to happen. You're going to hurt Quinn—that's a given. But worse, you're going to ruin her. You're going to take this girl who's funny and smart and unique—and you're going to try to change her. You're going to drag her into stuff she doesn't want to see, and you'll break her. You'll destroy her, and I just hope I'm still around to help put her back together."

I expected him to flip out at me. I expected him to rail at me, defend himself and swear none of that would happen.

But he didn't. I saw something in his eyes, an anguish and fear, that shocked me by its depth. And when he spoke, his voice was almost defeated.

"You're not telling me anything I'm not terrified about. Why do you think I pulled away from you guys? Why do you think I stayed away from Quinn, when I've wanted her? I know the potential's there. But God, Nate. I'm trying. I'm doing my damnedest to not do that. I don't want Quinn to change. I want to protect her, and see her keep growing and being who she is. Quinn's got the truest heart I've ever known. And that heart loves us both. Why can't we accept that?"

I shrugged. "I'm not fighting it."

"But if you're not on my side, Nate, I don't really stand a chance of making this work with Quinn."

"I'm on Quinn's side. If you can make her happy . . . then I won't get in the way of that." I managed to get to my feet. I was nearly a foot shorter than Leo, but I drilled him with a glare. "But the minute I see you doing anything other than making her happy, I won't hesitate to get in the way. To stand up for her. You might look at me as weak, Leo, but don't underestimate me."

His face tightened. "Believe me, I won't. But I'm not going to give you any cause to get between us."

I didn't drop my eyes. "We'll see."

★ Twenty-Seven ★

Quinn

AFTER THE EUPHORIA OF THE ROUND ONE GAME, THE rest of the conference playoffs felt anticlimactic. Eatonboro rolled through games two and three, and we were riding high when we reached the championship match up, pitting us against Franklin Township once again.

I saw Leo between practices and team meetings, brief snatches of togetherness sandwiched by football. On days when it worked out, he'd pick me up for school, and we'd sit in the car, in the parking lot, talking a little and making out a lot. We ate lunch together, still with the football team; most of the guys seemed to have accepted me, although I noticed that Matt Lampert didn't talk much when I was around. I knew he and Leo were close friends, so I tried to draw him out, but he kept stubbornly silent.

"Don't worry about him, babe." Leo nuzzled my neck, touching his tongue to the pulse that thrummed at the base of my throat. "Matt's just . . . he doesn't have a lot of people in his life he can count on. He's a little possessive of me, and there's never been a girl in my life like you."

I shifted so that I was a little closer to Leo. I lay on top of him, our legs tangled together. We were in the backseat of his car, parked at the playground. It was too cold to be outside anymore, but the dark lot here gave us the perfect spot to fool around in the car. We tried to take advantage of those opportunities whenever they came around—which wasn't often enough right now.

"I don't want to come between you and your friends." I cupped his jaw with my hand. "Most of them are sweet to me. I feel like I have a whole bunch of big brothers, and that's great. But I wish Matt would thaw a little."

"Hey, babe?" Leo slid his hands under my shirt to cover my boobs. "I'm so glad that you want to be friends with Matt, and we'll figure it out. But right now? My hands are on your tits. And I want to put my mouth on you. We only have about another twenty minutes before I have to get you home, and I'd like to get you off first."

I swatted him, feeling my face go warm. "You have a dirty mouth, Leo Taylor."

"Yeah, I do. And I want to put that dirty mouth all over your body." He lifted my shirt up, and his fingers curled over the cups of my bra, tugging them down so that he could get to the nipples. I hummed in appreciation when his lips touched one side, while one finger and thumb pinched the other.

I'd never thought I was very interested in getting physical with guys. Hearing stories about girls in school who'd hooked up in dark hallways, at parties or in cars had sounded kind of icky to me. But now I understood. And it turned out that when it came to Leo, I was all about the touching and the kissing. I might've been pretty ignorant when it came to making out, but I was a fast learner. Probably because my teacher was the sexiest guy I'd ever known.

We hadn't had sex yet, but I was pretty sure that was just lack of opportunity. Leo knew how to make me feel good, and he never hesitated to make it happen. And even better, he taught me how to make him feel good. I was endlessly curious about how his body worked; I knew it from a hypothetical, abstract point of view, but getting down and dirty in reality? Yeah, I'd learned that nothing beat hands-on experience.

I braced myself up with one hand so that I could sneak the other between our bodies, curving my fingers over the promising bulge in Leo's jeans. I was rewarded when he hissed, canting his hips up toward me.

"Hey, I said I was going to make *you* come."

"Mmmhmmm. But that doesn't feel very fair. And why can't we both get what we want?" I maneuvered until I got his jeans unbuttoned and slid my hand into his boxers. Desperate want surged in me when I touched him, already hard and ready for me.

"Wait a second." He reached down too, hiking up my skirt. I wasn't ashamed to admit that I tried to wear either dresses or skirts when I knew Leo and I might have time together alone; it gave him easier access to me, and I was all for that.

His clever fingers covered me over my underwear, stroking in just the right spot before he pushed aside the material, touching my wet folds.

"God, babe. Mia, you're so wet for me." His mouth was still on my breast, and the vibration of his voice heightened the sensation. I closed my fingers around his cock, circling the head with my thumb and moving my fist up and down with increasing speed. Leo matched me movement for movement, until I was panting and begging.

"There, baby? Right there? Is that where you want me?" His thumb pressed against my clit, and I cried out.

"Yes—there. God, Leo. Oh, God . . ."

"I'm close, Mia. I'm going to come. Are you—"

He thrust a finger inside me, and that was all it took. I pressed down, riding his hand, mindless in my pleasure as I chanted his name over and over. At the same time, my hand fisted his erection until he grunted, shooting wet warmth over both of us.

We were still breathing heavily, my body limp over his, when the alarm on Leo's phone went off. He groaned, cursing.

"Fucking curfew." He ran his hands down my back, squeezing my butt and kissing the top of my head. "I want more time with you. No, correction: I need more time with you. And not in the backseat of a car."

"Tomorrow's the last game, either way." I kissed him, tangling my tongue with his. "Then things should ease up a little, right?"

"Yeah." He framed my face. "We'll have a break on practices and games, until spring. I know it's been crazy, babe. Thanks for putting up with this."

I smiled against his lips. "I'm sure you'll find some way to repay me for my patience."

Nate had returned to school about a week before the championship game, and he'd agreed to sit with me at the stadium. I knew Sheri was worried about him being out in the cold, but the day had actually dawned a little more temperate, and although the air was still chilly, the sun was warm. I promised Sheri that I'd keep my eye on Nate and get him home if he began feeling bad.

It felt as though the entire school was crowding the stands, but Gia had saved seats for us. The girls greeted Nate as though they were all long-lost friends, although they didn't know each other well.

"Dude, about time you're here." Gia folded Nate into a hug. At first he stood stiff, but no one was immune to Gia, I'd found, and in a few seconds, he patted her back, smiling faintly.

I introduced him to Gia's friends, and then there wasn't time for anything else. We stood for the anthem and stayed on our feet for kickoff.

This time, there wasn't any drama on the field. Matt and Leo played the game as though they'd been born for this day, moving in perfect concert. The blockers were on fire, so that Franklin Township didn't get in even one sack. Our running game actually worked for once. And the passes? They were more completions than in any previous Eatonboro game.

Defense rose to the occasion, and amazingly, when the final seconds ticked down, the Eatonboro Eagles had shut out Franklin Township fourteen to zip to take the conference championship.

I turned to hug Gia and Nate. Gia was as excited as the rest of us, and I knew I'd tease her about that later. But Nate's face was strained.

"Are you okay?" I yelled over the screaming fans.

He nodded. "Sure. Just a little tired, I guess."

I glanced down at the field, where I knew Leo would be looking for me. "Can you just stay put until I go down to see Leo real fast? Then I'll come back and drive you home."

Nate began to answer, but Gia interrupted.

"Quinn, you're going to be down there a while with your guy. I can drive Nate home. I don't mind at all." She gave me a pointed look. "You have plans, don't you? An errand to run after you see Leo?"

I hesitated. "Yeah, I do, but . . ."

Gia gave me a little push. "Seriously. You're okay with that, right, Nate? I promise I don't bite." She winked.

"Uh, yeah. Sure." He stood up and smiled, but I could tell it was forced. "I'm fine, Quinn. Tell Leo I said congratulations."

"If you're positive . . ." I gave Nate a quick hug, glancing at Gia over his shoulder, telegraphing her my thanks. "I'll call you later. See you later, Nate!"

This time, it wasn't so difficult to push through the crowds. By now, everyone knew that I was Leo's girlfriend, and more than one of our classmates patted me on the back as I passed. The cheerleaders still weren't exactly my best friends, but most of them—aside from Trisha and her cohorts—were at least pleasant, nodding to me.

To my surprise, Sarah met me as soon as I stepped onto the field, greeting me with a hug.

"Wasn't that an incredible game? You must be so proud of Leo."

I smiled, although I felt a little uncomfortable chatting with the girl my boyfriend had dated right before me. "I am. Always."

She nodded. "I've wanted to tell you for a while, Quinn— I'm happy you and Leo finally got together. I think it was one of those things . . . I won't lie and say I wasn't disappointed when Leo broke up with me, but I get it. And if it had to be someone, I'm glad it's you. You're a nice person."

"Thanks." I fiddled with the strap of my purse. "I think you are, too. And I'm sorry for how things worked out. We didn't exactly plan it this way."

"I know." She laughed and shook her head. "Hey, easy come, easy go. It's all good." She glanced over her shoulder.

"You better get over there. Leo's going to wonder where you are."

"Yeah. I'll see you later, Sarah."

It was easy to find Leo. He was at the center of the crowd, and I grinned when I heard what they were all chanting.

"Go big or go home! Go big or go home!"

Brent, standing on the edge of the team, caught sight of me. "Quinn! Get in there, honey. The Lion is looking for you."

Before I knew it, I was being passed from one massive set of hands to another, gently pushed until I was in the middle, where the one set of hands I wanted caught me.

"Mia!" Leo pulled me to him, wrapping his arms around my waist and lifting me off my feet. "Babe, we did it!"

I laughed, burying my face in his sweaty neck. "Congratulations, baby! I'm so proud of you."

He lowered me until my face was even with his and took my mouth, kissing me with more aggression and desire than he ever had before. The bottom dropped out of my stomach, want and need filling me so that I couldn't think of anything but Leo's touch, his lips and his hands on me.

"Excuse me. Can a lowly mom get in on this hugging business?" Lisa tapped me on the shoulder, and I nudged Leo.

"Mom." He let me down, dropping me gently on my feet, and took his mother in his arms. He was so careful, so mindful of the picc line in her arm, and when I saw tears streaming down his cheeks, I started crying, too.

Lisa had already finished one cycle of chemo, and the plan was that she would begin the next one after Thanksgiving. The doctors hoped to put her into remission, after which they intended to begin her bone marrow transplant. We all knew there was a long road ahead, but Lisa never wallowed or let any of us do it either. She was cheerfully upbeat.

She whispered something in Leo's ear, patted his cheek and then turned back to hug me. "Wasn't he something, Quinn? I'm telling you. This boy of mine."

Leo slung an arm around each of us. "It was all for my two best girls."

"Sure it was, you big sweet-talker." Lisa poked her son in the ribs. "Now let your old mom go. I need a nap after all this excitement." She gave both of us a stern look. "Go out and have fun, you two. Celebrate. But please be careful. Be smart."

I blushed, pretty sure I knew what she was talking about. My own mother had taken to giving me the responsible sex talk at least once a week, even while she also cautioned me against making any impulsive choices.

"You and Leo are young and in love. I get that. Believe me. But Lisa and I are young, too. Too young to be grandmothers. And you two both have big, bright futures ahead of you. Don't screw them up."

I didn't intend to mess up anything. I'd grown up hearing all the warnings about safe sex, I'd gotten the lectures in health class, and I knew about condoms, birth control pills and abstinence. Just like the male body and how to give it pleasure, up until now, all of those things had been abstract. Hypothetical.

But tonight, that was changing.

★ Twenty-Eight ★

Leo

A TEAM PARTY AFTER WE WON THE CHAMPIONSHIP game was a given. Matt's grandparents had graciously opened their home to us, and the place was filled.

Now whether or not the elder Lamperts *knew* that they were hosting us was another matter. I knew that they'd been at the game; they'd congratulated both Matt and me on the field. But then they'd taken off for a huge benefit in New York. Matt swore that the party was their idea, but sometimes it was hard to tell where the truth ended and fiction began with Matt.

Still . . . I wasn't complaining. I was here, surrounded by all of my friends, beer in my hand, and even better? My girl, my Mia Quinn, was on my lap, her sweet little ass nestled over my dick in a way that was making me even hornier than I already was.

She'd been a little mysterious since we'd gotten to the party. Not in a bad way, but she'd refused the beer I'd offered her. That wasn't completely weird, because Quinn never drank that much, but she'd also asked me to stick to just beer tonight.

"I don't want you to pass out tonight." She'd kissed my

neck. "You know I have plans for my own celebration."

That sounded promising—definitely promising enough to keep me from drinking too much. Not that I was planning on getting wasted, anyway, but now I had even more incentive.

Since the game had ended around four, the party had been in progress for several hours when I noticed that Quinn was checking her phone more than usual.

"Mia, have you got another date tonight? You look like you're expecting a call."

She grinned. "I'm checking the time, you doofus. I promised Matt I'd let you stay here and party until nine o'clock, and then you belong to me."

I raised one eyebrow. "Uh huh. Now that sounds promising. What time is it, anyway?"

"Eight fifty. I owe Matt ten more minutes."

I shifted, bringing her core more fully over my dick. "Babe, Matt's upstairs doing God only knows what with Trish, Kaley and Lori. He's not going to be done doing them in the next ten minutes, and he's not going to know if I leave early."

Quinn sighed. "Yeah, but I'll know. And I promised."

I cocked my head. "When did you and Lampert come to this meeting of the minds? Weren't you just telling me last night that you thought he didn't like you?"

She nodded. "Yes. But we talked this morning when I took him out to breakfast."

I sat back, staring up into her face. "You did what now? With who?"

She smiled serenely. "I took Matt out to breakfast this morning. I told him that we didn't have to be best friends. He didn't have to treat me like the little sister he never wanted. But I'm in your life to stay, and so is he, so we had to figure out how to work together." She lifted one shoulder. "We compromised."

"Mia." I ran my finger down her jaw, tracing a line on her neck. "You never stop amazing me, you know?"

She grinned and widened her eyes. "You ain't seen nothing yet. Hey, guess what? It's nine. We're good to leave." She jumped off my lap and tugged on my hand. "You, Leo the Lion, are officially mine now."

"Where the hell are you taking me, Mia?" I peered out the window of her car at the passing lights.

She slid me a look. "Me to know, you to find out. Remember?"

"Okay, but do you know where you're going?"

Quinn rolled her eyes. "Of course I do. The sexy guy on the telephone GPS is telling me. Besides, I've been here before. I just need a reminder about where to turn—"

As if on cue, a deep voice with an Australian accent floated over the speakers. "Your destination is on the left in two-tenths of a mile."

Ahead of us, on the left, I saw only one tasteful, well-lit sign. I turned back to gape at Quinn. "Is that where we're going? That hotel?"

She bit the corner of her lip. "Yeah. It is. Is that . . . okay?"

I swallowed hard, suddenly just a little bit terrified. And incredibly turned on. "Uh, yeah. That's okay. But what . . .?"

Quinn turned the car into the parking lot, coasting along toward the back of the building. She found a spot, put the car into park and took a deep breath. "All right. Here's the deal. I made these reservations a week ago. I told my parents that I was going home with Gia after the party tonight. I drove down here this afternoon, after the game, while you were getting changed, and I checked in. I have the key in my purse." She patted the bag. "So we can go in there, and we can just hang out. Make out. Be together. Watch TV, chill." She raised her eyes to mine. "Or we can go up there, and I can take off my clothes, and yours, too, and we . . . you . . . we can have sex."

My heart was pounding so loud that I could barely hear her last words. She looked so nervous, so unsure of what I was going to say.

I unbuckled my seat belt, turned in my seat, and reaching across to Quinn, I slid my hands around to rake through her thick hair. Moving slowly, I touched my lips to her in the lightest brush of a kiss.

"Mia Quinn. You . . . you destroy me. Just when I think I know you . . . when I think you can't surprise me . . . you do this." I kissed her again, this time a little deeper. "There is nothing I want to do more than to make love to you tonight. If that's what you want, too."

Her eyes gazed into mine, shining with love and need. "I want."

The hotel room was simple and tasteful. A big king-sized bed dominated the space, and I glanced at Quinn, wondering if it made her nervous. But typical Quinn, having made up her mind, she was all in. She bounced on the end of the bed, grinning at me.

"They asked if I wanted a king or two queens, but I figured after all those nights in the back seat of your car, having more room would be a good thing."

I laughed. "You're not wrong. But how did you manage to even get this room? I thought you had to be at least eighteen to book at a hotel."

Quinn looked a little guilty. "Gia helped. She has a friend who works here, and she had it arranged for me to pick up a key. I paid extra as a gurantee that we wouldn't wreck the room."

"Quinn Russell. I'm impressed. That's some serious plotting you did there."

She flushed, but I could tell that she was pleased. "Okay. Now I'm going into the bathroom to get freshened up. You, get naked and wait here for me."

I saluted. "Yes, ma'am."

"Oh." She paused outside the bathroom door. "There are condoms in the nightstand drawer. I hope I bought the right ones."

I shook my head, amazed all over again. "You thought of everything, didn't you?"

She shrugged. "I tried."

Once the bathroom door had clicked behind her, I stripped off my Henley, kicked off my shoes and tugged my legs out of my jeans. And then, obeying orders, I slid under the cool cotton of the covers.

I'd only been lying there a few minutes when the lights in the room dimmed. She didn't turn them off altogether, but the lighting was definitely of the mood variety. I blinked a minute, letting my eyes adjust.

And then she was there. Quinn stepped around the corner, into my line of vision, and for a matter of seconds, I actually forgot to breathe.

Her hair was down, spilling around her face. Her arms and legs, still sporting a little leftover tan from the summer, were bare. And on her body, she wore my jersey.

It was huge on her, of course. Quinn wasn't tiny, by any means, but I was still half a foot taller than her and outweighed her by almost a hundred pounds, probably. The jersey hung low on her shoulders, dipping enticingly between her breasts.

She walked toward me, her eyes glued to mine, and then crawled onto the bed, kneeling at the foot.

"Baby." I breathed the word and held out one hand. "Look at you. How did you . . . where did you get this?"

She smiled and lifted one shoulder. The slippery material slid down one of her arms, baring the top of one gorgeous tit.

"I had help. And I wanted to be wearing it tonight. Because like you said . . ." She moved closer to me, until her knees rested next to my legs. "Go big or go home, right?"

I couldn't wait another moment. Sitting up, I reached for her, hauling her body over mine. "God, babe. You're beautiful. Absolutely . . . gorgeous." My hands touched the hot, bare skin of her flat stomach and traveled upwards to fill my palms with her boobs, loose beneath the jersey.

"You do realize I'll never put on this jersey without picturing you in it, right?"

She laughed. "I like that." She kissed my neck, moving her mouth up to my face and then my lips. "I like what you're doing to me even more."

"Good, because that's what I want to do. I want to make you feel incredible." I raised the jersey out of the way, baring her boobs to me, and took one pink nipple into my mouth. She arched toward me and held my head in place.

I'd never been with a virgin before. I'd heard stories, and since Quinn and I had been together, I'd done some reading on the internet. Research. What I knew for sure was that this might not be a fun night for her, not the way it would be for me. But I also knew I could make her feel damn good before the less comfortable part began.

"Lay down." I flipped her over onto her back and stripped the shirt off her. "This jersey? Best idea ever. But now it's in my way."

Once it was gone, I sat back on my heels, taking her in. We'd been messing around for a while now, making out in cars or in quiet hallways or on the sofa in her parents' house after they'd gone to bed. I'd made her come, and she'd done the same for me.

But I'd never seen her completely naked, laid out before me, and seeing her now? I had to take a couple of deep calming breaths so that I didn't embarrass myself by coming right there.

Her boobs were average size, but on Quinn, they were perfect. Her stomach was flat and her hips flared down into long and slender legs. In the middle of them lay paradise.

I was shaking a little as I bent over her, my mouth sucking gently on one nipple and then the other. She sighed and closed her eyes.

"If you're uncomfortable or need a minute, just tell me." I kissed a line down from her breasts. "But try to relax, and I promise I'll take care of you."

"Okay." She sounded so full of trust, and that responsibility weighed on me. I had to make this as perfect for her as I could.

I laid my head down on her stomach, my mouth just above the juncture of her legs. With one hand, I nudged her thighs apart, and she acquiesced, allowing me entrance.

I slipped two fingers into her folds, just tracing her seam, moving up and down until her breath started to come faster. I shifted to lie between her legs, parted her and covered her with my mouth. This was new territory for us; I'd made her come with my hand before, but oral sex was a challenge in some tight spaces. Although now that my tongue was licking her sex, I was pretty sure I'd figure out a way to make this happen much more often, no matter where we were.

As soon as my mouth touched her, she arched her back, gasping. "Leo—God—oh my God. That's . . ."

"Not good?" I found her clit and teased it with my tongue.

"No. I mean, yes, so good, but intense. I'm—it feels so good. I'm going to come too fast."

"That's what I want, babe. Go ahead. Relax and let it happen. Come against my mouth. It'll make everything easier for you tonight."

A small line formed between her closed eyes, and I reached up a hand to touch her arm.

"Hey. Don't hide. Open your eyes. Look at me."

She slowly raised her head, her eyes going wide at the sight of me with my mouth on her pussy. "Sometimes it's even more intense if you're watching. You know, involve all the senses. Touch . . ." I sucked her clit between my lips. "Sight . . ." I smiled at her. "Hearing me tell you how much you're turning me on . . ." I licked her again. "And taste. Baby, you taste so fucking delicious."

Without pausing, I slipped two fingers inside her and pressed my tongue against her. She cried out, pressing her core against my face as she rocked, her orgasm long and intense. It was the most singularly sexy thing I'd ever seen in my life.

I rode it out with her, touching her gently, kissing the insides of her thighs, until she tugged on my hair. "Too much. Too sensitive." Her hands reached lower for me as I crawled up her body. "And I want to touch you. I want you . . . I want you inside me."

"It's where I want to be, too." I kissed her, tangling our tongues, pressing our hips together so that my dick rubbed between her legs. "Do you know how beautiful you are when you come, Mia? If I had the talent to paint, that's what I'd do. I'd paint your portrait, right at the second when you're so caught up in the pleasure that you can hardly breathe, and your cheeks are flushed, and your eyes just shine."

"You make me feel beautiful." Her slim fingers closed around me, and I sucked in a breath. "When you're touching me, it's like there's nothing I couldn't do." She teased her thumb around the head of my cock, slippery with pre-come. "I want to make you feel just as good."

"You always do." I kissed her cheek, her chin, her nose. "Mia, you know, if you're not ready for this, we can wait. I don't want to push you. I don't want you to feel like you have to do it."

She smiled, her lips curving lazily. "Leo, this was my decision. I do feel like I have to do it, but not like you're thinking. I have to do it because I love you so much, I can't imagine not doing it." She tilted her head up to kiss me. "I want you to be my first and my only. I don't ever want anyone else touching me like you do. You're my best friend, and I want you to be my lover, too."

I smoothed her hair back, staring down into her bright eyes. "I love you, Mia Quinn. I will always love you, with everything I have."

Quinn touched my cheek. "Then make love to me. Make me yours."

I rolled over and reached into the drawer of the nightstand, fumbling with the box of condoms. Once I had one out, I ripped open the small package, as Quinn pushed up on one elbow.

"I want to see how you do it. Like, for real, not just with a banana."

I laughed. "Health class, huh? Okay." I held the rubber

over my dick and rolled it down over the shaft.

Quinn touched me, trailing the tips of her fingers over the condom. "It feels different. I like feeling you, bare."

I lay down next to her. "I've never had sex without a condom, babe. If you want to go on birth control eventually, we can talk about it, but for now, this is keeping you safe." I palmed one of her tits. "And don't worry. It won't feel that different once I'm inside."

"I guess you'll have to prove it to me." She rubbed her hand up and down my cock, cupping my balls.

"That sounded like a challenge." I pushed her onto her back. "I want your tits, babe. I want to suck on those pretty nipples until you're begging me to be inside of you."

Her laughter ended on a gasp as I closed my mouth over one tip, biting gently. With my hand, I teased the other boob, tantalizing and tracing circles with the tip of my finger until she was writhing beneath me again.

I raised myself over her, holding my weight on one arm and using my free hand to position my dick between her legs. Remembering something I'd read, I rubbed the head over her pussy, getting her used to the feel of me before I settled at her entrance.

"Tell me if you need me to stop." I was panting, but I needed her to understand that she was in control. "Okay?"

She nodded. "I'm all right. Really, Leo. I am."

I pushed in a little, gritting my teeth. Every molecule of my body wanted to pump inside her tight channel until I came, and going slow was an excruciating pleasure. Canting my hips, I slid in a little more, meeting some resistance.

"Okay?" I ground out the word.

"Yeah." She was breathless again, a little tense. "I'm fine. You can—you can move more."

I knew this was going to be the worst part. Taking a deep breath, I thrust into her, feeling the last barrier give way.

Quinn gasped and pressed her lips together, but within a minute or two, I could feel her begin to relax. "All right. Better now. Are you good?"

Good? I was in fucking paradise. She was so damned tight that I knew if I moved at all, I'd blow my load. "Yeah, babe, I'm more than good. You sure I'm not hurting you?"

"I feel very full." She shifted a little, which changed the angle of where I lay inside her.

I groaned. "Mia, I can't hold back any more. Sorry—" As though of its own accord, my hips began thrusting into her, pulling out and plunging back in, an exquisite form of torture.

Quinn murmured my name and wrapped those long legs around my waist. That was my undoing. I came hard, pushing into her body with everything I had, calling out her name as the orgasm gripped me.

"Babe. Mia." I couldn't catch my breath. "My God." I rolled her over with me, keeping her body as close to mine as I could. "Are you all right?"

"Mmmhmmmm." Her hands played over my back. "More than all right." I felt her sigh wash over my chest. "Was it—was I okay? I mean, I'm sure being with someone who doesn't have any idea what she's doing isn't great."

"Mia, I told you. This is you and me. There aren't comparisons, and I don't keep score." I tipped her chin up and kissed her nose. "But if I did, you'd blow away all my experience. Because you're mine. My Mia, only mine. All right?"

She nodded. "All right."

"Now . . ." I withdrew slowly from her body. "I'll be right back."

I stalked into the bathroom, took care of the condom and

ran the water until it was warm enough to soak a washcloth. When I came back to bed, I carefully helped her to clean up.

"Do we really have all night?" I slid back under the covers and pulled her against my chest.

"I do, as long as my parents don't go to Gia's house to check up on me. I don't know about you, though."

"Sometimes I flop at Matt's after parties. My parents won't worry."

"Then we're both golden." She smiled up at me sleepily. "What will we do with all that time alone?"

I growled against her neck. "Don't worry, Mia. You're not the only one with plans."

★ Twenty-Nine ★

Quinn

I'D SPENT MY FIRST TWO YEARS OF HIGH SCHOOL DREAMING about being Leo's girlfriend. I'd built some amazing fantasies about what that would look like.

None of those dreams even began to touch how wonderful it was.

Over that winter, after football ended, we fell into a routine. Leo picked me up for school each day. We ate lunch together, and if I didn't always feel entirely comfortable with his football friends, that was a very small price to pay.

Nate wouldn't eat with us, though. The first time I'd asked him, he'd looked at me like I'd sprouted a second head.

"You want me to eat with Mike Anders and Brent Collins? No, thanks."

I'd felt that familiar tearing sensation, the one that hit me whenever Nate wanted me to do one thing and Leo asked me to do another. I hated having to choose between them.

But before I could say anything else, Nate had added, "Don't worry about me. I'm going to start working in the computer lab over lunch anyway."

I convinced myself that he would've done that, anyway. As much as I worried over Nate, it wasn't unusual for him to do things without considering how they might affect me. He probably hadn't even thought twice about letting me eat lunch alone.

After school, I hung out in the newspaper office while Leo lifted in the weight room. Even in the off-season, he had to keep in shape, and he'd told me the coach was working with him especially, because there had already been several colleges expressing interest in him.

My parents had laid down some rules about when we could and couldn't go out during the school week. Leo was always welcome to join us for dinner, and he often did, although we ate with his family, too. Lisa didn't cook very much anymore, so once or twice a week, I'd usually make dinner for the four of us.

And on weekends, we'd go out, either to the movies, to dinner or to a party. If there was any part of dating Leo that made me uneasy, it was the parties he liked. Sitting in a crowded house surrounded by drunk kids, while a cloud of smoke from the people puffing weed hung in the air, wasn't my idea of fun. The closest thing we had to arguments were over those parties.

But even so, I was happy. Nate seemed to be recovering well from his last illness, and he and Leo had reached some sort of détente. Leo couldn't have been a more loving or attentive boyfriend. We didn't have many opportunities to be truly alone, so we did push a few boundaries; there were nights when Leo would sneak up to my bedroom after my parents had gone to bed. We'd turn on my TV or music to cover any noises, and then we'd make love on my bed. Afterwards, Leo held me in his arms, whispering into my ear.

"I hate that I can't stay all night with you. I like waking up with you next to me." He blew softly on the earlobe he'd just been nibbling.

"I know. Me, too." I turned to face him. "But we just have another year of high school left. Then we go to college."

Leo's mouth tightened. "What if we end up across the country from each other? I don't know where I'm going to go to school. It depends on who gives me the best deal."

"So once you know, I'll apply there, too." I snuggled up against him, my eyes drifting shut. "Unless you don't want me to."

"Of course I do. But things don't always work out. What if you don't get in where I do? Or what if your parents want you to go somewhere else?"

I sighed. Both sets of our parents had begun making noises about us being together so much. Mine reminded me often that I was too young to base important decisions like college on my high school boyfriend and where he was going. My dad more than once brought up the appeal of making smart choices for my future.

I did a lot of nodding and smiling. But I wasn't worried, because I knew Leo and I would work it all out. For now, life was too good to ruin it by obsessing over the future. The present was way too much fun.

"Look at us, going out on a date like real people." Leo smiled at me from across the table. "At a restaurant, even. Not just the pizza place."

"I've wanted to try this place forever." I glanced around the dimly-lit room. "It's supposed to be the best Italian restaurant around here."

"Yeah, the food's good. Coach had them cater one of our Twelfth Man dinners."

I held up one finger. "No football talk on a date in the off-season. Remember? This is when I get you all to myself."

Leo raised his eyebrows. "And you've been making good use of that time, too." He reached for my hand. "Which reminds me. My dad and mom stayed in the city tonight, since Mom's got an early doctor's appointment. Guess who has the house to himself?"

I pretended to think. "Hmmm. Who could it be? Maybe Dylan or Beau?" Of all the football team, those two were the friendliest to me. They both had steady girlfriends, but Leo liked to tease me that he was jealous of the attention they paid me.

"Ha, ha, ha. I guess I won't invite you to come have dessert . . . up in my bedroom." He leaned forward and lowered his voice. "I was going to get us canolis to go. And then paint you with the cream inside them."

I swallowed hard. "Can we skip the entrée?"

It wasn't surprising to me that our sexual chemistry was off the charts. Leo was a very physical guy, and he'd always been very tactile. And for someone who hadn't really been interested in sex before now, I'd found that I loved being touched and held, as long as it was Leo making love to me.

But I was relieved, too, that we had so much else in common. We could talk football for hours—pro and college, as well as high school—and Leo had taken an interest in the newspaper, too. He'd sat in on a few layout and folding parties, making the younger girls on staff swoon when he smiled at them. He and Jake had found that they liked each other; sometimes they even played video games together, while I sat nearby reading.

Nate still wasn't thrilled that we were dating, but slowly, he thawed enough that the three of us could hang out again. Leo and I were both careful not to make him feel like a third-wheel, and sometimes, it felt like the old days: the Trio back together again.

Best of all, Leo and I spent most of our waking, non-school hours together, and so far, neither of us was tired of the other yet. If everything could have stayed exactly as it was then, life would've been perfect forever.

In mid-March, though, things began to change.

Lisa had gone through two grueling cycles of chemo, and she was finally ready for her bone marrow transplant. Her sister, who lived in Philadelphia, was the donor, and everyone in the family had high hopes for her recovery once this procedure was over. But I knew Leo was anxious about it. His mom was going to be in the hospital for a long time, possibly several months, and there were risks. He didn't like to talk about it, and when I tried to bring it up, he changed the subject.

At the same time, spring football began. After months of relative freedom, Leo was once again committed to daily practices and weekly games. Of course, the spring session wasn't as intense or as important as fall was, but it was still time-consuming. It also meant that Leo was spending more and more time with his football buddies, and there were more parties, too.

Parties were on my mind one Friday afternoon in late March, as I sat in the newspaper office with Gia and Jake, brainstorming about our next several issues. Leo had told me that morning that Matt had invited everyone over Saturday night to celebrate the spring season. I was less than enthusiastic, and as Jake brought up story ideas that afternoon, I was still preoccupied, brooding.

"Q, you know, you've been sitting on that series about bullying." Jake quirked an eyebrow at me. "This might be the perfect time to print it. I think enough time has passed that no one's going to link anything to Nate's incident. And it's something that needs to be brought up."

"Yeah." I sighed, playing with a tiny scrap of paper on the desk. "I know, but . . . you know, the football players aren't going to like that. I know most of those guys now, and they don't see themselves as bullies."

"But it's not just them." Gia spun her chair around, turning in slow circles. "Bullies come in every shape and size. I say we do your series and then we start talking about cyber-bullying. That's becoming a real problem, too."

"Hey." We all three turned at the sound of Leo's voice. "Quinn, you ready?"

I frowned. Leo liked both Gia and Jake, and he usually came in and sat down with us for a few minutes when he stopped to pick me up after school. Today, though, he hovered in the doorway, his jaw tight.

"Uh . . . sure, I think." I glanced at Jake. "Are we done?"

"Yeah." Jake glanced at Leo. "How's it going, dude? Team working hard?"

"Yep." Leo's voice was clipped. "Quinn, let's go."

"Okay, okay. Sheesh. Give me a break." I smiled at him, so he'd realize I was teasing, but he didn't even meet my eyes. An odd sort of dread began to swell in my chest as I followed him out the door and down the hall. He walked so fast that I had trouble keeping up.

"Leo. Hey, slow down. Some of us aren't record-breaking runners."

He looked down at me as if he'd forgotten I was there. "Sorry. I need to get out of here."

"What's wrong?" I grabbed his arm. "Leo. What the hell's going on?"

He didn't stop moving, but he did slow his steps a little.

"Simon just texted. Something's going on with my mom. She's rejecting the bone marrow, or something like that. I don't know, I don't understand it. But I need to get to the hospital."

"Oh, God. Of course. Why don't you just go, and I'll call my mom to get me?"

He shook his head. "No, it's fine. You're on the way, anyway. I just—" He raked his hand through his hair. "I need to get there."

We drove in silence to my house, and I jumped out of the car as soon as it had come to a halt. "Leo, do you want me to go with you?" Only immediate family was allowed to see Lisa at this point in her treatment, so I hadn't been over to the hospital in weeks.

"No." His hands gripped the wheel. "Thanks. But they wouldn't let you see her anyway." He glanced at me and then back at the road. "I'll text you later, okay?"

"Sure." I leaned back into the car to kiss his cheek and then jumped back, slamming the door as he raced away.

I kept my phone close to me the rest of the night, but I didn't hear from Leo. My mom hadn't gotten any news from Leo's father, either, and we were all worried. Finally, the next morning, I messaged him.

Are you okay? What's going on with your mom?

Nearly two hours went by before he responded.

Not sure. Call you later.

Later turned out to be about seven that night, and when I heard Leo's voice through the phone, I wasn't sure whether to be hurt or furious.

"Heyyyyyy, Quinn. Come on over, babe. I'm at Matt's. It's a party."

I had been sitting at the dinner table with my parents when the call came in, and I marched out of the kitchen and up to my bedroom.

"Leo, what the hell? Are you drunk?"

"Maybe a leeetle bit." He laughed, and in the background, I heard the sound of music and other people talking.

"I thought you were with your mom. I've been worried about her. And you."

"Ah, no, babe. She's gonna be okay. But I miss you. Come on over here, 'kay? Guess what, Matt's grandparents are away and there're like, five empty bedrooms. We can use one of them."

Since we'd been dating, I'd seen Leo tipsy at parties. But this went far beyond that. He was drunk and slurring, and it scared me. This Leo wasn't the same guy I'd been dating for five months. He sounded like the person who'd ignored me for two years and forgotten about our friendship.

"I'm coming over there, Leo, but I'm not going into any bedrooms with you. You stay there, you hear me? Don't go anywhere."

"Waiting for you, babe. Always waiting for you."

Rolling my eyes and clenching my jaw, I picked up my handbag and jogged down the stairs. My mom met me in the foyer.

"What's going on?"

I heaved a deep sigh. "I don't know, really. Leo's at Matt's house, and he sounds . . ." I hesitated. I hadn't been completely honest about everything related to my relationship with Leo—I hadn't shared that we were having regular sex, for instance— but I tried not to lie to them about anything I could avoid. "He sounds drunk. I'm thinking something's going on with Lisa."

"And you're going where?" My mother cocked her head.

"If it's okay, I'm going over to Matt's to take him home. I'll try to find out what's going on."

My dad was standing in the doorway to the kitchen. "Are you sure that's a good idea?"

I shrugged. "I don't know what else to do, Dad. He needs me. I'd do the same for Nate."

"Nate would never make you do that." My father's voice was even, but his words still annoyed me.

"Leo's mother is in a life-threatening situation. I'm not saying he's reacting the right way, but I'm not going to judge him right now. I'm going to help him."

"Be careful. And if you need us for anything, call." My mother kissed my cheek.

I nodded and hurried out to the car, my anxiety levels rising the longer I drove.

The Lamperts' huge house was surrounded by cars, and I smothered a groan as I found a spot to park as close to the front door as possible. I could hear the thump of music even before I climbed up on the porch.

The door flew open, and Tim Stewart came stumbling out, his arm around Trish Dawson.

"Look! It's Quinn the queer. Come to find your little doggy, queer queen? I think I just saw him go upstairs with Sarah. You better find him fast." She lowered her voice, like she was telling me a secret. "He used to be Leo the Lion, but since he's been with you, he's just Leo the lapdog." She giggled at her own joke.

I didn't believe anything that came out of Trish's mouth, but she damned sure knew where to hit. Ignoring both of them, I went inside and began searching for Leo.

The living room was only dimly lit, and on the recliner in the corner, two people were hooking up. Not just making out; the girl, who I recognized as a senior, was riding the football player beneath her. Her shirt was off, and he was pawing at her breasts.

I turned away as fast as I could and made my way to the kitchen, where to my tremendous relief, Leo was sitting in a chair at the table. His face lit up when he saw me.

"Babe! You got here." He pushed the chair back a little and patted his leg. "C'mere and sit on my lap. I missed you." Only his words were slurring, and it came out, "I mitthed you."

I took his hand but didn't sit down. "Okay, Leo. Party's over, dude. Time to go home."

"Nooooo . . ." he wailed. "I don't wanna go."

I closed my eyes and counted to ten. "Leo, baby. Come on. I'm going to take you home and put you to bed." I skimmed my fingers through his hair. "Don't you want to go to bed?"

He raised bloodshot eyes to me. "With you?"

"Of course." I was willing to say anything to get him moving. "My car's right out front. Let's go."

Moving close to two hundred pounds of solid man—solid *drunk* man—through the house, across the porch and down the steps wasn't easy. A couple of times, Leo stumbled and nearly fell on top of me. But in the end, I managed to settle him in the car and fasten his seat belt. Before I could get into the driver's seat, I heard a shout.

"What do you think you're doing?" Matt Lampert stood on the porch, staring down at me belligerently. "Where are you taking him?"

I narrowed my eyes, scowling up at him, hands on my hips. "I'm taking him home, Matt. And I'm not very happy with either of you right now. Leo's mom is sick, and you got him drunk? What the hell?"

Matt smirked. "Dude wanted to forget. It was his decision. I just gave him a hand."

"Do you know how worried I was about him, all day?"

"Chill, Quinn. You're not his mother. You're not his fucking wife. You're just a girl, and you need to give Lion some room, or he's gonna dump your ass."

"You." I pointed at him. "Stay out of this. What happens between Leo and me isn't any of your business." I knew that even though Matt and I mutually tolerated each other, he didn't like how much time Leo spent with me. I wouldn't put it past him to try to sabotage our relationship.

"The Lion's gotta roar, sweetheart. You get in the way of that, and we'll see who wins." Matt chucked an empty beer can off the porch, narrowly missing my feet.

"Nice, Matt. Real nice." I turned my back on him and got into the car. Leo had already fallen asleep, and he stayed that way on the drive to his house.

When I pulled into the Taylors' driveway, I almost cried with relief. Danny's car was there. I ran up to the front door and leaned inside.

"Danny! Are you here?"

A slightly older version of Leo, with lighter hair, came padding into the foyer, in jeans and bare feet, blinking at me. "Quinn? What's up?"

"Your brother is in my car, passed out drunk. I need you to help me get him inside."

If Danny was at all surprised, he didn't show it. He also didn't waste any time before he followed me out the door, where he was able to hoist Leo to his feet with ease. I trailed behind them upstairs to Leo's bedroom.

Danny dumped his brother unceremoniously on the bed. "He'll be okay now." He yawned and rubbed his face. "What the hell happened? He left the hospital last night, and I thought he was heading to see you."

I shrugged. "I don't know. He called me from Matt's just

now. He wanted me to come party with them." I bent over and took off Leo's shoes. "I'm going to get him comfortable, and then I'll head home. Are you going to be around to keep your eye on him? Oh, and how's your mom?"

"I'm staying until tomorrow night. Mom's out of the woods now. She had some kind of host-graft deal, like a rejection. Doesn't usually happen so early in the process, but they caught it, and it looks like she'll be okay. But it was frightening as fuck." Danny gazed down at the sleeping form of his little brother. "Leo doesn't do so well with this kind of stuff, in case you haven't noticed. Try not to take it personally, Quinn, okay? We're all doing the best we can under some shitty circumstances."

I nodded. "I understand. I'll just get him undressed and then take off."

Danny held up both hands. "Hey, you know, you want to stay with him, no problem from me. Dad's sleeping up at the hospital tonight, and Simon's there, too. No judgment on this end."

I flushed. Talking about my sex life with a guy who'd known me since I was in diapers wasn't the most comfortable deal. "Thanks, but my parents would kind of freak out if I didn't come home. Just promise me you'll check on him every now and then."

"Will do." Danny turned and closed the door behind him.

I unbuttoned Leo's jeans and managed to get them off his legs. At least he'd be more comfortable sleeping, I thought. I covered him with a sheet and kissed his cheek.

"Mia?" His voice startled me as I stood with my hand on the doorknob. "Mia? Don't leave me, 'kay?"

My heart broke a little bit. "Shhhh. You're all right, baby. Go to sleep. We'll talk in the morning."

"Please don't go."

I sighed. "I can't stay all night, but I won't go yet. I'll sit here with you for a little bit."

He held out his arms. "Lay down with me, babe. I just want to hold you. I need you."

There wasn't a chance on earth I could resist those words. Kicking off my shoes, I pulled back the sheet and slid underneath with him. Immediately, Leo wrapped me in his arms, his lips skimming the top of my head.

"I love you, Mia. So much." His eyes didn't open, but his words were clear.

"I love you, too, Leo. Always."

★ Thirty ★

Leo

"**D**UDE, YOU ARE SO FUCKED."

I groaned, holding the pillow to my head. "Danny, get the hell out of my room. Leave me alone."

"Oh, you'll thank me later. Get up. Get a shower. Quinn's on her way over, and she's not going to be happy if you're still sleeping off your drunk."

I blinked in the sunlight streaming through my windows, as memories of the last few days filtered into my head. *Shit*. My mom. Driving to Matt's Friday night after I'd left the hospital and getting wasted. We'd both slept the next day away, and then he'd said, "Man, you have to stay for the party. We don't hang enough anymore, all the team together. We need you. Team building, buddy."

Somehow that had made sense, and I'd been drunk again by the time most of our friends arrived. I hadn't called Quinn, because I knew she wouldn't be happy; she hadn't wanted to come to Matt's tonight anyway. I was okay with putting off that conversation for a while.

But then I'd seen all the guys hooking up. Taking girls up to the bedrooms, fucking on the damn sofa, and suddenly I wanted my girl with me. Matt had tried to talk me into taking someone else into one of the bedrooms, but I wasn't interested in anyone but my Mia.

After that, everything was hazy. I had a vague memory of Quinn showing up. Had she hauled me home, or had I imagined that? I groaned again and rolled over.

"In case you're wondering, Mom's doing much better. She was asking when you're planning on getting your ass back over there to see her."

I nodded. "Good. I'm glad she's okay. Did you say Quinn was coming?"

"Yeah, she texted me fifteen minutes ago and told me she was on her way." I heard a door slam downstairs. "Well, that's probably her."

"Shit, Danny. Go talk to her while I get a shower."

He pointed at me. "You owe me big, bro."

When I went downstairs ten minutes later, freshly showered and mostly steady, Quinn was sitting at the kitchen table with Danny, drinking a cup of coffee. I came around and kissed her cheek.

"That's not the cheek you need to be kissing," Danny muttered, smirking, and Quinn glared at him.

"Shut up, Danny." I snarled the words.

"Shutting up. Actually, getting the hell out of dodge. I'm going to see Mom and then heading back to school from there. Later, dude. Quinn, go easy on him."

As soon as Danny was out of earshot, Quinn turned on me. "What the hell was that, last night? Actually, come to think of it, this whole weekend?"

I had come downstairs planning on begging her forgiveness, but something contrary seized hold of me. "Oh, you mean when I was hanging with my friends? That was called having fun, babe. In case you didn't know what that looked like."

"Really? To me it looked like an orgy. People were having sex in the living room, Leo. Out in the open. Everyone was drunk. Why would you want to be there, part of that? Why didn't you call me?"

I shrugged. "I did call you, didn't I? I asked you to come over."

She snorted. "Yeah, after you were drunk and horny."

"Could've been worse. I could've gotten horny and decided to scratch that itch with someone at the party. Believe me, there were plenty who were willing."

She stared at me, deep hurt in her eyes, and panic filled me. "Babe, I'm sorry. I'm so sorry. I didn't mean that. I wasn't even—I only wanted you. I only *want* you." I slid out of my chair and knelt in front of her. "Mia, God. I'm so sorry." I buried my face in her lap.

It seemed like an eternity before her hand came down to stroke my head. "Leo, you can't do this. I can't handle it. If you're hurting or worried about your mom, you need to come to me. Not to Matt. You don't run off and get drunk. We deal with it together, okay?"

"I just—I was scared." My voice was muffled against her. "I wanted you, but I didn't want to be scared in front of you."

"You can't think that way. I love you, Leo. Not just for the good times. Not just for the championship games. I want to be part of all of you. All your life."

I nodded. "All right. Yeah." I let out a deep breath. "I'm sorry."

"Yo! I'm heading out. See you guys later. Don't do anything I wouldn't do." Danny's voice floated back to us just before the front door slammed behind him.

For the space of a few minutes, we stayed still. Quinn combed her fingers through my hair, and I relaxed, my eyes closing as breathed in her scent.

"Hey, Mia?" I turned my head to look up at her.

"Hmmm?" She smiled down at me, and by the gleam in her eye, I knew she'd already guessed what I was going to say.

"You know what we haven't done yet? Makeup sex. I mean, I've never had it, and neither have you, so we're both makeup sex virgins. And right now, we have an empty house. And my bed."

Quinn lifted one eyebrow. "I'm still a little mad at you."

I snaked a hand up to cup her tit. "I can work with that. I'm willing to do anything to make you feel better. Think, like, multiple orgasms."

Her cheeks flushed and she rolled her eyes, but I knew I had her. "Well, I guess it would be mean-spirited of me not to give you a fighting chance to make it up to me, hmmmm?"

"Definitely." I stood up, congratulated myself silently that I didn't sway at all, and scooped Quinn into my arms. "Let me remind you how much I love you. Over and over again."

Quinn forgave me for fucking up that weekend, and on the surface things between us went back to normal. But deep down, something had shifted.

It felt like we were arguing more. Part of it was the time of year, I knew; football was taking up more of my time, and when I hung around so much with the team, I ended up wanting to go to parties. It wasn't that I needed to drink or that I wanted to spend time in crowded houses, watching other people get wasted and fuck each other. But not going to the parties meant I was somehow less part of the team. I missed stuff that happened.

Quinn didn't get that. She thought I was just making excuses to go, and that pissed me off, too. I didn't have to make excuses. If I wanted to go, I would. And if I thought there was something I should do to make our team better, hell, I'd do that, too. We were going into my senior year, and what happened in my future—where I went to college, which would then determine whether or not I went pro—could be determined by what happened on the football field this coming fall. Coach had drilled that into me. I was a leader, and the team needed me as much as I needed the team.

And if Quinn didn't understand that . . . well, I didn't want to think about the second part of that sentence.

My mom was doing pretty well, but the stress of her illness was weighing on me, too. I hated the uncertainty of everything. I worried that when the day came for me to go pro, my mother might not be with us anymore. I wanted to spend extra time with her, but I was afraid to get too close. Terrified of losing her.

I was fucking sick of being scared of everything. The only time I stopped thinking about being afraid was when I was drunk. Or when I was on the football field.

We'd just finished practice on a gorgeous afternoon in early May, and I was heading into the locker room with the rest of the team. We were messing around as usual, giving each other shit, and I was laughing with Matt when Brent punched me on the shoulder.

"Dude, you got a minute?"

I frowned. Brent sounded serious, which was unusual enough to make me nervous. Nodding, I stepped over to the railing that divided the field from the stands. "Sure, Collins. What's up?"

Brent shuffled his feet in the loose dirt. "Ah, maybe nothing. But um, I saw that stuff Quinn's writing in the newspaper. About bullying, you know?"

I nodded. "Yeah. What about it?"

"I was just checking—she's not going to write about me, is she? About Tim and Karl and me, and what happened with the gi—I mean, with Nate last year?"

I sighed and pinched the bridge of my nose. "No, of course not, Brent. Why would you even be worried?"

He lifted one massive shoulder. "Don't know, but I just got to thinking. About college next year and shit. If something like that was on my record, I could kiss my shot at a decent school goodbye. I can't take that chance."

"Okay, well, problem solved. I told you she's not going to include that."

"But maybe you should talk to her. Just make sure. I mean, Quinn's cool and all, but I'm not sure how much she loves the football team, you know? Will you talk to her for me?"

Great. This was going to be a big fucking deal, I knew. But to Brent I only said, "Yeah, I'll mention it. But don't worry, okay? Not going to be an issue."

"Aw, thanks, Taylor. I appreciate it." Brent whacked me on the back and went whistling into the locker room, clearly feeling much better. Me, on the other hand? Not so much.

After I'd showered and changed, I texted Quinn to meet

me at my car. I didn't feel like making nice at the newspaper office right now, and I was tired, too. I leaned against my car, my eyes closed.

"Boo." Laughing, Quinn circled her arms around my waist. "Are you asleep on your feet out here, you poor thing?"

"Pretty much." I opened her door and then got behind the wheel on my side and backed out of the lot. "Hey, Mia. Need to ask you something."

"Hmmm?" She turned to look at me, smiling.

"That bullying series you're doing in the paper. You're not going to talk about what happened with the guys last fall, are you?"

I could practically feel her good mood evaporating. "Why do you ask?"

I exhaled loudly. "Brent asked me today. He's afraid of what would happen to him if it came out. I mean, if the administration found out. It could fuck up his future."

"Oh, really?" I'd come to dread that tone of Quinn's voice. "Maybe Brent should've thought about that when he decided to physically assault another student. Maybe Brent should've stopped being such an asshole years ago. And maybe Brent should own up to his actions and stop being such a coward."

"Whoa there." I shot her a look. "I get that Brent made a mistake, but he's sorry and he hasn't bothered Nate since then. I happen to know he feels bad. So should one moment of poor judgment screw up the rest of his life?"

We pulled up in front of Quinn's house. She unlatched her safety belt and turned toward me. "Leo, the truth is, I don't have any intention of talking about Brent and what happened. But not because of what he wants—because Nate doesn't want me to do it. Nate's the victim here, so he's the one whose opinion I respect. But what really pisses me off is that you'd ask me not to do this. That you'd take Brent's side over mine. Did you ever once think about telling Brent that your girlfriend has the right to print what she wants? Did you think about me before you promised your football buddy that you'd take care of the matter?"

"Quinn, chill. It's not that big a deal. I told Brent I'd ask you, I did, problem solved. Don't make this into something it isn't."

She opened her door and climbed out of the car. "Fine. I won't. And you can go back to Brent and tell him you protected his precious future." She slammed the car door and dashed up the driveway, never even turning back to look at me.

I pulled away from her house, anger pulsing in my neck. But instead of going home, I took the turn that led to Matt's house. We spent the rest of the evening with our good friend Jack, who helped us forget all our problems.

★ Thirty-One ★

Quinn

ONCE UPON A TIME, I'D THOUGHT THAT IF LEO AND I ever got together, if he ever admitted to loving me like I loved him, life would be perfect. We would never fight, and everything would be sunshine and roses. We'd live happily ever after.

The last two months had opened my eyes to the absolute absurdity of that way of thinking. Leo loved me, I didn't doubt that. I loved him, more now than I had ever thought possible. Most of the time, he was sweet to me, funny and protective. Before spring football season began, I'd had no doubt that I was Leo's top priority. But lately, I felt like I'd been slipping down that list, until I fell somewhere below football and his friends.

And today? Well, today I was furious. I'd already been a little worried about the bullying series, for the very reason Leo had listed. But it was actually going well so far, and our local newspaper had even picked up one of my articles, highlighting a problem in the schools that most people preferred to ignore. I was excited to tell Leo about it, but before I could say anything, he'd launched into me about Brent and how his future could be ruined if I wrote the wrong thing.

I hadn't handled it well, I knew. But I'd been hurt when I felt that once again, Leo was choosing his teammate over me.

The house was empty when I went inside, and I remembered that my parents were at a planning meeting for their high school reunion that evening. I'd actually been looking forward to having precious time alone with Leo . . . and he'd ruined that when he brought up Brent. Just another reason for me to be upset.

I was too keyed up to stay home alone. I grabbed my car keys and drove back to the school, thinking that I might work on editing this week's columns if Jake was still in the office.

The parking lot was nearly empty, and I didn't see Jake's car anywhere. With a heavy sigh, I pulled the keys out of my ignition and dropped my forehead onto the steering wheel.

A knock at the window startled me, and when I turned, I saw Sarah Jenkins standing there, waving at me. I rolled down my window.

"Hey, Quinn. You . . . okay?" She frowned. "I just saw you pull in as I was coming out. I think the school's empty now. And locked. I had a late meeting with the prom committee, and I was the last one out."

"Oh. Sure." I nodded. "I was hoping maybe Jake was still in the newspaper office. No big deal." I began to roll up my window.

"Wait a second. Are you sure you're all right? You don't look like you are."

One side of my mouth curled up. "Thanks."

"No, you know what I mean. You just seem upset."

I blew out a breath. "I am. But I don't want to talk about it, if you don't mind."

She shook her head. "I don't." She took a step backward

and then paused. "So you're probably not interested in this, but
. . . I'm meeting some of the other girls at the Starlight. Want to
come with?"

I opened my mouth to say no, but then I thought . . . why
not? I didn't have anything better to do tonight. And if Leo
could have fun with his friends, why couldn't I? Sure, Sarah
and I weren't close, but I liked her. Maybe, if we got to know
each other better, we'd find out we had more than just Leo in
common.

"Yes. As a matter of fact, yes, I do."

As it turned out, the 'other girls' Sarah had mentioned were all
cheerleaders. If they were surprised to see me with her when
we walked into the diner, they didn't show it. And after we'd
spent an hour together, ordering food, chatting and giggling, I
realized that I was really enjoying myself.

"Hey, you guys, want to come back to my house? My dad's
away tonight and my step-mother is going to an all-night yoga
shut-in." Alicia rolled her eyes. "We'll have the place to ourselves."

"Sounds like fun." Sarah glanced at me. "Quinn, you in?"

I hesitated. "Um . . . I'm not sure. I should probably head
home."

"Oh, come on." Chelle leaned forward in the booth, smiling at me. "It'll be fun. Just come for a little while, at least."

"Yeah, just stay for like an hour." Sarah grinned, too. "Everyone needs to blow off steam now and then, right?"

She made a good point. Leo hadn't texted me or tried to
call me, and that stung, too. I wanted to forget about our fight

and everything else that was making me feel so unsettled.

"Okay, but just for an hour. Then I need to get home."

"Yay!" Alicia clapped her hands. "You can follow me, Quinn. Everyone else, see you there."

Alicia lived closer to the edge of town, not far from Matt Lampert's house. Thinking about him didn't improve my mood. He and I hadn't exactly made up since our spat when I was trying to get Leo home, and I got the sense more and more that he was actively working against me, when it came to Leo.

I pulled my car into Alicia's driveway and walked inside with her. The house was large and modern, the kind of place where I was afraid to touch anything. But that didn't seem to bother Alicia. She led us into the kitchen, and we all took chairs around the large table.

The first half-hour was fun. I laughed along with the girls telling stories about cheerleader camp, and we all ate popcorn Chelle made on the stove. I was just thinking that I should start to make my exit when the back door opened, and Trish Dawson came in. I noticed she didn't even knock, but no one else seemed bothered about that fact.

"Hey, bitches." She seemed to notice me for the first time, and her mouth dropped open. "Well, well, look who's joined the party, huh? What up, Quinn? Shouldn't you be at, like, a rally or something? You know, whatever it is you geeks like to do?"

"Shut up, Trish." Chelle rolled her eyes. "We invited Quinn. She's fun."

"Hmmm." Trish sat down, a small smile playing around her mouth as she gazed at me.

"What're you doing here, anyway?" Alicia leaned back in her chair, rocking it on two legs. "I thought you had better plans. Or that's what you told me."

Trish's mouth twisted. "Those plans fell through. Probably thanks to Quinn, actually. I was supposed to hang out with
Matt tonight, and I planned to make it a very special night.
If you know what I mean." She glanced around the table, her
eyebrows arched, and I was pretty sure we all knew what she
meant. "But then *her* little lapdog shows up, and Matt kicked
me out. Said bros before hos and shit like that."

Leo was at Matt's? My heart sank. When he'd left me at
home, I knew he was pissed, but I hadn't thought he'd go running to his QB for comfort. *Shit.*

"Oh, Trish, calm down. You can fuck Lampert any other
night of the week. Here." Alicia pushed the popcorn bowl toward Trish. "Have some nourishment."

"If I'm getting cheated out of a night of fun with Matt, I
want more than popcorn." She wriggled her fingers. "Break out
the good stuff, A."

Alicia giggled. "Okay, okay. Hold on." She jumped up and
went over to a large oak cabinet, opened the door and rooted
around for a minute, emerging with a large bottle. "Voila."

Trish unscrewed the lid and lifted the bottle. "Cheers,
bitches." She took a long swig, wiped her mouth with the back
of her hand and passed the bottle to me. "Here you go, Quinny
Quin Quin. Bottoms up."

I shook my head. "No, thanks."

Trish tilted her head. "Oh, but I insist." She leaned over,
dropping her voice. "Did I mention that Leo was knocking back
Jack pretty hard, even before I left?" She smirked. "I might've
offered to let him take a shot off my tits."

My stomach dropped. "He wouldn't touch you, Trish. So
you can just shut the hell up."

She shrugged. "Maybe he did, maybe he didn't. But I can
tell you that he was pretty mad at you. Matt was telling him

that he doesn't need a chick like you in his life. And I could be wrong, but it seemed like your boy was sitting up and paying attention."

I swallowed hard. I didn't trust anything Trish said. But this was sounding too close to what I'd feared might happen.

"Men are such scum." Chelle tipped the bottle back over her mouth. "Fuck 'em. Fuck 'em all."

Sarah reached to take a drink next. "Fuck 'em." She glanced at me and then held out the bottle. "Quinn?"

It wasn't peer pressure. It wasn't wanting to fit in. Tonight, it was all about the forgetting, making the hurt go away.

I accepted the bottle and drank deep.

★ Thirty-Two ★

Leo

I WAS STILL A LITTLE HUNG OVER THE NEXT MORNING WHEN my alarm went off. I texted Quinn that I was going in late to school, so she wouldn't be waiting for me to pick her up, but she never responded. I worried about that for about ten seconds before I went back to sleep.

By the time I woke up again, it was after lunch. It seemed pointless to drag my ass into school for two classes, so I stayed home, planning to play the sick mom card that had given me so much wiggle room this year. I'd learned that all I had to tell them in the office was that my mom was still in the hospital, and my absence or tardiness was excused. It was like a get-out-of-jail-free card. Not that I wouldn't trade that for my mother being healthy again, of course, but I figured I needed any break I could catch just now.

I'd just gotten a shower and was actually getting ready to go see my mother when the doorbell rang. *Quinn*, I thought. She'd gotten my text and was worried about me. I grinned a little, thinking that maybe she'd calmed down enough that I could talk her into another round of makeup sex.

But when I opened the door, it was Nate who stood there, leaning on the frame. I stared at him, frowning. He nodded to me.

"Can I come in?"

"Uh, sure. Come on in. Everything okay?" I shut the door behind him and trailed him into the living room.

"Yeah. I just wanted to talk to you."

"Sure. Shoot." I leaned against the side of the sofa, my hands in my back pockets.

Nate fixed me with a determined stare. "You remember back when you first starting going out with Quinn? I told you what was going to happen. I told you that you'd ruin her. You'd break her heart. And now you have."

I shook my head. "Nate, dude, what're you talking about?"

"It's been coming on for a while. I see her getting more and more unhappy. She doesn't want to go to your stupid parties. She hates your friends. But she's trying to change, to be better for you. She's turning herself inside out. But what are you doing? Going out and getting drunk every weekend? Not calling her, so she's worried and upset all the time? And then you tell her not to write an article in the newspaper. The one thing that's hers. You're making her choose between who she is and who you want her to be. And so you know what she did? She got drunk with cheerleaders last night."

"What?" I heard the words, but they didn't make sense. "What're you talking about?"

"Last night, Quinn called Gia around midnight and asked her to come pick her up at some girl's house. She was completely wasted. Gia was afraid Quinn's parents would freak out if she came home drunk, so she texted from Quinn's phone that she was spending the night with Gia."

"Shit."

"Yeah. Quinn missed school today. She told her mom that she thought she had food poisoning." His lips thinned. "Does that sound like the Quinn we both know?"

I shook my head. "No. But she's all right, isn't she?"

"You mean, is she safe and not still puking? Yep. But nothing else about her is right anymore. This is the end, Leo. The last straw. You're wrecking her."

"No. She got drunk, okay? Kids do that all the time. Just because you don't—"

"*Quinn* doesn't. And you know, if she drank a little with you, had a beer, that's one thing, but she's drinking whiskey with girls like Trish Dawson—that's totally different."

"Trish Dawson?" I felt stupid, repeating everything he was saying, but it just didn't compute. "Why Trish? How?"

"Maybe you should ask Quinn about that. But according to Gia, Quinn was upset about something you'd done, and Trish goaded her, and I guess one thing led to another."

I felt like I was smothering. Quinn hated Trish. I knew that. Trish was always a bitch to her. And then abruptly, I had a flash of memory of Trish at Matt's house the night before. I saw her through the haze of booze, lifting her shirt up to display her impressive rack. And she was asking me if I wanted to do my next shot off her tits.

I'd said no. I was sure I had. God, I hoped I had.

I stood up. "You know what, Nate? Get out. Go home. Get the hell out of my house. You don't know what you're talking about. You're jealous because Quinn loves me. You're jealous because it's *me* she wants. I got there first, and it's killing you, isn't it? Well, fuck you, Nate. You don't know shit."

"I know Quinn. I know you're forcing her to change. For once in your life, Leo, think of someone other than yourself. Do this for Quinn." He hesitated. "Quinn didn't tell you about the scholarship from Evans, did she?"

I searched my memory. It sounded a little familiar, but . . . "I don't know. I guess not."

"Ms. Nelson, the newspaper advisor, nominated Quinn for the scholarship. It's huge, and it's prestigious. If she won it, she'd get a full ride to Evans, for their journalism and media program."

I remembered now. Evans was a small, exclusive college in Massachusetts, and when Quinn had mentioned it and the scholarship, I'd remarked that they didn't even have a football team.

Maybe Nate had a point about my selfishness.

"It's not too late, is it? For her to get the scholarship? I'll tell her—"

"She didn't want you to know. She's turning down the nomination, because Evans isn't anywhere near the schools you're looking at." Nate's lip curled. "No decent football schools in the area."

I covered my eyes with one hand. "Fuck."

"You need to think about her future. Not just how it relates to yours." Nate's voice softened. "Quinn used to be this quirky, happy person who didn't care what people thought of her. She was . . . just *her*. And now she's not. It's like I said, Leo. You ruined her."

"That's bullshit, Nate. I love her. I'd never—"

The front door slammed, and we both turned as my dad came in. "Boys." He frowned at both of us, and I thought distractedly that he looked tired. "Everything okay?"

"Yeah. Nate's just leaving." I walked toward the door, and after a minute, Nate followed.

Just before I slammed the door behind him, he turned back for a minute. "Think about it, Leo. If you love her like you say you do, if you want her to be happy . . . think about it. In the long run, what's the kinder thing to do?" He gazed at me, eyes steady, and then stepped awkwardly down the steps of our porch.

"What was all that about?" My dad was in the kitchen when I went in, opening and closing cabinets at random. It was his nightly ritual; I suspected he thought one night he might come home to find a meal magically prepared. We'd eaten so much pizza and Chinese takeout since my mom had been in the hospital that just thinking about that food made me queasy.

I dropped into a chair. "Nate thinks I should break up with Quinn. He says I'm not making her happy."

"Ah." My father nodded.

"That's all you have to say?"

Dad sighed and sat down across from me. "Leo, son, I'm not surprised Nate thinks that. Matter of fact, I'm only surprised it took him this long to say it. And I'm sorry that he thinks you're not making Quinn happy."

"But . . .?"

My father smiled a little. "But. But I've been planning to talk with you for a while about Quinn and what you planned to do. Listen, Leo. I like Quinn. Hell, I love her like the daughter you were supposed to be." He smirked at his own joke. "And I know you kids think you're in love. But you're young. God, you're so damn young. You, particularly, have the kind of future ahead of you that would make maintaining a long-term relationship at this point . . . difficult, if not impossible. You'll end up putting stress on yourself and on Quinn that neither of you needs. And in the end, the result might be a lot messier and more painful that it would be to just end it now."

Panic gripped me. "But I don't want to break up with Quinn, and she doesn't want to break up with me."

Dad cocked his head. "That's what you tell yourself, but I've noticed a change in you lately. And if I notice it, you can be damn sure Quinn does. I think maybe there's a part of you that already knows what you have to do, and that part is making decisions to force the issue."

My throat was tight. "So you think—what do you think I should do?"

My dad got to his feet and patted my shoulder. "I'm not going to tell you that, son. I think you're smart enough to figure it out." He paused before he left the room.

"But I'm here if you need me. Remember that."

I didn't sleep well that night.

Every time I closed my eyes, I saw Quinn's face. I heard her voice. I felt her body under mine.

And then I heard Nate's words, and my father's, too. I wanted to stop hearing them. I wanted to forget what they'd said. They were both wrong, I knew they were. They had to be. Quinn and I were right together. We belonged with each other. We'd both made that clear.

But I thought about what my dad had said. College was going to be hard. College football was going to be a full-time job, if I wanted to get into the pros. How would I juggle that along with making Quinn happy, if I couldn't even manage to do that when we were only in high school?

And Quinn wanted to be a writer, wanted to be a journalist. Was I justified in denying her that chance, just because I needed to go to a college that would help funnel me into the pros? She could still study journalism wherever we went to school, and I was sure that was what she'd tell me if I brought up the scholarship. But we'd both know that she'd be giving up something huge. For me.

Everything went around in my head, until the sun rose. By then, I'd given up. I knew what I had to do. It was going to kill me, but I knew I had to do it.

I walked into the school the next morning, feeling oddly removed. Everything around me seemed far away, and not quite real. People spoke to me, but I had trouble responding. I was only focused on getting through the day.

I hadn't heard from Quinn, and I hadn't texted her again. I made a point of avoiding her during the school day; I came in a little late, I didn't go to the cafeteria at lunch, and I went right to practice after school.

After practice, I didn't stop to chat with anyone. I walked down the hallway, straight to the newspaper office and stuck my head inside.

Quinn was there, of course, sitting with Jake and Gia and two other people I knew only vaguely. They all looked up when they saw me. Quinn's eyes brightened for a moment and then shuttered, as though she'd remembered our last conversation.

"Hey, Quinn. You got a minute?" I couldn't believe how normal my voice sounded.

She frowned and then nodded slowly. "Yeah. Sure." She stood up and walked toward the door, following me as I moved down the hall a little way, far enough from the office that no one would overhear us.

I'd put a lot of thought into where I was going to do this. I'd heard of guys who planned out proposals with such precision, who chose the spot where they'd first kissed or had their first date. I could imagine that the place was important, because years later, they'd remember—that was where our real life together began. Place was important.

It mattered to me that I didn't ruin any place that was special to Quinn. For the sake of privacy, I'd considered the playground, the place where I'd given into her and to myself, where we'd become us, but I couldn't do it. I couldn't sully that memory.

So here we were, in a nondescript hallway of the high school we'd be leaving in about a year. This was where I was going to say the words I didn't mean, where I was going to break her heart. Where I was going to end us.

"What's up?" She was still pissy from the spat we'd had the other day, and that worked in my favor. If she'd come to me with smiles and kisses, I'd have lost my nerve, for sure. But she stood there, arms over her chest, scowling.

I still wanted to kiss her senseless, but it was easier to keep my distance when she looked prickly.

"Quinn, listen." I mirrored her pose, arms folded. "I've been thinking. And the thing is, this isn't working." *I sounded so calm. No one would ever guess how much this was hurting me.*

Her forehead wrinkled. "What isn't working?"

"This." I pointed at her and then at myself. "You and me. We gave it a good shot. It was fun for a while. But the reality is, I've got big plans. I need to focus on football, on getting into the right college, and even then, when I'm there, my whole life is going to be about football. I want to play in the pros. That's my dream. I can't have any distractions."

Realization was beginning to dawn on her. I could see it in her face. "And I'm a distraction?"

I sighed, as though I was dealing with a small child. "Honestly, yes. I know that sounds cruel, but it's the truth. And you don't understand me. You don't understand what I need, what my life is going to be . . . you're not a good fit, Quinn." *There it was. The brutal cut, the one that would make her hate me.*

She took one step forward, stopped, and lifted her hands to her mouth, covering it. Her chest was moving up and down rapidly. "You don't really mean this, Leo. We had a fight. We'll get over it. We need to talk—"

"No, we really don't." I shook my head. "This isn't about a fight. This is about . . . both of us getting on with life. You're not like me, Quinn, and I'm not like you. We were friends in grade school, but then we grew apart. That was natural, and when we tried to force it—it was fine for a while, but it's not a long-term thing."

Her face was wet now with tears streaming from her eyes. "You're serious. You're ending us."

"Yes." I couldn't speak any louder than I did. And when she turned, her face in her hands as her back shook with sobs, I knew I had to get out of there, fast, before I dropped to my knees and begged her to forget what I'd said. Begged her to forgive me. Begged her to love me forever, no matter what.

"I'll see you around, Quinn. I hope . . . well, I hope you can be happy."

"Happy? You hope I'm happy? You just destroyed my life, and threw everything I ever said to you back in my face, and you hope I'm fucking happy? Fuck you, Leo. Fuck you." She spun around again, and I fled, sprinting down the hall and out the nearest doors I could find. I felt like I couldn't breathe. I couldn't think. Every fiber of me screamed out how wrong this was and told me to go back and tell her the truth.

But I couldn't, because I loved her too much.

I got to my car and lifted my phone with trembling hands. "It's me. I'm coming over. For the love of God, have something strong waiting for me. And line them up. It's going to be a long night."

★ Thirty-Three ★

Quinn

THE CRAZY THING WAS, LIFE WENT ON.

I wasn't sure it would, or that I could. I left the school that day, walked home—I'd walked to school that morning, since Leo hadn't texted about picking me up—and I locked myself in my room. I cried until my eyes were too swollen to see out of. When my mother knocked on my door to tell me dinner was ready, I told her I didn't feel well and didn't want to eat. That was understandable, given that I'd claimed food poisoning the day before. When she pushed the issue, worried, I claimed killer cramps, which I knew would buy me as much alone time as I needed.

I slept badly that night, when I did sleep. Since the next day was Saturday, I didn't have to go to school. I had another two days to hide and figure out what my life was going to look like now.

Once the shock wore off and the tears had stopped, I came to a few decisions. I wasn't going to tell my mom and dad what had really happened. I couldn't. I loved Lisa and Mark, and I didn't want my parents to feel awkward around their friends, particularly when Lisa needed all her friends so much right now. I'd handle it casually. We'd decided to take a break. We needed space. That was all. If they guessed the truth, well, there wasn't anything I could do about that. I didn't think Leo would say much to his own parents.

I wasn't sure I could sell it, but I was damn sure going to try. I couldn't stand the idea of everyone feeling sorry for me, for poor Quinn who got dumped by Leo. I didn't want to see my parents to think less of him, either. I wasn't sure why that mattered to me, but it did.

I finally went downstairs at lunchtime on Saturday. My parents were already at the table, eating subs, and they looked up at me in surprise.

"You okay, honey?" My mom pushed out a chair with her foot. "Feeling better?"

"Mostly." I sat down. "Look, I'm going to tell you both something, and I don't want either of you to freak out or make it a big deal, okay? I'm fine with it, and you should be, too."

They exchanged alarmed glances, and I imagined what my words must've sounded like, especially when I'd been sick the day before. They were going to think the worst. I hurried to go on.

"Leo and I decided to take a break. We're not . . . together anymore. I'm fine, so is he, everyone can still be friends. But we're not dating. Not anymore."

My mother let out a long breath. "Oh, honey. I'm sorry."

"Mom." I held up a hand. "I don't want to talk about it, and I don't want sympathy. I don't need to eat chocolate ice cream and listen to Alanis Morissette. I'm fine. Now let's just move on, all right?"

There was a beat of silence, and then she nodded. "All right. We understand."

"Good." I stood up. "I'm going over to see Nate. I'll be back for dinner."

If Nate had been able to break into a happy dance without falling over, I was sure he would have when I told him that Leo and I had broken up.

He tried to keep the look of sympathy and sadness on his face, but he'd never been very good at hiding his emotions. Finally, I threw up my hands.

"Nate, I know you're glad Leo and I broke up. That's fine. You have your reasons. But I can't deal with those right now, okay? I need some time. I need you to pretend for a little while that you understand why I'm sad. Can you do that?"

"Of course." He touched my hand. "What can I do?"

I thought about it for a minute. "You can watch *Buffy* with me. Season two, after Angel turns. And don't make fun of it. And if I cry, you just hand me tissues and don't make comments."

That's how we spent the rest of Saturday. I let Buffy be my substitute, and I cried for her pain and loss, because it was easier to do that than to cry about my own any more.

When we finished the final episode of season two, I wiped my eyes and stretched. "Now there was a girl who knew how to kick ass and get over heartache, huh?"

"By sending her boyfriend to hell?"

"Whatever does the trick." I stood up. "Okay, I need to get home. I told my parents I'd be there for dinner."

Nate stood with me. "Want me to walk you home?"

I shook my head. "I'm fine. I'll see you on Monday. Should

I pick you up for school?"

"Uh, sure. But Quinn . . ." He took a deep breath. "I know my timing sucks. But I feel like I need to tell you this, or I might not get another chance. I might not get up the nerve again."

I groaned. "Nate, please don't."

"I have to. Quinn, I love you. I've wanted to be more than friends for . . . well, since junior high. I've been waiting for you to notice. For it to be the right time. But I think we could be good together. I'd never treat you like—"

"Stop." I growled the word through gritted teeth. "Just stop, Nate. I can't do this. Not now. You're my friend, and I need you to be that. Nothing else. Please. Can we please just do that?"

I thought he might push me, but after a moment, he nodded. "All right, for now. But you'll keep it in mind? You'll remember, in case things change? Once you're over Le—everything, you might feel differently."

"I won't." I tried to sound definite without being hurtful. "I'm sorry, Nate."

"You don't know that. Right now, you're upset. But when you're not, maybe . . ."

"Sure, Nate. Whatever you say." I kissed his cheek. "See you Monday."

I got through dinner with my parents and managed to keep my shit together until I could convincingly say I was tired and wanted to get ready for bed. Pretending that everything was fine was exhausting, so that wasn't much of a stretch.

I'd just changed into sweats when there was a knock at my bedroom door. I called out an invitation, and my dad stuck his head into the room.

"Hey, sweetie. Got a minute?"

I shrugged. "I guess. I'm really tired, though, Dad."

"Yeah, I know. I just wanted to say . . ." He leaned against the door frame. "I'm proud of you, honey. I get the feeling there's more to what happened with Leo, and you could've made a big deal of it. But you're thinking of other people. You don't want to get between us and the Taylors, am I right?"

I sat down on the end of my bed. "Does it matter, Daddy? It is what it is. Leo—" Those stupid tears threatened again. I'd thought I was all cried out after Buffy. "He's made his decision, and I'm moving on. Like we all should."

"Hmm." He nodded. "Teenaged boys are notorious for being idiotic and short-sighted. I sure was. But I'm not convinced that's what Leo's doing here. Not that it's going to change anything, but maybe someday, it might help for you to remember Leo a little more kindly, if you realize you might not understand all his reasons right now."

I snorted. "I don't want to remember Leo at all, Dad. I'll see him when I have to, until we graduate, and then I never want to hear his name again." I hunched my back over my knees. "Boys are jerks. Do you know, I went over to Nate's today for a little bit of distraction, and he actually tried to tell me that he's in love with me? Why would anyone *do* that? God."

My father began to laugh. "Oh, sweetheart. I'm sorry. You're right, boys are idiots and jerks. You should stay away from them until you're at least forty, and even then proceed with caution."

"Thanks, Daddy." I stood up and crossed the room to give him a hug. "For a boy, you're kind of cool."

"That's because your mom's been whipping me into shape for years. This doesn't come naturally, you know. You ever meet a good man, you'll always find out there's a better woman in his life somewhere. Eventually, you'll meet a guy who has potential, and you'll take the chance to be that woman."

I shuddered. "Not for a long, long time. I don't want to feel this pain again. Not ever."

★ Thirty-Four ★

Nate

MY LAST YEAR OF HIGH SCHOOL WAS MY BEST ONE.
First of all, my health was better than ever.
Good old Dr. Randall came through with a new
protocol, and while I was on that, my energy and strength were
boosted. My immunity was increased, too, so I didn't pick up
every bug that came around the school. That was a relief, to me
and to my parents.

And then there was the fact that we were now at the top
of the high school food chain. There was no one older to pick
on me, and the guys in my own class had matured enough that
they didn't mess with me anymore. Brent Collins had even become almost friendly, out of guilt, I assumed.

But best of all, Quinn wasn't with Leo.

I'd worried for a while that they might get back together. I
was aware, even if she wasn't, that Leo was suffering from their
distance as much as Quinn was. When she didn't know it, he'd
stare at her, his eyes hungry. He gave her lots of space, but I
also heard that the Lion wasn't roaring so much anymore. He
partied, yes, and he drank, but he wasn't sleeping around. The

cheerleaders complained that Quinn had broken their football star. Whether Quinn heard about that or not, I didn't know, because she never mentioned him. And I didn't ask.

All of that extra time on his hands paid off, though, because Eatonboro walked away with the conference championship for the second year in a row. Leo was MVP, interviewed by the Philadelphia papers, and courted by a bunch of colleges.

Quinn never talked about football. She didn't go to any of the games. On the night we won the championship, she persuaded our friend Gia Capri to steal her a bottle of wine from the Capris' liquor cabinet, and the three of us sat together outside at the old playground while Quinn drank the whole thing and then cried for hours.

She'd changed, too. She didn't laugh as much as she had before Leo. She smiled sometimes, but she seemed shut off. Like there was a part of her that I'd known before that didn't exist anymore. I tried to do everything she liked, tried to get her excited about something, anything, but it never made a difference. She was just going through the motions of life, and sometimes, it was painful to watch.

I'd asked her to go to prom with me in senior year, but she'd adamantly refused to even consider it. As a matter of fact, she almost seemed upset that I'd suggested it. I'd enlisted both Gia and Quinn's mom to try to change her mind, but it didn't work.

She never mentioned my declaration of love, and neither did I. But I hadn't given up, because I knew someday, Quinn and I would be together. Someday, she'd be over Leo and she'd see that life could be good again. And then I'd have my chance.

I knew one thing for sure. Once I had Quinn, once she was mine, I was never going to let her go. I was never going to make the mistakes Leo had. I'd love her with everything I had, for as many days as I had.

★ Thirty-Five ★

Leo

"LEO ROBERT TAYLOR."

At Mrs. Colby's not-so-gentle nudging, I stumbled across the grass, earning snickers from the row of guys sitting to my right. I shot them the finger as I crossed in front of them, earning a gasp from Mrs. Colby. I glanced back over my shoulder at her and grinned, shrugging. What was she going to do to me now? Sure, she was our history teacher and class advisor, but I was graduating. Like, now. As in, out of here. Forever. And good fucking riddance.

Dr. Rider, the superintendent, stood at the podium, watching me approach. He offered me his hand to shake and a black cardboard folder to take. It was supposed to look like it was the diploma, but we all knew the folders were empty; the diplomas would come via mail next week. We might have been high school graduates, sure, but we weren't quite trustworthy yet.

"Mr. Taylor." He didn't let go of my hand right away, as he'd done with everyone ahead of me. "Congratulations. We expect great things from you in the future. Good luck at Carolina State."

"Thank you." I felt the heavy weight of expectation fall on me, chasing away all the laughter from a few minutes before. The way Dr. Rider was looking at me, if I didn't lead the Carolina Cougars to a championship all four years *and* win the Heisman, I'd be letting down the whole town of Eatonboro.

He released me, nodding, as the principal announced the next name. I made my way around to the back of the senior class and filed into the half-empty row, dropping into my seat. The guy next to me, Greg Talb, offered me his fist to bump. I managed a smile and pounded it.

"Taylor. Yo, Lion!"

I raised my eyes to a few feet in front of me, where Matt was turned around in his seat.

"Dude, Shang's parents gave him the beach house for the whole fucking weekend. We're there, right?"

My chest tightened, even as I nodded and gave Matt a thumbs up. Partying the weekend away should've sounded like the best idea ever, but everything felt empty. Hollow. I thought of how often I'd imagined high school graduation—finally being free, finally being done. But every time I'd pictured it, I'd seen myself with one elbow slung around Quinn's neck, her arm wrapped around my waist, and a summer of fun mapped out in front of us. I'd thought Nate would be giving me his typical crooked smile, the one that told me he saw through all my bullshit but still considered me his best friend anyway.

Instead, Quinn sat two rows in front of me, but she never looked back. She'd pulled her hair up into some kind of twisty deal today, probably to keep cool as much as to look good, knowing Mia. I'd been staring at the back of her neck since we'd sat down, all during the droning speeches by the president of the school board and the valedictorian, and the whole time they'd been calling other students' names. When it was her name announced—*Amelia Quinn Russell*—I'd cheered, whistled and cat-called, mostly because she wasn't close enough to know it was me doing it—but I was sure she'd known anyway.

After all, I deserved to celebrate my girl, even if she wasn't mine anymore. Even if she never would be again.

The row of graduates behind us stood up and filed toward the front. Nate was toward the end, stepping carefully as he always did. He glanced back at me and caught my eye when the line paused for a minute. I smiled and nodded, and after a second's hesitation, he returned the nod. Then the line began to move, and the kid behind him shoved his shoulder. Nate rolled his eyes and started walking again. I noticed he paused by Quinn's chair to squeeze her hand. I could see her in profile, smiling up at him, and with a pang that felt like a stab wound, I closed my eyes and wished this fucking ceremony would end already.

Finally, it did. The principal dismissed us for the last time as students of Eatonboro High School, and then everyone was doing the whole throw-the-hat-in-the-air deal and talking at once. All the chicks were hugging each other, some of them crying, and I snorted. I was willing to bet most of them would never leave town. They'd stay here, get jobs, get married and have babies, popping out the kids who'd be standing here as graduates in about twenty years.

I couldn't wait to leave this fucking town. The happiest day of my life would be when I was looking at it in my rear-view mirror, when I'd know I didn't have to live through every day dreading the possibility of seeing Quinn. Of being close to her without being able to be near her. When I could put everything about us behind me.

"Lion!" Trish barreled into me. Two other cheerleaders stumbled next to her. They were all giggling and weaving, bumping into each other. They reeked of alcohol.

I held Trish away from me. "Hey, Trish. You okay?"

"Never better." She slurred her words and laughed again. "Drunk graduation is so much more fun than . . ." She squinted at me. "Stand still, Leo. You're making me dizzy."

I set her away from me, not as roughly as I wanted to. "Good luck, Trish. See you later." *God, I hoped not.*

"But I want a kiss from the Lion! This is my last chance to bag the Lion." The other two girls giggled again as they hung on each other.

My head hurt. "Not going to happen, Trish. Not now, not ever. You better go find someone else who'll hold you up." I started to turn around and then stopped. "You're not driving, right? Where are your car keys?"

Trish blinked. "Not driving. We're all going back on the bus. The parrrrrrrty bus!" She raised a fist in the air and yelled.

"Cool. Later." I felt like I'd done everything I could. Watching them act like fucking idiots made me sick to my stomach. I pushed through the milling students, dodging parents who were searching for their new graduates, glancing around for my own family, when I heard my name again.

"Leo! Leo Taylor. Give me a hug, you big oaf." Carrie Russell caught up with me and put her words into action, wrapping her arms around me tightly. "Congratulations, sweetie! Can you believe it? You guys are all done . . ." Quinn's mom fumbled in her bag, sniffling as she dug out a tissue. "It doesn't seem possible. I swear it was just yesterday all three of you were playing naked together in your baby pool."

An image of Quinn, naked beneath me, flashed across my mind. I gritted my teeth and pushed it aside as Bill Russell joined his wife, clapping a hand on my shoulder.

"Don't mind her, Leo. She's been crying all week. You'd

think she's never going to see all you kids ever again." He gave my arm a quick squeeze. "We're all proud of you, son. I can't wait to see you playing down in Carolina."

Carrie brightened. "There's Sheri and Mark. Oh—and Quinn, finally. Come here, honey! Daddy and I've been looking for you."

And then she was there, standing in front of me, as her mom hugged her tight, leaned back to hold her face and then drew her close again. Nate's parents beamed at all of us, with Nate between them. He spared me a glance before returning his attention to Quinn.

"Carrie, I'm glad to see you're emotional, too." Sheri craned her neck, scanning the crowds. "Where's your mom, Leo? And your dad?"

I shrugged. "They'll meet me up on the bleachers. This is kind of same old, same old for them, you know? Plus my mom . . . my father didn't want her in the middle of all these people."

"She's doing okay, though, right?" Carrie frowned at me.

"Yeah. She's in remission, but she still has to be careful."

An awkward silence fell over us. Quinn had stepped back away from her mother and balanced on the balls of her feet. She was wearing sandals with high heels, and I could tell she was trying to keep them from sinking into the ground. Nate watched her so intently that I was pretty sure his eyes were going to bore a hole right through her. Neither of them looked my way.

"I better go find my parents." I forced a smile. "I'm sure we'll see you around."

"Oh, wait!" Sheri laid a hand on my chest, stopping me. "I want to get a picture of you three before everyone heads off in different directions." She pulled out her phone and gave Nate a little nudge. He hesitated before he ambled over to stand next to me.

Quinn took longer. She was gripping her square cap in one hand, playing with the silky tassels with the other, and her lips tightened.

"Honey, get in the picture. C'mon, we want something we can put in a frame next to your first-day-of-kindergarten photo." Quinn's mother turned her daughter by the shoulders. "There you go. No, Quinn, you get in the middle. It looks better that way."

I wanted to laugh at that. Yup, no doubt Quinn should be in the middle in a picture, because that was where she always was. In the middle, between Nate and me. Our buffer, and the one heart each of us wanted. As though he could hear my thoughts, Nate fastened his eyes on me over Quinn's head, only turning away when his mom instructed us to all look at the camera.

"Get a little closer, you guys. Geez, you'd think you didn't know each other." Sheri motioned to Quinn. After a moment's pause, Quinn and I both moved closer, until the side of her body was pressed up against mine. Even through the layers of clothing and robes, I could feel the heat of her. And my dick hardened, making me grateful for the first time all day that I was wearing the stupid robe.

I took totally advantage of the situation, sliding my arm around Quinn's waist and snugging her to me. If I had to go through hell, so did she. She stiffened for a moment, and then it felt as though she melted into me. I felt her exhale, and her eyes drifted shut briefly.

"Okay, say . . . graduation day!"

Both Sheri and Carrie took a bunch of pictures before they let us go. I was amazed that they didn't feel the thick tension that surrounded Nate, Quinn and me; we didn't joke around or laugh the way we used to. We didn't even talk to each other except when Quinn lost her balance for a second and clung to my arm, muttering, "Sorry."

"Me, too." I breathed out the words, but I wasn't sure if she heard them or not.

When the parents were finally finished, Quinn didn't lose any time putting distance between us. I bit down on the inside of my cheek until I tasted blood, just to dull the ache of her loss. Again.

"I'll send these to your mom, Leo." Carrie stood on her tiptoes to kiss my cheek. "Give her my love. And listen, kiddo, don't be a stranger. I know you're a big shot college football player now, but don't forget who used to change your diapers."

Sheri laughed. "That's true, and same goes." Her eyes traveled over the three of us, and for the first time, she seemed to be picking up on the awkwardness. "You three . . . you've been friends too long to let anything come between you. I hope you realize that. This is your last summer together before you all go your separate ways. Don't . . . just don't waste it." She blinked, and Mark slid his arm around her shoulder, pulling her to him. I remembered what I'd overheard when Nate had been in the hospital last year—*We don't know how long we have him here with us*—and I felt like scum. Here I was resenting Nate, and it was possible that he was living on borrowed time. I swallowed hard and turned to him, offering my hand.

He stared at me for a beat before gripping it firmly. I had the feeling he was letting me know this didn't change anything. Still, I held his gaze, willing myself to see no one but my old friend in front of me, instead of the guy who'd helped talk me into a decision that had basically destroyed my life. He gave me a little nod just before he released my hand.

After that, it would've been weird if I hadn't turned

to Quinn. She lifted her face to me, and for the first time in months, her eyes actually met mine, open and vulnerable. I wanted to look into those eyes forever. I wanted to sweep her into my arms and tell her I'd been a fucking idiot to ever let her get away, no matter how messed up I was, no matter how many times I'd told myself I was doing it for her.

I wanted to tell her how much I still loved her.

But I didn't. She let me pull her into a hug—shorter than I wanted it to be, but probably longer than made her comfortable. And then she pushed gently at my chest and moved away from me.

"See you around."

It was clearly my cue to exit, stage left. I sketched a wave to the parents and pushed my way through all the people, heading toward the bleachers. I saw my dad standing at the railing, waving to me, and my mom, sitting on a bench next to him, beaming.

I'd just about reached them when I was body-slammed from the right side. Matt grinned at me and smacked me on the back of the head with his graduation cap.

"Dude, we did it! We're done." He wrapped one arm around my neck and squeezed, nearly choking the life out of me. "Come on! Let's get out of here."

I ducked away from him. "I gotta go see my mom and dad first. I'll talk to you later, okay? I'll text you, and we'll meet up at a party or something."

Matt studied me for a few minutes. A frown creased his forehead. "What's going on, Taylor?" He cast a glance toward my parents and lowered his voice. "Is it . . . is your mom okay?"

"Yeah, man. She's fine. I just—" I rubbed a hand over my face. "I'm tired. I need to chill a little bit, catch up with my parents, do the family thing." I punched his shoulder. "I promise,

I'll get with you tonight. We'll knock back some beers."

"And this weekend, right? Down the shore? You're in?" He was watching me closely. "It's going to be epic. It'll make you forget all about . . ." Matt jerked his head in the direction I'd come from, and I knew he was talking about Quinn. "Distant memory, Lion. We'll make it happen."

I forced a grin. "Forgetting all about high school isn't going to take much, bro. I'm there. We'll drive down together, okay? I'll text you."

Matt nodded. "You got it. Later, man."

I watched him meander away, bumping into another small clump of people. Turning, I took the stadium steps two at a time and rounded the railing, making my way to my folks.

"I can't believe my baby—my last boy—is a high school graduate." My mother threw her arms around me. "Look at you."

"Yeah, yeah, yeah. Look at me. You saw me this morning. I'm still the same old handsome, brilliant and humble son you've always known and loved." I kissed the top of my mom's head. "You feeling all right? The sun wasn't too hot?"

"Nah. Dad kept an eye on me. I'm fine." She held my face in her hands, studying me. "But are *you*?"

I winked at her. "Golden just like always. I'm just glad to be done. Glad this is over."

"Graduation, you mean? Or high school?" My dad crossed his arms over his chest and cocked his head.

"Both." I managed a smile. "Let's blow this joint, huh?"

"Yep." My mother lingered, looking out over the field. "I know it sounds silly, but I feel like I'm graduating today, too. Leaving behind a whole era of my life. I've had a kid in these schools for . . ." She cast her eyes up, thinking. "God, twenty years. And now it's over."

Over. Yeah, that was the key word. It was all over. Finished. I followed my mom's gaze to where Nate and Quinn stood with their parents, and I knew with certainty that she was right. I was leaving behind an era of my life, too. The Trio had been over for a long time, but today . . . this was the official end. I wondered if I'd ever see Quinn and Nate again. Even if I did, nothing would ever be the same again. I'd destroyed my friendship with them, and in doing so, I'd buried any chance I ever had with Quinn. I'd broken her heart. What she didn't realize was that I'd done the same to my own.

"Let's go home. Simon and Danny said they'd see you there." My dad linked his hand with my mother's, smiling down at her. "One era ends, and another begins." He gripped my shoulder. "For you, too. Onward and upward, son. Time to tackle world."

I took a deep breath and turned my back on the field, on my friends. The finality of everything sent pain knifing through me so deep and so ripping that I wanted to curl around it and groan.

Instead, I kept walking, moving farther away from the girl who I knew I'd always love and into a future that felt uncertain.

Alone.

★ Epilogue ★

THERE WAS AN ANNOYING BUZZING SOMEWHERE NEAR my head, and still mostly asleep, I frowned. The wrinkling of my forehead sent an ache through my head, and for a moment, I was pretty sure I was going to puke.

The buzzing sounded again. I'd thought it was a mosquito, but as awareness seeped in, I realized it was a telephone vibrating somewhere. Close to me? I couldn't tell. A distant part of my brain considered moving my hand so I could grope around for the damn thing, but apparently some of the synapses had been damaged, because my hand didn't do anything. After a few seconds, the buzzing stopped again, and I drifted back into some kind of pseudo-slumber.

"Taylor! You in there, dude?" The voice was loud and unfamiliar. I groaned and covered my head with one bent arm.

"Taylor. Leo. C'mon, man, you gotta wake up." The guy I didn't know sounded upset. And then he shook me, and bile rose in my stomach.

"Stop." I ground out the word. "I'm going to fucking hurl on you, whoever the fuck you are. Get out of here."

He sighed, and the sound held a world of banked anger. "Bud, I would if I could. But your mom is on the phone, and she's been trying to call you all night."

I opened my eyes, groaned again, and attempted sitting up. It wasn't a good idea, since my head pounded harder and my gut roiled, but hearing that my mother was trying to get in touch with me kind of superseded all that. I knew my mom. She wouldn't be calling me unless it was an emergency.

"Where's my phone?" I fumbled around on the bed, and my hand hit soft, warm flesh. Blonde hair covered the side of her cheek, but shit. I had no idea who this chick was. I had a sinking feeling that this fact wouldn't change even if I could get a look at her face.

"I don't know where the hell your phone is, buddy, but your mom's on this one." The guy held up a black and green phone case that I recognized. It was Matt's. My parents had his number, just as his had mine, from back during football season, when we'd sometimes share rides.

"Okay." I held out my hand, and he gave me Matt's phone. "Thanks. Sorry about that. Um . . ." I had no fucking clue what his name was.

He rolled his eyes. "Tate Durham. We met yesterday." He paused, and when I didn't say anything—I honestly didn't remember him—he added, "I'm from Gatbury. We're playing ball together this fall at Carolina. I met Lampert at a camp last year, and he invited me this weekend."

"Oh." I nodded. "Okay. Well, sorry. I'm not at my best . . ." I glanced at the sleeping girl again. "Do you happen to know . . .?"

Tate smirked. "Nope. When I got here yesterday, she was sitting on your lap and you had your hands—well, let's just say I figured you knew her pretty well. But I was never introduced."

"Shit." I looked at the phone in my hand, remembering too late that my mother was probably hearing this whole conversation. "Hey, Mom. Sorry about that, but—"

"Leo." Her voice was rough and stuffy, like when she had a cold. "God, Leo, I've been trying to get through to you for over twelve hours. What the hell?"

"I'm sorry." My own tone went up a few octaves. "I was— uh, sorry. I can't find my phone. What's wrong?"

"God." For a few moments, she didn't answer me, but I could hear her sobs through the line, and my fear ratcheted up a few notches. "It's Bill. God, Leo, he's dead."

"Dead?" I repeated it stupidly, as though I'd never heard the term before. "Bill? Quinn's dad? No, I saw him the other day at graduation. What're you talking about, Mom? What—" Realization and horror began to creep in, finally seeping through the cocoon of alcohol. "What happened?"

"It was an accident. A horrible—oh, my God, Leo. He just went to pick up dinner for Quinn and Carrie. A truck hit his car head-on, and they said he was killed instantly."

As wasted as I'd been five minutes before, I was stone cold sober now. "Mom—no. *No.* That can't be right. Quinn—she's going to—she can't—she loves her dad. She's always talking about him—and he said he was going to come see me play football. I saw him right after I got my letter from Carolina, and I told him—he said he was going to come see me play. I thought—after everything with Quinn, he wouldn't want to. But he didn't say anything but that he was going to come down."

I was babbling, but I had to do it. I had to keep talking so I could drown out the sound of my mother's sobs on the other end of the phone. But then there was nothing left to say, no other reasons I could offer for why my mom might be wrong. Or lying. Or . . . anything but what my mind was beginning to accept was true.

"What do I do, Mom?" My eyes darted frantically around the room, searching for the clothes I must've discarded the night before. "What should—how can I help?"

"You need to get home. Is there someone there—someone sober—who can drive you? I don't want you to borrow anyone's car. I don't want you behind the wheel."

"I'll figure it out. I'll find someone." I thought of the guy who'd brought me the phone. What the hell had he said his name was? Didn't matter. He didn't look like he was drunk at all. "Don't worry. I think I know someone who can do it."

"Just come home, honey. Be safe, but come home. I need you, and—Quinn. She's going to need you."

I never remembered afterward what I said to my mother before I hung up, but it was probably more assurances. Once I'd hit the disconnect button, I sat there, Matt's phone still in my hands, staring at it as though it might have answers—better answers. Answers that would make sense of what I'd just heard.

I knew I had to get moving. I had to find my clothes, get dressed—I sniffed my pits and almost gagged. Yeah, grab a quick shower and then get dressed. Find someone to drive me home. Get home, so I could be there. For Quinn.

Quinn.

Not The End Yet
Leo, Quinn and Nate's story
Will continue in
HANGING BY A MOMENT
Coming May 24th

And will conclude in
DAYS OF YOU AND ME
Coming September 27th

★ Acknowledgements ★

This series has been a long time coming, and if you want to know its full history, I suggest you visit my website (tawdrakandle.com) and read all about it. Let's just say it was inspired by a real-life set of circumstances, began its life during NaNoWriMo2011, and evolved into something wholly different over the last four and a half years.

It's also very different from anything I've written before. As you've probably guessed, Quinn and Leo and Nate (and some of their friends) still have quite a journey ahead of them. I hope you'll come along.

Thanks to the fabulous Robin Ludwig for the beautiful, haunting covers she's designed for this series. She rocks my socks. Thank you to Stacey Blake of Champagne Formats for making this (many chaptered) book so pretty. Big hearts to you, my friend! Thanks for Kelly Baker for her superb proofing and editing, and for catching things I might not.

Thank you to Kara Schilling and Julianna Santiago, Temptresses Extraordinaire, for beta reading! You are fabulous, ladies.

Jen Rattie and Maria Clark, thank you so much for your patience, your grace and your humor. I adore you both. Also thanks to Dylan Clark for making sure I was up-to-date on high school football details. I appreciate it!

To all my readers, for their love, support and enthusiasm—my eternal gratitude.

★ About the Author ★

Photo by Heather Batchelder

Tawdra Kandle writes romance, in just about all its forms. She loves unlikely pairings, strong women, sexy guys, hot love scenes and just enough conflict to make it interesting. Her books run from YA paranormal romance through NA paranormal and contemporary romance to adult contemporary and paramystery romance. She lives in central Florida with a husband, kids, sweet pup and too many cats. And yeah, she rocks purple hair.

Follow Tawdra on Facebook, Twitter, Instagram, Pinterest and sign up for her newsletter so you never miss a trick.

If you love Tawdra's books, become a Naughty Temptress! Join the group for sneak peeks, advanced reader copies of future books, and other fun.

Printed in the United States
by Baker & Taylor Publisher Services

.